CROWNS

James B Lynch

ISBN-13: 9780991522118
ISBN-10: 0991522117

Cover design by: James B Lynch
Library of Congress Control Number: 2018675309
Printed in the United States of America

BOOK 1: SEE ME AFTER CLASS (PART 1)

CHAPTER 1

It was Thursday, and, for Joe, the last day of the school week. This was why he'd taken an overload first semester; now he had a three day weekend to look forward to every week.

Not that he did much with it, but it was nice to know it was there if he needed it.

Sitting in the lecture hall, he still found himself sometimes listening for a bell to dismiss him, rather than the teacher.

Professor. In college they were called professors. And it was history class, not social studies.

Joe gathered his things – notebooks, pens, computer, sweatshirt, charging cable – and waited at the log-jammed doorway to escape out into the hall, then into the world.

Joe wasn't a short guy, yet moving through the crowded hallway, it was like he wasn't even there, towering over nine-tenths of the people around him. It had caused him to develop a natural instinct to take up as little space as possible to navigate through; his shoulders always pulled in, his spine never quite upright – it was possible he imagined his slightly-lowered head as a sort of battering ram for pushing through public spaces.

Once out the school doors, he rhythmically trotted down the short concrete stairway at the front of the building. He tried to recall what lot he'd parked in, but Thursday classes started early and he was not a morning person. He was pretty sure he remembered, but this might have been one of those days where he'd need to ride the shuttle bus around to a couple of stops before he found it.

He'd, of course, noticed the girl at the bottom of the steps. Pale, athletic, her platinum hair cropped short. She seemed as oblivious to the other students as they were to him.

She wore tight jeans and a long gray cardigan, open over a black tank top. Was it cold enough to need a sweater, Joe wondered? He was fine in his t-shirt. His hooded sweatshirt, coincidentally also gray, was stuffed into his backpack. Probably getting all wrinkled, but since it had only cost about eight dollars, he wasn't too careful with it. He'd needed it this morning, but by afternoon it had warmed enough to go without. Maybe this young woman had been here long enough that the weather had changed on her, as well?

He tried not to stare as he walked past.

Accidental eye contact. Time for the polite, awkward smile, and then he'd go about his day.

"Hey."

Holy crap.

"Hey," Joe replied.

Okay, a one-word greeting. Not far beyond the awkward smile. It probably didn't mean anything.

"I'm Val."

"Uh, cool," he said. "I'm Joe."

He held out his hand just above waist height. In high school, one of his teachers had set aside a day for instruction on social protocol. It was ostensibly meant to prepare for things like job interviews, but the teacher had been fond enough of many of his students, and they awkward enough, that the guidance may have been intended to prevent any of them from making too much of an ass out of themselves in social settings.

Palm up meant friendly: open. Give it a firm grip, but not a tight squeeze. Two pumps and release. If your palms are sweaty...

He'd already blown past what to do for sweaty palms.

"Nice to meet you," he said. He hoped she wouldn't notice his palms.

She gave a quick glance down at his outstretched hand. "You wanna hang out?" she asked.

"Sure."

"Cool." She grabbed hold of his hand and gave a gentle tug as she headed off down the street. "Follow me."

Joe had to jog the first few steps to keep up. "You're not gonna, like, harvest my organs or anything, are you?"

"Why would I want to do that?"

"I don't know. Why are we hanging out?"

She gave a glance back over her shoulder.

"Maybe there's another organ of yours I'm interested in."

"Haha," Joe said. "Yeah. What?"

Joe had not previously been aware that there were warehouses within walking distance of the school. Though, to be fair, he wasn't sure how far they'd been walking. He was mostly enjoying the awkward silence and appreciating the girl who still held tight to his hand.

Val led him to a corner, far off the main road. He didn't even see any workers back this far, and the pavement and grass definitely hadn't been kept up.

Quite intent in her stride, she found a section of fencing where the chain-link had come loose. If Joe hadn't known any better, and he hadn't, he'd have thought the building it surrounded was abandoned.

She shoved the fencing aside and pulled him onward, towards the crusty brick structure.

"Okay, but this is weird, right?" Joe asked. Val simply smiled and shrugged. "I mean, it's not that I don't find you attractive. I do. I weirdly do. It's like..."

Val spun around, grabbing hold of his belt and pulling him towards her. Tall as she was, she still had to prop herself up on her toes to bring their lips together.

There was something about the kiss he couldn't describe, something unlike anything he'd felt before. It wasn't passion or raw attraction. Whatever it was, the kiss itself felt nice. Almost… technically proficient? Was that seriously how he was describing a kiss to himself? The lips were full and soft, mouth slightly open. Not too wet. Just the right amount of tongue. And all he could think of to describe it was "proficient."

"We good?" she asked.

"Yeah." He sucked for breath. "Yeah, we good."

She pulled him on.

"I good, anyway," he said. "I hope you good."

The interior of the building did nothing to dissuade the notion that the place was disused. The thick greasy buildup on the warped old windows only added to the difficulties with the illumination. It was too dark for Joe to even see Val ahead of him, though she pressed forward as though walking through broad daylight.

The floor seemed to tilt upward beneath them. The texture changed, too. Where his sneakers had been crunching against uneven, cracked concrete and sandy gravel, there was now only a soft padding. He found himself in surroundings that were somehow darker than before, with only the dimmest of lights along… was it a floor? A hallway? Where would a hallway have come from in the middle of a dilapidated warehouse?

And that's when the comforting grasp of the pretty girl he'd just met was gone. And he was alone. In the dark.

She was definitely nowhere within arm's reach. He wasn't even sure if he could hear her anymore, and something told him she liked it that way.

"Uh, what's going on?" he finally asked.

If he'd had the presence of mind to do so, maybe, just maybe, he could have turned right around the way he'd come and found his way back out again. The window for that opportunity closed on him in a literal sense, as the ramp he'd just climbed rose up flush to the walls.

The lights coming up did little to assuage his confusion. The floors, ceiling, and walls of the hallway - it was definitely a hallway - looked like brushed metal. He couldn't tell exactly where the light was even coming from, other than it was above him.

"Hey, Val..."

He was at least finally able to see well enough to spot the doorway just a few yards to his left. The back of a chair and of Val's head could be seen from his vantage point, so that's where he headed.

Before he could get to her, the ground beneath him lurched. His hand shot out to brace him against the wall. The feel of it didn't seem to match the look. It felt more like a matte rubber than metal.

He refocused on getting to that room at the end of the hall.

As he moved along, swiftly as he could, he was able to make out a window just in front of Val. Being in the center of a dark building, there wasn't much to see out of it.

Until there was daylight.

And clouds.

Clouds that seemed to be getting closer.

CHAPTER 2

It didn't help much when Joe finally made it to the small room at the hallway's end. He found Val there, seated, as he'd suspected, but spread out in front of her was some sort of instrument panel. He'd only see that sort of thing in video games. There was even a... not a joystick, but something along those lines... directly in front of Val. Whatever it was required both hands to manipulate, and she kept having to reach for other controls on the board.

The console spanned the width of the cabin's front, which was just barely wide enough to accommodate the two chairs tucked beneath. A third seat was further back, just off to his right as he entered the room. He could stand upright, but just barely. The walls were all the same metal as the hallway, with dark inset panels; they didn't seem to be colored black as much as they simply swallowed light.

"What the hell's going on?" Joe asked.

"Give me a second. Getting out of the atmosphere is always the trickiest part."

"What?"

Joe leaned over her to peak out of the forward "window." He was just in time to see the land below them completely disappearing into clouds. He couldn't make out a single building before the ground vanished into the soft white haze. It wasn't long before the clouds themselves started to fade into the distance.

Val looked up at him, perched directly over her shoulder.

"Do you mind? I just said I need to get us out of the atmosphere."

Joe took a step back, his hands up in front of him.

"Sorry."

"I *just* said it."

"Sorry," he repeated. "It's my first time in a... this is a spaceship."

"Yes."

"And you're... are you an alien?" he asked.

"Huh. I hadn't thought about it like that. I guess from a certain viewpoint I would be."

"Oh, God, are you gonna probe me?"

"What? Probe you?" she asked. "Why the hell would I probe you?"

"I'm just saying, I'm pretty open-minded. I'm willing to give most anything the ol' college try."

Her eyes narrowed at him.

"I'll take that as a no."

Her attention returned to the controls in front of her.

"I'd appreciate it if you'd stay quiet until we've engaged the space-fold drive."

"The what what?" Joe asked.

Val let out a sigh.

"Right. You grew up in human culture," she said. "The space-fold drive bends the fabric of space to create a shorter distance between two points, allowing for faster-than-light travel without the risk of time dilation."

"That sounds dangerous."

"It's pretty safe, as long as no one distracts the pilot while they're engaging the drive."

"Are you hinting that you want me to be quiet?" he asked.

"I'm pretty sure I've said it outright already."

"Okay, I'm shutting up now."

"Announcing that you're doing it completely defeats the

purpose."

"Well, in my defense..."

Her head snapped around.

His mouth shut and his jaw tightened. His hands found the chair just beside her and he dropped down.

Her focus once again went back to the complex, multi-layered bank of translucent panels in front of her.

"Entering space-fold in five, four..."

Just at the edge of Earth's solar system, space warped in front of the small ship, like a canvas of the universe being bent.

There was no visible component for the drive's energy on the ship's streamlined exterior. Rather, the entire pearlescent hull served as a broadcast array for the distortion effect.

Propelled by the four cleanly glowing engines towards the aft, the vessel shot forward, swallowed in the folds of the starscape. The instant it disappeared, everything once again appeared normal.

Within the cockpit, Val let out a short breath and turned to her traveling companion.

"And we are in the fold," she announced. "We're just coasting now until we get to the other end. So, if you have any questions, this would be actually the right time to ask them."

Joe stared at her. "Who, me?" he asked. "No. Nope. No questions."

"Seriously?"

"I don't think I have a frame of reference from which to start this conversation," he said.

"Okay."

She turned back to the controls.

"I've just been abducted by an alien woman who looks

like an attractive blonde," he said, his voice rising in both volume and pitch.

She spun back to face him again.

"You haven't been abducted," she said. "You're being retrieved."

"Jah?"

"I can let your mother explain once we've gotten to Kaia."

"My mother?" He gripped the sides of his head. "Oh, God, my mother. She's gonna be so pissed."

"No, Joseph, I'm talking about your real mother."

"Excuse me?"

"Catherine and Jason Hammond may have adopted you," Val said, "but they're not your real parents."

"Hey, those people raised me." He wasn't even conscious of his small, aggressive move in her direction. "They're my real family."

"Alright, don't get sore. I didn't mean anything by it. I meant, I guess, that the humans who raised you had no idea who you really are."

"What the hell is that supposed to mean?" he asked.

"Your real - your birth family is still alive."

"What?"

"Well, your mother, anyway," she said. "Your father and your older brother, that's the reason I had to come get you."

"You're trying to tell me that I'm an alien?"

"It would probably help if you'd stop thinking of yourself that way." Exasperation was beginning to leak into her tone. "From your point of view - our point of view - the humans are the aliens, and, honestly, a painfully underdeveloped species."

"No," he said. "I mean, I look human."

"I guess. I'd say it's more that the humans look Kaian."

"What are the odds that two species in, like, different galaxies would evolve almost identically?"

"Better than you think," she said. "Most sentient species we've met tend to look a lot like us. Maybe some minor cosmetic differences, but mostly."

"And why do you want me?" he asked.

"I don't. I'm here on orders of the queen."

"The queen."

"Yes," she said. "Your birth mother, the Queen of Kaia."

"I'm a space alien prince?"

"No," she said. "Your father and older brother are dead, and your mother married into the family, so she can't inherit the Crown. You're the king."

"This is insane," he said. "Space aliens and other worlds and... do you have any proof of this?"

Val's eyes turned to narrow slits as her lips pursed. She gestured at their surroundings.

"Yeah, okay, I guess," Joe said.

Somewhere, far from where their voyage began, space wrinkled itself in the opposite manner in which they'd entered the fold. The galaxy spat the tiny vessel out and they were once again in real space.

It wasn't long before they'd reached deeper into the nearest star's orbital pull, approaching a planet colored very much like Earth. The landmasses and oceans were shaped differently, but it was otherwise a close match.

In orbit, their diminutive shuttle was found upon by a group of heavier, angrier looking ships.

Joe caught a glimpse of them out the window, though they were far too large for him to see even one of them in its entirety.

"Those do not look friendly," he said.

"Those are Kaian warships," Val said.

"That makes me comfortable."

She smiled, knowing what was coming next.

The bellies of the warships above split. A series of brilliant flashes, each like a miniature star going nova, dropped out.

Joe recoiled from the sudden, harsh light. He threw his hands up just a moment too late to protect his eyes.

"Gah!"

"Relax," Val said. "Those are just signal flares. Everyone in the eastern hemisphere now knows that their king is with them."

"You could've warned me?"

"I could have."

They were well below the cloud line by the time Joe was able to blink his vision clear enough to take in their surroundings. Val's ship was very nearly within the gleaming capital city, heading towards the towering palace at the center of it all.

The warships remain a respectable distance behind.

Not always one for aesthetics, Joe was impressed by the architecture around them. The buildings weren't quite like anything on Earth, though the engineering principles remained the same. Some design elements even echoed periods from Earth's history, from ancient times to the twentieth century. Old world spires mixed with art deco and a touch of gothic but melded together in ways that felt unfamiliar.

Joe soaked in what he could, though it wasn't much, as Val's ship whizzed through the artificial valleys. Aside from the escort ships, air traffic was cleared for as far as the eye could see.

The royal palace loomed ahead of them. It was at once the seat of power on the planet, a guarded stronghold, and an opulent residence: a collection of gleaming, engraved towers, turrets, and keeps synched together by a network of bridges and walkways. Once inside the buildings, in fact, there was virtually no way around at ground level. Movement from structure to structure was all accomplished via the pathways raised high above the city floor.

Nearly everything about the place, from the shapes of

the buildings to the etchings on the walls, favored a circular aesthetic. It was as though the architect of the place, some long-buried and forgotten engineer, had so wanted the castle to be the heart of the city that no line or corner could be allowed to be closer to the center than another.

Within the main wall were acres of land that mostly served as recreational spaces and gardens for the residents. Calling the area around the outer ramparts a moat did it no justice. It was a chasm running the full circumference of the grounds, the bottom of which had not been glimpsed by anyone living.

As they cleared the walls, their ship took a sharp spin before descending vertically onto the rounded landing pad. Only a long, suspended walkway separated them from the nearest keep.

Surrounded by her retinue, the sole remaining royal occupant exited the castle, hustling towards the ship that still had disembarking protocols to observe before its occupants could emerge. That should have given the elderly woman plenty of time to cross the expanse. Val's efficiency being what it was, she and Joe still beat the queen to the pad's surface.

As hesitant as he'd been back on Earth, Joe was exponentially more so now. For the first time in his life - the first time in the life of anyone from Earth, as far as he knew - his feet set down on a planet that wasn't his own, wasn't the one he was raised on.

The warships continued to hover above.

It took a few moments of stunned admiration before Joe recognized that there was a crowd heading towards them, headed by a broadly smiling woman. She was dressed almost entirely in a deep red, with only some fringe offset in white. Her tightly pulled hair was nearly the same color. Not an inch of skin was visible from beneath her chin, her frock reaching down to her feet, and yet it didn't seem to drag.

"*My queen.*" Val's voice suddenly took on an accent Joe hadn't heard before. He certainly couldn't make out any of the words.

"Valentina," the queen said. *"I'm so glad to have you back. And quicker than I expected."*

Val looked over at Joe.

"The mission went smoothly."

Loving eyes feel upon Joe.

"And this is my son?" she asked. Her voice betrayed not a whit of the quivering she felt in her chest.

"Yes, your highness," Val said. *"You didn't need to make the trip out here. I could have brought him to you. After what you've been through…"*

"Nonsense." Val fought the urge to recoil as the queen tsked at her. *"I've been separated from my son since his birth. I wouldn't have tolerated being apart for one second longer than I had to be."*

She moved towards Joe, her arms outstretched. She wrapped them around him as tightly as she could manage.

"May I present to you, King Joe, your queen mother, the reigning regent of Kaia," Val said.

The queen released her hug but kept her hands on his shoulders. She scanned him over and again.

"My god. I haven't seen you since you first left my womb. I cannot tell you how much I've missed you. I never thought to see you again. I wish it were under better circumstances, but it's still joyous to have you back in your home. Back where you belong. I wish you'd never left."

Joe nodded.

"Uh-huh. Uh-huh." He leaned towards Val. "So, uh… what?"

The queen's brow furrowed, her smile fading.

"What?" Joe asked. "What'd I do?"

"I believe you've disappointed your mother," Val stated.

"Yeah, that tracks," Joe said.

"What's wrong with him?" the queen asked Val.

"I'm not sure you truly want me to start that list."

The queen's brow grew ever sharper.

"*The foster parents you sent with him were killed in an accident when he was an infant,*" Val said. "*He was adopted by humans and raised in their culture. He doesn't know anything about us, including our language.*"

The queen lifted her hands from Joe's shoulders, sharply drawing them in towards her.

"*Well, that is distressing,*" she said.

Though he knew very little of the world he now stood upon, the forced, awkward smile that Joe saw on the queen's face was universal.

"*But, nothing that can't be resolved in time.*" The queen beckoned to be followed. "*Come.*"

CHAPTER 3

No time was wasted upon entering the palace. For an older woman, the queen sure could move. Joe's sightseeing would have to be put on hold. A pity, he felt, for the architecture within was just as impressive as that without. Though it didn't shine the same way without the sunlight, it was still something to behold. High ceilings, wide floors, everything precisely crafted from stone of complimentary cut and texture. Yet, it retained the same sense from inside the spacecraft. Nothing was quite the same feel or illumination Joe expected of it.

"So, wait," Joe said to Val, "how come I can understand you, but they're all talking Klingon?"

"Because I spent several weeks on Earth learning English before approaching you," she said.

"Okay." Joe accepted the answer. "Wait, several weeks? You became fluent in English in a few weeks?"

"Yes."

"Jeez," he said, barely grumbling aloud. "And I learned like five words in two years of Spanish."

"As you said, that tracks."

"Hey, so, can I ask you something?"

"I believe you just did," said Val.

It took a moment for that to land with Joe. "Oh, okay, I get it. No, I'm being serious, though."

"What's your question?" Val asked.

"It just seems weird to me that a civilization advanced enough to, like, travel between galaxies and stuff would still have a monarchy," Joe said.

"*What is he saying?*" the queen asked.

"*He's asking why a civilization as advanced as ours would have a monarchy,*" Val said. "*On the world he grew up on, monarchies are considered archaic and represent a repressive class divide. How would you like me to answer?*"

The queen smiled at her.

"*Honestly.*"

They crossed into the throne room as Val gave her answer, the retinue remaining dutifully outside the doorway.

"The people elected it," Val said.

The throne, large and ornate, sat on the far side of the room, elevated on a tiered platform. It stood higher than any man who would stand beside it, much less sit upon it. A golden scepter, property of the last person to inhabit the seat, leaned against one of its arms.

"They did what?" Joe asked. "They – that doesn't make any sense. Is something getting lost in the translation? How could people elect a monarch? That's not what a monarchy is."

"They didn't elect the monarch, they elected to maintain the royal family," Val said.

"And why on..." Joe stopped short. "I was about to say 'why on Earth would they do that,' but I guess that doesn't quite apply."

"*He wants to know why the people would elect to maintain a royal family,*" Val said to the queen. "*I'm not sure I studied enough of the philosophy of his world to give an eloquent answer.*"

"The people wanted to maintain the royal family because only the royal family can access this." With a grace only a longtime royal could exhibit, the queen gestured towards an emblem at the center of the floor. Joe had no time to register what it was and had no opportunity to decrypt the blue and tan shapes, before it split, each half sliding away into the surrounding stone.

A column rose from beneath, capped by a transparent display case. Atop a cushion within the clear box sat a crown. It wasn't fancy. There were no jewels or ornate carvings. It looked to have been pounded into shape rather than carved or molded. The metal was of a warmer color, not quite gold but not bronze or copper.

The protective covering retracted.

Far more gently than seemed necessary for such a blunt looking piece of ironware, the queen lifted the crown with the tips of her fingers and held it out towards Joe.

"The Crown of the Five Point Star," she said.

"Cool." Joe nodded. His head shook. "Wait, what? Are you speaking English now?"

"No. You're speaking Kaian," the queen said. "The Crown bestows many gifts on its owner, including the gifts of languages. Just by being so near it, you're already feeling its effects. Your bond with it will be strong, I can tell."

"Neat," said Joe.

The queen took a deep breath, ready to savor the moments ahead.

"The Crown was forged in our civilization's earliest days by our most powerful mages."

"Mages." Joe pulled his head back, one eyebrow rising. "You mean like wizards?"

"Exactly."

"There are wizards involved now?" He shrugged. "Okay. Should I be writing this down?"

"Writing this down?" his mother asked. "I don't understand what that would mean."

"On his world, they take slices of large plants and inscribe language on them with handheld tools," Val said.

"Oh. How quaint." The queen barely skipped a beat before continuing. "The Crown of the Five Point Star was imbued with the power to grant its wearer special abilities. Strength, speed, stamina…"

She was interrupted by both of the young people before

her bursting into laughter.

"Stamina," Joe chuckled.

"Right?" Val giggled.

The queen couldn't help but smile.

"I said very much the same thing when I was told the story. As I was saying, the Crown also grants the wearer wisdom and understanding. The caveat is that the Crown was bound to the bloodline of the royal family. Only they can access its power." She took a breath. "Centuries ago, during a period of extended peace, the king and queen of that time offered the citizens of our star empire a choice: keep the monarchy, or remove them from power. They could freely choose their leaders, but without devoting resources to maintaining the royal family, they'd risk losing the protection of the Crown forever. For their own safety, the people chose to keep the Crown and its bearers as their rulers."

Joe finally reached out and took the crown from her hands.

"So, I just put this on and get, like, smarter and stronger and stuff?"

He placed the Crown on his forehead. Through some unseen force, it held in place.

"Am I smarter yet?" he asked.

"Very much no," said Val. "Do they not have crowns on your adoptive world?"

"Not magic ones, no," Joe said. "And it's not like I'd have ever worn one. Not one I didn't get free with a kid's meal, anyway."

The queen placed a fingertip against the top horn of the Crown and pushed downward. The crown slid until the bottom edge covered his nose.

The Crown expanded, wrapping itself partially around the shape of Joe's skull. An impossible amount of armored sheets slid from somewhere within it, forming around his body. The underlying bodysuit that materialized was dark in color, with a thicker layer of warm metal plating of varying shades protecting the most vital areas.

Joe looked at his hands, then further down. Traces of energy still ran across the seams where the pieces of armor met.

"Whoa," was all he could muster.

He lifted one foot, then another.

"It's surprisingly comfortable."

"It forms itself to your exact shape. Why would it not be comfortable to wear?" the queen asked.

"I don't know. It's big and bulky," Joe said. "I mean, they molded the Batman suit to Michael Keaton and he couldn't turn his head in the damn thing."

"Who is this Michael Keaton?" his mother asked.

"Oh, uh, he was Batman."

"Explain Batman," she demanded.

"He's a superhero," said Joe. "I guess I'm kind of one too now, right?"

"Why was his armor not properly forged?" the queen asked.

"What?"

"Earth isn't as advanced as us, by a long ways," Val said. "Their grasp of metallurgy is probably centuries behind the curve."

"I don't think it was metal," Joe said. "More like rubber or something. And it weighed like 80 pounds."

"I'm sure their armorers did the best they could," Val said.

"Yeah, I think Christian Bale's suit was like a third the weight. And he could turn his head." Joe bounced on the balls of his feet. "Huh. How much does this suit weigh?"

The two women shared a confused look.

"I'm not sure anyone's ever thought to ask that before," Val admitted.

Joe continued putting his new armor through its paces, twisting from side-to-side.

"Because it feels pretty light," he said. "I'm just

wondering how good of protection something that feels weightless can be."

"The power of the Crown propels itself," the queen told him. "If anyone else tries to move you, they will find it tremendously difficult."

She gave a nod to Val.

Val leaped into the air. Her vertical was impressive, high enough that she could thrust out both legs and impact Joe's chest with the soles of her sneakers.

Her momentum stopped dead, she fell straight downward. Prepared for this, she caught herself and sprung back up, landing solidly on her feet.

"Alright, so that's how that goes," Joe said. "What about a tank or something?"

"Beg pardon?" the queen asked.

"Like, if a tank shot at me, what would it do?"

"Can I?" Val asked.

"No," the queen said.

"Aw."

"We'll save that for another time," said the queen.

"I've got your word on that?" Joe asked.

"No. I'm just trying to dissuade you from allowing yourself to be shot at by a tank," his mother said.

"You can't stop me forever," Joe muttered beneath his breath.

"Alright, remove the Crown for now," the queen said.

"But, don't I, like, own it?" Joe asked.

"Yes, but until you've been tutored in its proper usage, it will be better for everyone if it remains here."

"Alright, fine." Joe lifted the Crown. Immediately, the suit disappeared and the Crown itself shrank back to its original size.

He handed it to the queen, who set it back in its display.

This coincided with a sudden commotion from outside the room. Through the heavy – Joe wanted to say they were wooden – doors, there was a definite sound of muffled shouting followed by at least one thing breaking.

"What's going on out there?" Val asked.

"Wait here, please," the queen said.

She rushed to the door, opening it just far enough to slip herself through before letting it slam shut again.

Joe looked at Val. She gave the tight, polite smile, this time with a flaring of the eyes thrown in.

"So, what are we doing?" Joe asked.

"We're waiting," she said. "Like the queen mother said to."

"Do you always do what you're told?" he asked.

"Sometimes."

"Really?"

"Usually."

"Yeah, me, too."

"The queen brought me to the palace, put me in the training program," she said. "I basically owe her everything."

"Plus, she's the queen. So, you probably owe her everything you have anyway."

"What?"

"You guys don't have taxes here?" he asked.

"Oh. Yeah, we do," she said. "We just don't get all weird about them, and the government doesn't act like a bunch of prigs about it."

"Cool." He tapped out a quick rhythm on his jeans. "So, you wanna get out of here?"

"And go where?"

"I dunno. We're in space…"

"We are securely within Kaia's atmosphere."

"I have a space castle…"

"The castle is firmly rooted to the ground."

"I'm the king…"

"Eh, I can't argue with that one."

"And I want to see this other planet here."

"For your safety, no one is going to let you out of the castle anytime soon," she said.

Joe looked around the throne room. There was a second story to it, he noticed, and a number of smaller doorways, stairs, and passages dotting the outer wall.

"Yeah, okay," he relented. "Hey, how tall is this place?"

"The palace is the highest structure in Olivert."

"Okay, so if I just..." He took off running for one of the doors.

She squeezed her eyes shut for a moment, her head gently shaking, before giving chase.

"Dammit."

Down the hall, past overturned furniture and light fixtures, the queen found the source of the disturbance.

A group of guards, their backs to her, blocked the path of a dark-eyed man. His hair and beard were black, and the only things keeping his coat from sharing that color were the gold trim and some flecks of red where the light hit it.

Between the guards, in their black, red-edged uniforms, he saw the queen charging up the corridor.

"What is the meaning of all this?" The gentle, loving tones she'd used with Joe and Val had vanished, replaced by the growls of a defensive mother.

"Ah, a simple misunderstanding," the intruder replied.

"A misunderstanding didn't knock over a six-hundred-year-old vase, Angelo. What are you doing here?"

The guards parted, allowing her to face him directly.

"I wanted to see for myself."

"You weren't summoned."

"When my brother was king, I didn't need a summons to enter the palace," said Angelo. "I'm sure your memory stretches back far enough to recall that I even had chambers very near to yours."

"Your brother isn't king anymore," she said.

"I'm painfully aware." He took a step towards her. She

didn't flinch. "Don't make the mistake of assuming you're the only one in grieving."

His eyes darted up in time to spot two young people in unusual clothing coming up the hallway. He took a step back from the queen and around to one side.

"Hey," Joe said. "Who's this?"

"Wow." Angelo marveled at the sight, his smile and eyes glistening. "Look at you."

"Uh, okay. I asked a question." Joe leaned towards his birth mother. "Can I order someone to answer me?"

"This is your Uncle Angelo," Val said.

"Huh." Joe stared back at him.

"And what did they name you?" Angelo asked.

"My parents? Er, my human parents?"

"Yes."

"Joseph," he said. "Or, Joe."

"Go by Joseph." Angelo gave him a wink. "It's always better for a king to go more formal."

"Yeah, okay." Joe leaned away slightly.

"Sorry, I just... last time I saw you, I could hold you in one hand." Angelo held up and pointed to his palm.

"But he didn't," the queen said, "because we warned him he had to support your head."

"Right, I get it," said Joe. "Because I was a baby."

"What are you doing here?" the queen asked.

"I wanted to..." Joe began.

"I was speaking to Val."

"The king wanted to see the view from the top of the castle," Val said. Her voice was just a touch softer than Joe had ever heard it before. "I was taking him to one of the northern towers."

"Well, you would know all the best spots," the queen mused. "Very well."

Angelo nodded to Val as she and Joe worked their way past the crowd of guards.

"Valentina," Angelo said.

"Prince Angelo," she replied.

Once he was sure they were out of earshot, Joe looked to Val.

"Wow. Are they always like that?" he asked.

"No," she assured him. "Sometimes things get tense."

Likewise, Angelo and the queen waited until the younger ones were away before continuing their conversation.

"Don't you worry how the people will react?" Angelo asked.

"Since when do you care about what people think?"

"Since it could destabilize the kingdom," he said. "The people might not stand for this."

"Don't presume to speak for the entire population."

"He is an outsider," Angelo said.

"He is my son."

"Who you haven't seen since his birth."

"Because of laws and tradition," she reminded him. "Not because he's illegitimate."

Angelo stepped towards her again.

"You know, according to that same law, with my brother dead, I should take you as my wife."

"If the bloodline needed to be continued," she said. "There is an heir, and my childbearing years are well behind me."

"I'd still be willing to give it a try."

"You may petition the courts if you like," she said.

He moved back, his body language loosening.

"My point I was trying to make is that, in all of history, no reserve monarch has ever taken the Crown," he said. "I don't know how the citizenry will respond. I was once my brother's Guardian. It was my job to maintain the peace. If needed, I can perform the same function for our new king."

"As always, it will be up to him to name his council," the queen said. "If you want to keep any sort of job here, perhaps you should start trying to earn his trust instead of plotting behind his back."

All Angelo could manage was a tense, flat mouth and a slight dip of his chin as he turned to leave.

"And, Angelo," the queen called after him.

He paused and looked back.

"Making untoward advances on someone's mother is seldom a good way to earn their favor."

He sneered and strode off.

"And it doesn't always sit well with the mother, either," she grumbled.

CHAPTER 4

True to Val's word, the third northern tower of the palace offered the best view in the capital. Standing just behind a knee-high restraining wall at the edge of an open-air balcony, Joe could see for miles. It was the first glimpse he was getting of the natural land. It wasn't just the people on Kaia. Were it not for the distinct cityscape before them, the hills and forests could have been mistaken for a remote spot of untouched countryside on Earth.

"Whoa. Cool." Joe inhaled a lungful of the crisp air. There was something different about even it. It wasn't just cleaner, but sweeter, too. "Everything the light touches is my kingdom."

"I was on Earth long enough to know you're quoting a children's movie." Val leaned against the archway separating the balcony from the interior hall.

"Oh, The Lion King's got layers." Joe gestured at the view, from the palace grounds to the cloud-shrouded mountains in the distance. He'd thought it was either sunset or sunrise when he'd arrived based on the sky's tint, but time had passed, the sun remained high above, and there was still a warm glow to the atmosphere. "Seriously, though. This doesn't impress you?"

Val shrugged.

"I suppose it did. Once."

"What does that mean?"

"What?" she asked. "I grew up in the castle. Believe me, I'm well aware of the lifestyle it's afforded me, but things like the view... I guess they just don't hold the same luster they used to."

Joe turned back to the edge.

"Well, damn. I hope I never get that jaded."

"I'm not jaded."

Joe cocked an eyebrow at her.

"Okay, maybe I'm a little jaded."

"Hey, you said you grew up in the castle?" he asked.

"Yeah."

"What do you do around here? Exactly? I mean, besides retrieving crown princes?"

"I don't usually do that. That was a special assignment. Mostly I've been a member of the palace guard. I went through the military training program. I was good enough to make it into the guard, which, believe me, is a big deal around here."

"Right, but, how did they pick you?"

"I earned my spot."

"No. I mean, yeah, I'm sure you did," he said, "but how'd you get picked for the palace in the first place?"

Joe looked down at the grounds.

"My palace," he mumbled to himself.

"It's a... kind of an outreach thing that the royal family does," Val said. "Every year they take in a bunch of young orphans, give them a better life."

"That doesn't answer how they're picked, though."

She shrugged again.

"Luck of the draw, I guess."

"Huh. So, it was just random luck, then?"

"The odds are still slightly better than the random luck of being born into the right family," she said.

"I guess, yeah."

Joe planted a heel on the stone and spun himself.

"So, as part of the palace guard, your job is to protect me, right?" he asked.

She stood upright and inched closer to him.

"Yes," she said, "why?"

He let his arms flail out and flexed a knee, tilting back ever so slightly.

"So, if I start to slip…" he teased.

Val's hand lashed out with cracking speed, gripping him by the collar.

"Don't." Whatever softness he'd thought he'd noticed in her voice was gone.

Nodding as much as he was able, he slapped at her tensed arm.

"Okay, okay. Please let me go. You're choking me." He glanced back over his shoulder. "And I'm actually a little afraid of heights."

She easily pulled him in, letting him stumble to the floor.

"Don't do that again," she said.

"Okay." Joe rubbed his throat. "You make a very convincing argument."

"Come on," she said before disappearing back into the palace.

With no one to offer a hand, Joe pulled himself up to his feet and followed.

"As king, eventually I'm going to get to decide something, yeah?"

Flanked by several servants, the queen reached the bottom of the tower stairs just in time to meet her son and his companion.

"There you are," the queen said. "Did you enjoy your little outing?"

Val gave Joe a dirty look.

"Uh-huh," he said.

"Good. Would you like to settle into your quarters?" his mother asked.

"Oh, yeah, sure."

The queen motioned to one of her attendants. Like all members of the retinue, she dressed in layers of shimmering crimson to match her queen.

"We'll get you settled in and cleaned up before we go any further with your duties," the queen said.

"If you can believe it, for his planet, he's considered clean," Val said.

The young woman took Joe's arm and led him off.

"Oh, hey," he said to her. "Hi. I'm Joe."

"Valentina," said the queen, once the pair was out of sight, "I would like for you to serve as Joe's Guardian."

"Really?"

"You sound surprised."

"That's probably because I am," Val said. "The Guardian is usually a high-ranking general."

"There's no rule that says it has to be," the queen said. "You're a level six operative. You're more than qualified. But I can ask the Ministry of Defense to promote you if the title is going to be a point of contention. Is that what you're angling for?"

"No. But... are you sure?"

"Are you questioning my judgment?" the regent asked.

"No, of course not." Val spoke quickly. "It's just that, with everything going on, activating the hidden heir, so much change, do we want to throw even more upheaval into the mix?"

"Do you feel Angelo should stay on as Guardian?"

"God, no."

"Exactly."

"I..." Val cut herself off.

"What is it?"

"Nothing," Val said. "I nearly spoke impertinently."

The queen chuckled. "Please do."

"I..." Val took a pause. "I honestly never got why your husband kept him around."

"Andor had his uses for Angelo," said the queen. "I don't."

"And you're sure about this?"

"Val," the queen said. "I'm asking you, as a mother, to take care of my son. There's only so much I can do for him. But his Guardian can be there for him, always. There's no one I'd trust more with this horrible privilege than you."

Val nodded slowly, her eyes not focusing anywhere in particular.

"I'll do what I can," she conceded. "Try to get him into shape."

"That's another thing," the queen added. "I don't want you to train him."

"What?" Val asked. "Why not? That's something I'm actually qualified for."

"Until he decides otherwise, you're his Guardian. His right hand."

"Please don't phrase it to him like that."

"Your job is to protect him."

"The best protection would be to make sure he knows how to handle the power he's being given," Val countered.

"You'll oversee his training. You don't need to get into a cage with him and brawl to make sure he's being properly instructed," the queen said. "At some point, you have to realize that the picture is bigger than that."

"Why?"

"Beg pardon?"

"I'm just a soldier," Val said. "My job is whatever the royal family puts in front of me. You all see the bigger picture. I paint whatever little part of it you tell me to."

"You're more than that," the queen assured her.

"More than just a commoner?"

"Yes," the queen said. "So much more. If nothing else, you're part of the royal court."

"Until the king realizes he has the power to replace me."

"Well." The queen nudged the younger woman with her hip. "I'm not in a hurry to tell him."

If she'd had a moment to herself, Val would have broken out in a smile. Perhaps even a grin. But they were quickly interrupted by one of the royal stewards.

"Pardon the interruption, your highness." The steward spoke softly, barely able to be heard over the constant din of castle life. "The king has requisitioned the use of a tank..."

"No."

"Very good." The scrawny man scurried away.

The door to the monarch's private chamber opened. The queen's attendant entered, followed by the new occupant.

"Holy crap."

"Is everything alright, your highness?" the attendant asked. She stared at him with widened eyes. Her hands lay flat across her lap. He couldn't be sure, but she might have been pouting her lips.

Joe slowly turned around the circular space. There were mirrors, cabinets, and water fixtures along the continuous wall, all stone or marble and inlaid with precious metals. The center of it all was consumed by what seemed to be one massive cushion, layered with sheets, blankets, and pillows. The posts and curtains that surrounded it were as opulent as anything else.

The lighting was somewhat dim. Was it always like this, he wondered? No, that couldn't be right. No one would intentionally leave their living space this dark, especially not the aging pair of royals who'd previously occupied the room. If he thought it was dark, they wouldn't have been able to see a thing.

"Alright?" Joe asked. "The bed is bigger than my room back home."

"I don't understand," the attendant said. "This is your home."

"Right, right. Everyone else seems to be having an easier

time getting on board with that than I am."

The young lady in the glistening gown sauntered towards him.

"Is there anything we can do to ease your transition?" she asked.

Her thick hair brushed against his face, leaving a hint of perfume behind.

"No. No." He winced. "I'm not that kind of guy. At least I never have been. God, I wish I was right now."

"Once again, my king, you have me at a loss for understanding."

"I'm not the kind of guy that meets a beautiful woman and can just, you know, do something about it. I never have been. I mean, I tried earlier today and look where it got me." He glanced at his surroundings again. "I might be defeating my own point, I think."

Her eyelashes fluttered. "The only point I got from all of that is that you think I'm beautiful."

Joe sighed. "Yeah. You are. And I know I'm a complete knob for not being able to take advantage of the situation."

"Perhaps in time, you will learn to be less of a 'knob.'"

With a smile, she was gone, leaving him alone in the cavernous room.

"Don't bet on it."

He plopped down on the oversized bed. It was squishier than he'd anticipated, sending him flailing for a moment as he sank in. It took him only a second to regain his bearings.

He'd give the bed another try later on, he decided. Springing back to his feet, he headed towards the rather sizeable wardrobe off to the room's side. Was it a side, he wondered? Does a circular room have sides or just one side? If he'd needed furniture brought in, where would he tell the movers to put it? He couldn't very well tell them "against the right wall" or anything like that. Would he need to micromanage that sort of thing?

The doors to the wardrobe were heavy, made from a

wood denser than anything he'd felt before. Upon opening it, he found an assortment of clothing and accessories hung in place.

His arm slowly went out, his fingers touching a velvety tunic. As he pinched the soft material, he wondered if this was his father's – his birth father's. Then he pulled it out and looked at it.

The garment was tailored to his size. And it seemed to be new. All the clothes in the wardrobe did. It was either an amazing coincidence, that his birth father as a middle-aged man had been the exact same body shape as a teenager and had just ordered an abundance of fresh attire, or a whole new set of clothing had been crafted in anticipation of his arrival.

And they'd somehow gotten hold of his dimensions already.

He flipped through the rack, glancing over every shirt and jacket that hung there. They were all rich in color – predominantly shades of red and black, with white and gold trimming – and displayed fine needlework.

His suspicions were supported by the realization that there was no sign of the queen's belongings. As the late king's wife, surely she'd have shared a room with him, but there wasn't a trace of her here. Not a stitch of clothing in the wardrobe or the dressers, no pictures or personal effects displayed anywhere.

One thing he did find, curiously, was his backpack, already tucked away at the base of the wardrobe. Thinking back, he wasn't actually sure when he'd lost track of it, but here it was.

He unzipped it to confirm that everything was exactly where he'd left it. His computer, notebooks and pens, the balled-up sweatshirt.

The laptop was removed and set on one of the shorter dressers. It was opened: the rest of the bag was tossed to the floor at the foot of the bed.

Joe stood before the screen, his fingers hovering over the

keys.

He clicked the email icon.

Dear mom...

He froze for a second.

and dad,

By now, you probably haven't even realized I'm gone since it's only...

He glanced down at the corner of the screen.

6:48 PM, local time. You probably figure I just stopped somewhere on my way home. I did not. I was taken into outer space to meet my birth mother because I am a space prince from space.

He tapped the backspace key.

I am a space king from space.

I am fully aware of how insanely stupid that sounds, and I'm sure you wouldn't believe it, but it doesn't matter, because you'll never get this message, as the castle where I am now living lacks adequate wifi. And standard American wall outlets. So, I guess even typing this out as a journal for myself isn't worth the effort, since it'll only last as long as the charge on my laptop holds out.

He slowly lowered the screen and set himself back down on the bed. His head hung low, his eyes barely open.

He kind of wished he knew where the light switches were.

CHAPTER 5

The space designated for the king's training was, predictably, large and round. A second level, used for observational purposes, ran around most of the outer edge.

Exercise equipment was pushed out to the walls, including racks of weaponry, of varying types. Markings and shapes, used for various training drills, dotted the floor.

Much like the throne room, there was a pedestal to house the Crown of the Five Point Star.

Val and the queen waited. Nearby stood a mountain of a man. His body was broad. Each arm was thicker than his head. Hairier, too. Oddly, there still seemed to be a lightness in his movements. Older than either of the two women, he wore his years of military service on his face and across his exposed arms. He dressed in a dark uniform that strained against his chest; it was similar to the one Val now wore, though hers had sleeves, and with a different color of trim along the body, cuffs, and collar. His was red, rather than white. Both wore tall leather boots and short gloves.

"And where is the king now?" he asked.

"Oh my God!" They heard Joe's voice echoing in the stone entranceway before he even appeared, looking back over his shoulder as he strode in. "There's a laser bidet!"

The queen cleared her throat.

Joe snapped to attention.

"As the king, as the bearer of the Crown, you're more than simply a figurehead, more than a statesman, more than someone who gets to tell others what to do and have his orders carried out without question," she told him.

"I still get to do that, though, right?"

"The king must also be a warrior," she continued. "He must be at the frontline when our armies go into battle. The person who wears the Crown does not lead from behind, they do not send others to fight in their stead, they do not seek safety while others are in danger. Do you understand?"

"You're not being real subtle about it," Joe said.

"How are your archery skills?" the queen asked.

"Ah... nonexistent?"

"Swordsmanship?"

"A guy in my math class once accused me of 'playing swords' in the bathroom with another dude, but... no."

"Then I'll leave you to your Guardian." The queen stepped back and walked away, her footfalls echoing with the same ring Joe's words had.

Joe looked to Val.

"So?"

Val looked at the unmoving Trainer.

"Maybe it would help if you became acclimated to the Crown's power?" Val suggested. "It might bolster your confidence."

Trainer shrugged.

"Who says I have a problem with my confidence?" Joe asked.

Val's eyes squeezed shut; her head shook.

"Yeah, okay," Joe said.

Val retrieved the Crown from its display case. She handed it to Joe.

"Put it on."

The king complied, allowing the armor to again envelop him.

"I am never going to get tired of this." He breathed in

awe.

"You wouldn't have thought I'd have gotten tired of the view from the tower, but, here we are," said Val. "Now, Trainer here will be responsible for your actual combat conditioning."

Joe waved to Trainer.

"Hey," he said. "I was wondering who you were. I'm Joe. Or Joseph, if you prefer."

"I know who you are, my king." His voice was as heavy and rough as his body was.

"Right, yeah, this is usually the part where you tell me who you are," Joe said with a nervous laugh.

"I'm the trainer, as your Guardian just said."

"Right, but like, what's your name?"

"I'm the trainer."

"That's not a name," Joe said.

"It's as much of one as I've ever needed. Sire."

"What kind of nonsense is that?" Joe asked.

"Much like Val, I was adopted by the palace and brought up to fulfill a role," Trainer said. "Being the trainer is what gives me purpose."

"Okay," Joe said. "Intense."

"Shall we begin?" Trainer asked.

"Yeah, sure, go for it."

Joe took a step back at raised his hands in front of him. A generic fighting stance, probably something he picked up from a film or television show.

"I was talking to your Guardian," Trainer said.

"What?" Joe asked.

"I'm in charge of your training," Val said. "And yes, Trainer, you may begin."

From a dead stop, Trainer launched at Joe with a flying knee. Joe punched back several times, but each of his swings was batted away. A boot between his retreating legs was enough to trip the king up. He was able to remain upright but was sent so far off balance that Trainer was able to clasp onto the horns of the Crown, swing him around, and toss him into a far column.

"Dude," Joe said. "Respect the Crown."

He pushed off the column and stumbled back towards Trainer. Reaching for his head, his fingers gently touched the tips of the Crown's spikes.

"Huh."

"What?" Val asked.

There weren't as many mirrors in the training room as in much of the rest of the castle, but there were still a few. Joe found one on the opposing wall; he took a good look at himself in full armor for the first time. His fingers continued to slide around the edges of the Crown.

Val reticently followed behind him.

"It's still there," Joe said.

"Of course it is," Val said. "Where would it have gone?"

"I didn't get a chance to look at it before," Joe said. He turned from his own reflection, though couldn't seem to stop poking at his own face. "Hey, uh... I can't see it."

"See what?" she asked.

"The Crown."

"What?" asked Val. "It's - it's over your eyes."

"Right. Like, I can feel it. I think."

She waved her hand in front of him.

"Can you see this?"

"Yeah," Joe said. "I just..."

"If the Crown remained opaque to your vision, you wouldn't be able to see at all, would you?" Val said.

"I guess not," Joe said. "But this is still weird."

"You'll get used to it."

"How would you know?"

"Because your father did, and his father before him, and his mother before him, and on and on down the line," Val said. "There's no record in any of the songs about the king or queen moaning about not being able to see."

"Wait, songs?"

"Yes. Operas and operas full of them," she said.

"Seriously?"

"Yes."

"Okay, but, if they did bitch about the Crown, is that really something they'd record into an opera?" Joe asked.

"The operas are pretty detailed."

"How detailed?"

"I can tell you what your great great great grandmother had for breakfast the morning of her coronation. And what color it turned her stools."

"Ugh."

"Yeah, so, maybe focus on your training a little bit," she suggested.

Joe headed back to his training.

"Hey, do you think they'll write operas about me?"

"They will," she said. "I'd suggest not giving them a reason to write the Ballad of King Joseph the Moaner."

"Hehe. Moaner."

"Okay, I walked into that one," Val admitted.

"How about you walk into the dining hall tonight?" Joe asked. "With me, I mean."

"If the king requires an aid to assist him with eating his dinner, I can arrange for someone to be with you," she said. "I'll make sure they know to cut your meat into tiny little bites so you don't choke."

"Come on. You know what I meant," said Joe. "Wouldn't it bolster my confidence if you said yes?"

Val sighed. Heavily.

"If my king would like his Guardian to dine with him, I suppose I can't deny that request."

"Cool."

Joe squared up to continue sparring.

He backed up, signaling to an impatient Trainer for one more moment with his guardian.

"Wait. How far does me being able to order you to do stuff go?"

"I wouldn't suggest trying to find the limit," she said. "I'll be watching. Trainer, put him through the paces."

Trainer smiled. It didn't seem to suit his face.

Joe's shoulders slumped. He groaned.

By the time Trainer began wailing on Joe again, Val had already moved herself to a perch on the upper deck.

A man approached from an adjoining hallway, wearing a common soldier's uniform. The fit wasn't customized, the fabric not as wrinkleless. The pants were baggier, with more pockets. Everything was in a dull, greenish-brown color. It was worn with a standard-issue garrison belt and a heavier jacket.

He glanced Val over.

"Nice uniform," he said.

"Thanks, Rik."

"Is it going well?" he asked.

"No," she laughed.

Were it not for the armor he wore, it would have been unlikely that anyone would have thought Joe the regal one out of the pair of him and Trainer. Even with the Crown's protection, Joe was still dwarfed by his instructor.

"The thing to remember is that when you wear the Crown, everything you touch becomes a weapon," Trainer told him.

"Is that, like, a metaphor?" Joe asked. "Like a Jason Bourne, 'I can beat you to death with a magazine' kind of thing?"

"I do not know this man, but if he can kill so easily, he must be a formidable warrior."

"You know, he really is."

"But, no, I mean it in a literal sense," said Trainer. "The Crown's armor doesn't just envelop you, it connects with whatever it is you hold. For example."

Trainer produced a knife from his belt, deftly cascading it between his fingers until the handle pointed out towards Joe.

The younger man took hold of it.

Growths from his armor wrapped around the knife's hilt. Raw energy moved in waves across the blade.

"Whoa," said Joe. "Neat."

"And that's just a small knife. We should begin your training in earnest. You're far behind where other monarchs would be at your age."

"Gee. Thanks."

Trainer plucked his knife back from Joe's grasp.

"Remove the Crown, please."

"Uh, why?" asked Joe. "Val just told me to put it on."

"We have to assess and grow your skills before accentuating them with the Crown's power."

"How would you know?"

"Beg pardon?" Trainer asked.

"I mean, you've never worn the Crown, have you?"

"I am not of the bloodline," Trainer said. "The Crown would not speak to me."

"Right. So, what makes you the expert?"

"Having knowledge of a thing does not require that one wield that thing," said Trainer. "My order has descended from the original mages who forged the Crown millennia ago. Though their magic has been lost to us, understanding of how to wield the artifacts they left behind remains strong. Now, please, remove the Crown."

"Alright." With great reluctance, Joe pushed the Crown up, retracting the armor, and lifted it off his head.

"Let's see how you handle a sword." Trainer flung a saber from a weapons rack towards his pupil.

Joe was just a fraction of a second too late, missing the handle and bringing his fingers together around the cold metal of the blade.

"GAH! Son of a bitch!"

"We'll start with a practice sword," Trainer said.

"Yeah." Joe held up his bandaged hand. "Good idea."

Trainer handed him a simple metal pole with a handguard on one end.

"Hey, though, quick question," said Joe. "Why do I need to know how to use a sword?"

"Because you wield the Crown," Trainer said. "You are King of Kaia and defender of the Empire."

"Right, but could I just use, I don't know, a gun? Or, don't you guys have, like, super space guns? Or something?"

"Alright," Trainer conceded. "Let's examine that."

Trainer drew a pistol from the rear of his belt and popped open the chamber, letting a bullet fly into the air. He snatched it and held it out for Joe to see.

"When firing a gun, this is what you are sending at your enemy," he said.

"You guys still use bullets? Not lasers?"

"There's a matter replicator in the magazine to keep the ammo full," Trainer said. "Laser weapons powerful enough to use in combat are comparatively inefficient."

"Could it make a pizza?" Joe asked.

"A what?"

"Food," Joe said. "Can it make food?"

"A gun? No, a gun cannot make food. It only makes bullets."

"What good's a matter replicator that only makes bullets?"

"There's no need..." Trainer paused and composed himself. "The more function you add to a device like this, the larger it would need to be. That its function is as simple as creating one type of small, simple object is why it can fit within the handle of a gun. But, please, focus." He shoved the bullet towards Joe. "This is your weapon. This is what you hit your enemy with. The Crown will charge this with energy, the same way it did the blade."

"Right right. So..."

Trainer's speaking quickened slightly.

"The Crown charges the same way, regardless of what the item is. A cubic inch of bullet holds the same amount of charge as a cubic inch of sword blade. The Crown's energy is much more powerful than the force of any bullet. If you need a ranged weapon, I'd suggest you brush up your archery skills. An arrow packs far more matter than a bullet."

With that tangent of the lesson over, Trainer returned the sidearm to its holster and hoisted his own practice sword.

"Now, come at me," he beckoned, "and let's assess your skills."

Joe again took a fighting stance he'd likely seen in a movie, holding his sword out just a bit too far in front of him, swinging just a bit too widely. At this stage, Trainer was content to let it pass without comment and just deflect the blow.

An echoing clang was produced as the two metal poles connected.

Joe dropped his practice weapon, yelping as he tucked his wounded hand beneath his other arm.

"Oh, right, be careful," Trainer said. "The training swords don't have grip cushions."

"Why would they not have grip cushions?"

"Well, we don't use them that often. When we do, we tend to wear gloves." He held his own hands up as an example.

"Then why am I not wearing gloves?"

Trainer shrugged.

Around supper time, Val donned her dress uniform and headed to the royal dining hall. Since her promotion to the position of Guardian, her new uniform was more formal anyway; the dress uniform was even more ceremonial than that, with layers of shirts, vests, and a longer coat.

Like most rooms in the castle, the king's dining hall

seemed needlessly grand, both in size and décor.

When she arrived, she saw that Joe was already seated at the end of the table, platters of food and pitchers of drink laid out before him. She knew she wasn't late. Had he intentionally arrived early? Moaned until Trainer cut the practice session short?

Joe worked at his dinner the best he could, cradling his knife in his injured hand.

The castle physician had put it into some kind of boxy machine filled with flashing lights to knit the flesh and muscle back together but warned that it would still be tender and stiff for a while. She was right.

Val took a seat next to him and promptly had a full place setting before her. The servers were nothing if not efficient in ensuring that she had a loaded plate and full cup within seconds.

"Thank you," she said.

The servants smiled and nodded before making themselves scarce.

"Oh, uh, yeah, thanks," Joe said.

"Are you enjoying your dinner?" Val asked.

"Yeah, it's good." He poked his plate with his fork. "I'm actually not sure what it is."

"It's a tri-meat platter," She laid her napkin in her lap. "Garuso, ventan, and suupar. I hear the suupar is fresh from the Kettle Mountains this afternoon."

"Cool, cool. I've never heard any of those words before."

"It's a flightless bird and two kinds of larger livestock," she said.

"Cool cool."

"How are you adjusting to all this?"

God. Smalltalk.

"Honestly?" Joe asked. "I'm not."

"What do you mean?"

"I'm on another planet," he said. "I'm, like, a king."

"You're not like a king, you are the king."

"Yeah. Of another planet," he said. "And I have a super-powered hat, and all my family and friends are back in another galaxy. I am not processing that at all."

"You can send for them if you like."

"Really?"

"You're the king," she said. "You can have anyone you want brought here. Almost anyone. If they're a citizen of a sovereign star empire, that could get messy. Still not impossible, though."

"Huh." He tapped his fork against his plate several times, before realizing it was probably considered rude.

"It's not like we're planning on keeping you a secret. We obviously know Earth's location. Bring friends, family, whoever. As your Guardian, my job is to see to your needs and comfort. And before you say anything, don't."

"Okay."

"Now, if you wanted to annex Earth, then you'd need permission from the war council."

"What?"

"Not really permission, I guess, more just that you'd need to coordinate with them," she said. "Occupying a planet takes a lot of resources, at least initially."

"I'm not occupying Earth."

"Totally up to you."

"Jeez."

"But if you wanted to add the planet where you were raised to the empire, I don't think anyone would bat an eye," she said. "It's not like Earth could mount much of a defense."

"No," he said. "I don't think anybody on Earth is really ready to find out aliens exist, much less be added to a star empire."

"As you wish. The soup's good."

More training was scheduled after dinner. As Joe made

his way to the room where Trainer awaited, Val took her place above.

She kept her focus on Trainer's brutalizing of the new king, even as the queen mother entered the balcony.

"Valentina. Walk with me," the queen said.

The pair of them began slowly pacing the gallery, occasionally glancing down at Joe's progress.

"What do you think of my son?" the queen asked.

"I think - it's not really my place to say."

"We've talked about this."

"Yes, we have," Val said. "And it still makes me uncomfortable."

"I'm not currently concerned for your comfort level. Tell me what you think. And speak plainly."

"Do I know any other way?"

"And what's that supposed to mean?" the queen asked.

"It means – it's exactly why I'm uncomfortable with this," Val said. "I'm from a common background."

"You received a fine education."

"But not a royal one."

"And what do you think the royals learn in their schools that you didn't in yours?" the queen asked.

"I've always presumed it was mostly about what the different types of towels are for."

"Well, imagine for the moment that he's not a king," the queen said. "Or, if it helps, imagine that you're a princess."

"Why not a queen?"

"For one thing, I'd have to be dead for that scenario to play out," the mum said. "I'd rather like to avoid dwelling on that right now."

"I'm sorry. You're right."

"Yes, I find I usually am. And you're stalling."

"Well, I've never seen a king go through training as an adult before," Val said. "Most kings and queens start from childhood so that by the time they're young adults, they're already adept."

"You recall when my oldest son began his training?" the queen asked. "The first time my husband let him wear the Crown."

Val nodded solemnly. Prince Thoome had been kind to her. And he was the queen's firstborn. She hadn't allowed herself to dwell on his fate much. Throwing herself into her duties had helped. But now...

"Yes," Val said.

"Is Joseph more or less adept than Thoome was in the beginning?"

"My queen, Prince Thoome was six at the time," Val answered.

"Yes. And?"

"I suppose I would have to say that Joe is better now than Thoome was at age six, yes," Val said.

Below them, Joe stumbled and knocked into a rack of weapons, sending blades and staffs clattering to the hard floor.

"Grudgingly," Val added.

"My bad!" Joe raised his hand as he hollered up to them.

"Well, then we're on the right path, aren't we?" the queen asked.

Due to time constraints, Val had neglected to change out of her formal uniform before returning to her duty overseeing Joe's training. Once Trainer had given her the signal that they were wrapping up, she'd made her way to the nearest dressing room.

She sat on a bench, fastening up her second boot when the door opened.

"Oh, sorry," Joe said. "I thought – Trainer said, I mean – I thought this was the boy's locker room."

"And you're a boy?" Val asked.

"A men's... men's locker room. Trainer said. For where the manly... men... Sorry to have bothered you."

Joe turned back towards the exit.

"It's not designated for either," Val said.

"Either what?"

"Sex."

Joe's lips clamped shut, desperately trying to hold back the spasming chortle building in his throat.

"Don't even say it."

"What?" Joe asked.

"Whatever you were going to say."

"Me?" Joe placed the fingertips of one hand against his chest as his neck tilted back. "If you thought I was about to make some sort of innuendo, then you wound me, madam."

"I could," Val said. "You don't have the Crown on right now, but, apparently there are rules against assaulting the monarch."

"Yeah, wow, who'd have thought?"

"Whatever." Val huffed. "Anyway, it's a private dressing room. Usually reserved for royals, so, if anything, I'm the one that doesn't belong here."

She rose from her seat.

"I mean, you don't have to go," Joe said.

"I'm not going to stay and watch you change."

"Oh, no, I really don't want you to," said Joe.

"Really?"

"If you ever do see me, you know, undressed, I'm hoping it's after these workouts really start kicking in."

"So you haven't taken care of yourself before now?" she asked.

"I guess not, no."

"Why not?"

"Probably because I suck," Joe said.

"Well, I can't help you there," Val said. "You're just going to have to, you know, try sucking less."

"Oh, okay, thanks. Because I totally wouldn't have already done that if I knew how."

"What did we say earlier about confidence?" she asked.

"I think we agreed I don't have any."

"Well, work on that, too."

"Thanks," said Joe.

"Women like a guy with confidence."

"Great."

"And people like a leader with it, too," she added.

"I think most leaders tend to have more arrogance than confidence," said Joe.

"On Earth, maybe. Things are a lot different here on Kaia," she said. "Besides, arrogance is just confidence that you can't actually back up."

"It's just, I don't know anything about ruling a planet." His arms swung out. "I probably won't be very good at it."

"The Crown will give you the wisdom it takes to rule."

"Will it?"

"In the millennia since its creation, it's never failed to."

"Well. That's good to hear," he said.

"Granted, I don't know if it's ever had to work so hard before."

"Why do you keep doing that?" Joe asked.

"Doing what?"

"Ragging on me like that. We already agreed I have confidence issues."

"Because, if I'm being honest, I'm worried, too, about what's going to happen," she said. "In all of Kaian history, a reserve heir has never been called up."

"Well that sucks for all of them."

"What do you mean?" she asked.

"Well, like, that means there're just all these royal babies sent off to Earth..."

"It's not just Earth," she said. "It would be really poor strategy to hide all reserve monarchs in one place."

"Well, whatever," he said. "I mean, those are your people. Were your people."

"Our people."

"Right, yeah. And you all just send them off to live out

their whole lives in some other place, without ever knowing who they even are?"

"You were supposed to know," she said. "You were supposed to live a life of comfort and spend your upbringing being steeped in our culture."

"Well, I wasn't."

He turned away from her and reached for a towel from a nearby shelf.

He turned back to her. "Wait, why wasn't I?"

"As far as my research could tell me, your royal guardians, who should have been responsible for all of that, were killed when you were young," Val said.

"My parents? I mean, my birth parents? I guess they're not my birth parents," he said. "But, yeah, I was adopted. So, the people I thought were my birth parents were actually... who?"

"Members of the royal court. Advisors meant to train you for a day they thought would never come. A day we all hoped would never come. Which is pretty much today."

"Hey, I didn't ask for any of this," he said.

"The Crown should grant you the wisdom to know not to care quite so much what every commoner thinks."

"And, is that what you are?" he asked. "Is that how you think of yourself? You're just a commoner?"

"There are a lot of politics involved in ruling a star empire. You can't concern yourself with what everyone thinks of you. People will disagree with you. People will think you're wrong."

"Right, but can't I just have those people beheaded?" he asked.

"Beheading your enemies doesn't tend to make a monarch very popular."

Her eyes only flicked to him as she left the room.

◆ ◆ ◆

Val shut the door behind her on her way out. Turning, she found herself face-to-face with her charge's uncle.

A quick gasp escaped her lips before she was able to catch herself.

"We need to talk." Angelo's eyes were as cold as she'd ever seen. The dim lighting in the hallway didn't help, nor did his pressing so close to her.

"Not here," she said. "Not now."

She pushed past him and walked off, not even sure if she was going to right way.

Joe opened the email program on his laptop again.

He'd never learned the so-called proper manner of typing. He couldn't have listed what the home keys were if his life depended on it. He'd had more than one teacher in school try to drill it into him, but it never took. Somehow he was still a proficient typist, easily able to pass any speed test he'd needed to for class or work. He just never did it the "right" way. A classmate had once remarked that he'd turned two-finger typing into an art form.

That was a little difficult now. His left hand was fine, but with his right, it took much more effort to not mash the keyboard with his bundle of fingers. He could barely jab at a key every few seconds, and the gap in dexterity between his two hands only served to frustrate him more.

Dear mom and dad,

I don't even know how far away from Earth I am. Once you hit a certain distance does it even matter?

You're probably wondering where I am by now.

I spent a lot of today with a guy who doesn't have a real name. He likes to hit me.

And there's this girl.

He deleted that last line. He glared at the screen.

And there's this girl.

I don't even know what it is about her. I feel like I connect with her better than anyone here. Maybe that's just because I met her first. Or because she learned about Earth culture. For three weeks. She learned an entire language in three weeks. She's crazy smart. I guess...

He groaned to himself.

I guess technically I'm her boss? I don't know. I'm the boss of the whole planet if I want to be. But she doesn't make me feel like I'm in charge.

I don't even know what I mean by that. And it doesn't matter, because you'll never read this. My battery's already at less than fifty percent. I wonder if I'll have any of this figured out at all by the time it dies. Probably not.

He took a breath.

I don't even know if she likes me. Not even likes me likes me, but I mean at all. Sometimes I think she does, but then she'll say something and I'm just like, I just need someone to help me get through all this. Really.

I'm sure I come off sounding nuts. Probably better that you'll never read this. Or her. Hell, if I reread this a little while from now, maybe even I'll cringe at myself.

I'm already cringing at myself.

I suppose I should get some sleep now. I have to be up bright and early to get hit some more.

CHAPTER 6

Training continued shortly after the next sunup and was scheduled to last throughout the day.

By mid-morning, Trainer had finally begun to sweat, while his king hunched in front of him: red-faced, dripping, and gasping for air.

"So, it's time for lunch, right?" Joe asked. "Lunchtime? Now?"

"Lunch isn't for over an hour, and we still have a lot of work to do," Trainer said.

"Right, yeah," Joe said, "because I suck at this."

"You don't 'suck' at this, but you are a novice."

"But, protein, right?" Joe asked. "Protein is good for working out."

"I don't know how much it would help right now."

"Aw, come on, man. We can break for lunch," Joe pleaded. "I didn't even bring up second breakfast, 'cause I know nobody here would get the reference."

"Technically, you are the king. If you decree a meal break, then you'll get a meal break."

Joe managed to rise to a full standing position, holding his hips.

"Do I need to make an official decree?" he said, still huffing for breath. "Like in writing? Do I have to get in front of a big crowd and announce that I'm having lunch?"

"I don't think that's necessary. Though you may want to

check with your mother on matters of protocol."

"I was kind of joking," Joe said.

"So was I."

Joe pointed back and forth between himself and the larger man. "We don't seem to be communicating well."

"You are aware of course, that the Crown strengthens your endurance," Trainer said.

"So I've been told."

"And you laughed when the queen said it?" Trainer asked.

"Yes."

"The Crown doesn't just boost your endurance," Trainer said. "It can replenish you as well."

Joe scooped the Crown off the pedestal and gave it a look. He held it before his face.

"I will keep that in mind."

Trainer's brow and mouth both flattened.

"If you would actually listen for a moment. Not hear, but listen..."

The rest of the sentence was lost in the deafening roar of the fiery explosion that tore through the room.

The entire space seemed to be ablaze. After several tense moments, the only shape that could be made out was that of an armored body staggering in the dense flames.

BOOK 2: SEE ME
AFTER CLASS
(PART 2)

CHAPTER 1

The Council Chamber room was identical in appearance to the dining hall. They were probably designed by the same person for the same reason: hosting large groups of people in a formal setting.

Angelo, the queen, and a pair of robed viziers sat waiting, each surrounded by a small group of attendants. The head of the table was left open for the king, always.

Joe entered the room, flanked by Val and a contingent of armed guards. Each member of the guard carried a firearm at the ready and wore extra body armor. The reinforced vests and limb guards were colored black, with red trim helping them blend into their uniforms.

There was something different about Joe. Not just that, for the first time since arriving on Kaia, he was seen wearing something besides the clothes he'd brought from Earth or sweaty workout attire. A red, sleeveless tunic, the gold-embossed hood pulled back, sat atop a white shirt and trousers. An embroidered recreation of the family's crest, a stylized rendition of the Crown of the Five Point Star in a series of rings, was stitched to the right breast. Black boots and a wide matching belt completed the ensemble.

But it wasn't just the clothes. No, he carried himself with a greater sense of seriousness, a greater maturity. The feeling spread to his entourage.

Without a word, he crossed the room and took his place

at the table's head. Val seated herself to his right. The guards remained standing and ready.

"So, someone tried to kill me," Joe said. "I'm not a huge fan of that."

"Do we have any clues as to who planted the explosives?" asked the first of the crimson-cloaked viziers.

"No," said Val. "Not yet. The training area is deep within the castle, so…"

"Trainer." The second vizier piped up. "It must have been him."

"Why on Kaia would you think that?" the queen asked.

"He had access to the training room. Who else did?" the second vizier reasoned. "We all know how meticulous he is. How would he not have noticed anything out of the ordinary?"

"Trainer is the one who insisted King Joseph take his training today without the protection of the Crown," the first vizier said.

"That hardly proves anything," the queen said. "My husband and elder son were instructed the same way."

"Trainer was caught in the explosion and is barely holding on right now," said Joe.

"It's not beyond radicals to sacrifice themselves for what they believe in," said the second vizier.

"Yeah," Joe said. "I guess that's true even on my world."

"This is your world," Val said. "You really have to accept that."

"Well, whatever." Joe brushed her off.

"Trainer has loyally served the royal family for decades," the queen said. "He tutored my late husband and my eldest son."

"Both of whom grew up under his tutelage," Angelo said. "King Joseph is an outsider. I warned you there would be people unhappy with someone ignorant to our ways taking the Crown."

"Trainer knew better than most how the royal successors were handled," the queen said, a sharp snap entering her voice. "I refuse to believe he would lose his mind over activating the established contingencies."

"Who of us ever know what someone is truly capable of?" Angelo asked.

"Perhaps we should ask the king's Guardian?" the first vizier suggested.

Val sat upright.

"Well," Angelo began, "as I said..."

Val interjected. "They were talking to me."

"Oh. Of course," said Angelo. "Old habits, as it were. It may take me a while to acclimate to my new role."

"And what role is that?" the queen asked.

"Beg pardon?"

"What role is it you think you have in Joseph's government?" the queen asked. "You're no longer Guardian."

"I am available to my king to serve in any way I'm needed."

"So is every citizen of Kaia and its colonies," she said. "Yet they don't find themselves with a seat at this table, nor attempt to put their voice into official matters."

Joe leaned towards Val. "Is this getting awkward to anyone else?" he asked her.

"Super awkward," she replied.

Joe straightened himself back up.

"Am I dismissed, then?" Angelo asked his nephew.

The queen looked to Joe.

"Oh. I have to decide?" Joe asked.

"This is your council," the first vizier said. "The choice of who sits on it is entirely yours."

"Well, I don't really know you..." Joe said to Angelo.

"Know that I faithfully served as your father's Guardian for more than twenty years."

"Hey, don't interrupt," Joe said. Angelo's head snapped back. "Now, I was saying, I don't know you. You're my family, so I'm hoping you're not a complete crapbag. My mom seems to think you are."

"I don't know what that term means," Angelo said. He nevertheless shot a quiet glare in the queen's direction.

"It's not a good thing," Joe said. "But I don't know. So, here's what I'm going to do. I'm going to assume you're an okay guy until you prove otherwise."

"A prudent decision, my king." Angelo nodded approvingly.

"Cool," said Joe. "So, we good?"

"Yes," Angelo assured him, "we're good."

"We'll have to see," said the queen.

"Good." Joe turned his attention back towards the larger group. "Okay, where were we before someone got us sidetracked?"

He pointed around the table. No one spoke.

His finger landed on Val.

"Val, right?" he said. "You're my Guardian, or whatever, so they were asking what you thought."

"Right." She drew herself up again. "Well, the burn patterns are consistent with a trinot-based explosion. That's a military-grade incendiary…"

"It also has industrial uses," Angelo said.

"Excuse me?" Val asked.

"Angelo…" The queen's voice was a low grunt.

"Trinot is also used as an industrial herbicide," Angelo explained. "It's not just for military purposes."

"But it's illegal for use as an herbicide on Kaia, and should probably be banned throughout the empire," Val stated.

"Alright, fine, that's not the point," said Angelo. "I was just saying, as a military man for decades, it's important that we not just cast aspersions."

"You just can't help yourself, can you?" asked the queen.

"Like I said, trinot is illegal on Kaia," said Val. "No one could get it onto the planet without customs knowing."

"Right. Just like no one could get it into the castle?" Angelo asked. "Into the king's private training room, no less? Don't throw customs under the rails…"

"I'm not…"

"…when your own security force has done no better."

"My security force?" Val balked. "I've been the king's Guardian for less than two days. The force I have now is the one I inherited from the last Guardian. Maybe I should give some serious thought to personnel changes if the quality of security is going to reflect on me."

"Or maybe you should stop looking to pass blame…" Angelo was nearly growling at her.

The group was brought to a stunned, silent order by the bang Joe's palm made against the slick wooden tabletop.

"Okay, you know what, no," he barked, pointing around the table. "None of this, this, is helpful."

"He started it," Val murmured.

"Yeah, he did," said Joe. He jabbed his finger in his uncle's direction. "I said you could stay until you proved you weren't a good guy. You are dangerously close to making that happen."

"My apologies, my king," Angelo said sincerely. "It won't happen again."

"I'm not the only one you need to apologize to," said Joe.

Angelo's head tilted, his eyes squinting.

Joe pointed to his right.

"Her?" Angelo was truly startled. "You want me to apologize to her?"

"You don't have to," Joe said. "But it's what a good guy would do."

Angelo's tensed knuckles vibrated against the table for a moment.

"Apologies, Guardian." He didn't even look in her direction as he shot the words from his lips.

Val glared at him.

"Okay, now that we've got that cleared up. Angelo, you need to talk to security," Joe said.

"Me?" Angelo asked.

"Him?" Val echoed.

"Yeah," Joe said. "Make sure they understand that you're

not their boss anymore. Val's in charge of all that now."

Angelo took a pause before nodding his compliance. "Understood."

"And Val," said Joe, "Your job is to make sure they understand you're in charge now."

"I don't even know what that would mean," she said.

"Then maybe you shouldn't have this job," said Angelo.

"Hush," the queen said.

"And what exactly is your official position, now?" Angelo asked her.

Her eyes locked onto his.

"I'm the queen."

CHAPTER 2

Angelo waited alone in the dim, secluded hallway outside the council room, barely able to stand in one place. As he tried to stop himself from shuffling, stop himself from shaking, he was approached by the second vizier.

"Is everything alright, my prince?" the vizier asked.

"Who does that boy think he is?" Angelo said with a voice that could curdle the stone of the walls around them.

"I believe he thinks he's the king."

"My brother was the king. He knew well enough to heed my counsel."

"With all due respect, sire, your brother knew you," the vizier said. "Joseph does not."

"And that's my fault?"

"No," the shorter, balding man said. "But I believe we all need time to adjust. Had the order of succession gone as usual your eldest nephew would be on the throne, and he'd know you. As stressful as it is to see what is, for all intents and purposes, a stranger wear the Crown, please remember that it's even stranger for him. In less than two days he's left what he thought of as his homeworld, had royal duties thrust upon him, and had an attempt made on his life. I believe he finds comfort in having Valentina by his side."

Angelo sneered at the mention of her name.

"And I believe he finds your level of familiarity to be unsettling," the vizier added.

"My familiarity?"

"As I said, he doesn't know you," the vizier said. "Yet you presume to have his ear, because you had your brother's, and would have had your nephew's. Your other nephew's, I mean to say. Show Joseph he can trust you the way they would have. I've watched you handle royal duties for years. He'll come 'round."

"My sister-in-law said much the same thing," Angelo conceded. "But time is something that we don't have in abundance. Our former king was killed, and his rightful heir. The empire is under attack. The Crown needs to be at full strength. There's no way that can happen with it in the hands of a novice."

"I share your concern. More than perhaps you realize. But, the order of succession is clear. The law is clear. Joseph is the heir to the throne, and to the Crown. There's nothing in the universe that can change that law." The vizier bowed and backed away. "By your leave, my prince."

Angelo dismissed him with a wave of his hand. He was left alone in the darkness to contemplate.

Joe wasn't sure how long he'd been sitting on his bed - damn that thing was huge - staring into nothing at all, really.

Really, nothing. If pressed, he couldn't even say for sure if his gaze had been on the wall or the ceiling. He might not have even been able to give the color of either.

A knock came on the door. It opened just a bit and Val's head slunk in. "Hey. Can I come in?"

"Yeah, sure." Joe sat upright. "Come on."

She stepped in and shut the door behind her.

"Hey." Joe perked up. "Finally got you into my room, huh?"

"Joe..."

"Kidding, kidding." He raised his hands apologetically. "Unless, you know, you're not?"

She glared at him.

"Right, right," he said. "So, what can I do for you?"

"I had wanted to tell you that you handled yourself well out there," she said.

"Oh really?"

"But I'm reconsidering that now."

"Aw."

"I also wanted to thank you for supporting me."

"Ah, no problem." He stood and walked off the side of the bed. "That Angelo seems like kind of a douche."

"A what?"

"A... it's like a feminine hygiene... thing," he said. "Do you have those here?"

"Feminine hygiene products?"

"Yeah."

"Yes, we have those here."

"Oh. Cool," he said.

"So, 'douche,'" she said. "It's not a compliment?"

"Very no," he said, before adding, "Seriously? You never came across that word when you were on Earth?"

"But why did you put up with him?" She folded her arms. "Why make a deal with him?"

"I don't know." He shrugged. "Strategy?"

"And what's your strategy here?"

"Well, he said he's been in charge around here for like twenty years, right?" asked Joe.

"You say 'like' an awful lot."

"Habit," he said. "We do it a lot on my planet. Or, they do it a lot on... you know what, never mind. Okay, so, I had this one job for a few years. It kind of sucked, but every job sucks. Except being king. Anyway, after a couple years, the store manager got fired and a new guy came in. Like, half the store walked out."

"If their loyalty to the manager was more important than their loyalty to the store, then that was probably for the best," she said.

Joe winced. "No one should be loyal to a store. Okay, so, the analogy isn't perfect."

"Why would the new manager have wanted to keep them on, anyway?" she asked. "Wouldn't they be resentful?"

"Because a lot of them were good workers," he said. "They'd been there a while, they knew their jobs, they knew the customers, they showed up on time and almost never called in sick. Plus, since they lost like... since they lost half the staff all at once, the store was shorthanded for weeks. The people who stayed were miserable, it was a pain in the ass to train new people with how slammed we were, customers were pissed off. We probably lost a lot of business."

"Why did you stay?"

"Well, I honestly started looking for a new job pretty soon after that. But the job market sucked and I needed money, so... anyway, that's not the point," said Joe. "If I just out-and-out fire Angelo, isn't that going to piss off a lot of the security people?"

"Most likely, yes," Val said. "I would like to think they're more loyal to the Crown than they are to their supervisor, but, you might be right."

"Maybe that Crown thing is actually working on my brain like my mom said."

"Maybe," Val said. "Trainer said it's usually a slow process. It takes a while for the Crown to make you smarter."

"So, you're saying I'm this smart on my own?" he asked with a smile.

"Let's not get carried away."

"How is he?" Joe asked.

"Trainer?"

"Yeah."

"I haven't heard any updates," she said. "Which is actually probably good. If someone dies in the castle infirmary the Guardian would be one of the first people to know."

"He seems like a good dude," Joe said. "Kind of uptight, but good."

"He is," she said. "I hope you get a real chance to see that."

"Yeah. Me too."

Val smiled and nodded.

"But, you know, I had this neighbor back on Earth whose kid was in the army," said Joe. "The dude was like a friggin' real-life superhero, but he got really messed up by an IED and he was just never the same."

"Okay, that wasn't reassuring."

"I mean, he lived and everything, but he had all kinds of health issues." Joe's face scrunched up at the recollection.

"Joe."

"He needed one of those robot wheelchairs with the off-road tires."

"Please, stop," she implored. "You had a good closer there, and you kind of blew past it."

"Yeah, maybe I need to let that Crown do a little more work on my head."

"Probably," she said. "I'm gonna go now."

"Yeah, okay."

Val turned towards the door.

"Val, wait."

"What?"

He summoned his courage and stepped towards her.

"I really do value you." His voice shook just a tiny bit. "Your opinion. Your friendship. And... I like you."

"I know."

"I mean, not just like that," he said. "But you're the closest thing I've got to a friend, and, I need to get used to the idea of this being my life now. Do you think... I mean..."

"I think... now's not the time," she replied softly.

He closed his eyes and nodded. Swallowing had suddenly become difficult.

"Okay."

Val reached up and gently held the back of his head.

She kissed him on the cheek. If asked, she might not have been able to explain why. Even a display of affection as simple as that was not something she was in the habit of.

As she pulled away, their lips lightly grazed against one another. Barely touching, and yet enough to elicit a breathy grunt from Joe. Val's eyes flittered away from his. She had enough self-control that no sound escaped her lips.

"Goddamn," he exhaled.

"I have to go."

And she was gone.

CHAPTER 3

Val retreated to her own chambers. Still reachable if the king needed her - it was the Guardian's job to be at the ready around the clock - but she required solitude at that moment.

Upon entering her room, her spirits sank.

"What the hell do you think you're doing here?" She spat the words like a curse.

"Here?" Angelo stepped towards her, away from the shadows cast by the bed's canopy. "In my chambers?"

"You know damn good and well this is my room now," she said. "It belongs to the king's Guardian."

"And the queen was in quite a rush to get me out of it, and out of the castle, wasn't she?" He began pacing around her.

"Take that up with her." She didn't budge. Didn't flinch. "And get out of here. Now."

"Maybe I just wanted to talk to you for a bit."

"I definitely don't want to talk to you," she said.

"Your old boss is barely out the door and you can't wait to tell him how you really felt, can you?"

"I'm trying very hard not to right now." Her voice had become breathy.

"I just wanted to see if you still remembered where your true loyalties lie."

"Where they always have."

"So, I have your support," he said matter-of-factly.

"No," she said. "And you never did. I worked with you…"

"For me."

"…because it was my duty. The duty the queen assigned me. Now she, and the king, want me to be the Guardian. If I never see you again, my life will be better for it."

He took a step towards her. Still she was unfazed.

"You know, it could be my room again." His voice had gone disturbingly quiet and calm for such a brash individual. "The Guardian may share their quarters with whoever they like."

That got her to recoil.

"Out," she demanded. "Now."

Angelo moved closer still.

"Make me," he said.

Without another word, her fist came at him. His palm deflected her hand, but her elbow caught him across the jaw. A spin in place allowed him to bring the back of his forearm across her face, and her momentary stumbling gave him an opening to get behind her and bring his arms around her throat, cutting off her airway.

"Don't forget who it was who taught you everything you know," he said. His speech became halted as he was forced to put effort, more effort than he would have liked or anticipated, into holding her still.

"I haven't," she managed to choke out. "He's in the palace infirmary right now. And if I find out you had anything to do with it…"

His head jolted back as he released her.

"You think I had something to do with what happened to Trainer?" His jaw hung slack. "He was like a… well, not like a father. More like a very angry uncle. I love that man, probably far more than you do."

"I wouldn't put anything past you." She rubbed her throat.

"Then you don't really know me at all," he said.

"I wish that were true."

He made for the door. Passing her, he leaned in to whisper, "I'm sure there are still a great many things I can teach you."

And finally, he complied with her first request and left her alone.

After the door shut, silently, Val let out a deep growl. Her hands flew up the front of her jacket, undoing the buttons from the collar down. Once a few had been unfastened, she shrugged the garment loose and slung it onto the bed. Her fingers reached out and found the lever next to the sink. She threw it on, cold, at full blast, and dunked her head under.

After a few numbing moments, she pulled herself upright, splattering water across the countertop, the stone floor, and down her own spine. The strands of hair that stuck to her forehead were swept back.

Alone - unseen, unheard – she leaned against the counter, desperately gasped for air.

It took Val some time after that to get her head together. But, she knew, she was the king's Guardian, and she had duties to perform, expectations upon her head.

And so, once dried, groomed, and changed, she ventured back out into the castle. Even if new information about the attempt on the king's life couldn't be found just yet, she could still make her presence known.

"What've you found?" she asked Rik, barely within earshot as she approached. That gap was quickly closed.

"Nothing you're going to like," he said.

"How about you don't tell me what I will and won't like and just give me the report," she said. "Operative."

"Yes, ma'am."

As it happened, Joe had also felt the need to make himself known around the castle. Show he wasn't afraid, perhaps? And he also just so happened to reach the same stretch of corridor as Val, just moments after. He poked his head around a corner just in time to see her finishing her conversation with another man, one he didn't recognize. One who seemed awfully familiar with his Guardian.

"You're right," Val said. "I don't like that."

"I told you," said Rik. He stiffened up, standing at proper attention. "Am I dismissed?"

"Yes," Val said. "Go away."

"Aye aye, Guardian."

He made a sharp about-face and marched off.

"What was that all about?" Joe finally approached her.

"The ministers of law enforcement have been collecting forensic evidence from the training room," she said. "We were going over what they've found."

"And how's that going?"

"Not well. Trinot's a pretty powerful incendiary. It burns very thoroughly, so there's no evidence left of the actual bomb itself."

"That sucks."

"Yeah, it does."

"It also sends off what are called 'poppers,' where pieces of the incendiary are randomly shot out at the moment of denotation. In a contained area like the training room, it's meant to obscure the point of origin of the original blast," Val said. "However, based on the very fact that Trainer survived, we have to believe you were between him and the bomb. That narrows the point of origin a bit."

"Don't you guys have security cameras and stuff, though?" Joe asked. "We even have those on Earth. I'd have to figure you guys have, I don't know, hologram video cameras?"

"Not inside the palace," she said.

"Seriously?"

"No," she said. "I mean no, they don't have them. Yes, seriously."

"Wouldn't the place where the royal family lives be the place you'd want to be most secure?" he asked.

"And the perimeter is," she said. "But the royals like their freedom and they like their privacy. That's how they're able to do all that stuff, like having kids in secret and sending them off to other planets."

"I guess that makes sense, yeah," he said.

"Yeah, it wouldn't really work if there was a recording of it."

"Jeez. I wonder how many more of me there are out there right now," Joe said. "How would we even know?"

"What do you mean?" asked Val.

"Are there any more hidden princes?" he asked. "Or princesses, I guess? Could be either-or."

"The queen assures me there aren't."

"Does she always tell you everything?" he asked.

She didn't immediately respond.

"I'm gonna take that as a 'no,'" said Joe.

"The succession plan only requires one heir to be hidden off-world," she said.

"But who told you that?" Val didn't answer. "Was it the queen?"

"Yes."

"I'm not accusing her of anything," Joe said. "I'm just curious, is all."

"I can find out."

"How? I thought it was a big secret."

"I have some ideas," she said. "I'll let you know."

"Naw, c'mon. It's not as important as figuring out what's going on around here."

"I promise it won't interfere with the investigation."

"Yeah, okay," said Joe. "Whatever."

It wasn't just the royals and their advisors that operated out of the palace. Every aspect of their lives, from transportation to security, required a dedicated on-site support staff. Those people, who devoted themselves to the safety and comfort of the royal family, lived, worked, and communed in other parts of the castle.

Rik had just arrived in the mess and taken a seat across from a young lady when he caught a blurred glimpse of Val rushing past the doors.

"Someone's in a hurry," Rik said. "At least she still knows where this part of the palace is."

"I bet the king gave her a proper reaming out after what happened," Elle said. She was roughly the same age as Rik, with a slightly lighter complexion.

He wore his wavy hair neat and tight while her thick tresses were pulled back and tied into a bundle larger than her actual head. It remained elevated off her shoulders, which kept her within uniform regulations.

She broke off a piece of bread and shoved it in her mouth.

Rik chuckled. "He wishes."

"Come on," Elle said. "Her first day on the job and she bungles something like this?"

"What was she supposed to do?" Rik asked. "The trinot got past every security measure in the castle. She can't be held responsible for that."

"She's the Guardian. The coin stops with her."

"Well, whatever." Rik stabbed a hunk of meat off of his tray. "The king isn't about to say anything to piss her off."

"Oh, the king should be worried about not pissing his Guardian off?" Elle asked. "Is that how it works now?"

"I'm not saying he should. But..." Rik glanced around before leaning over the table. "Okay, don't tell anyone, but, I think the king fancies her."

"Oh, really?"

"What's that supposed to mean?" Rik settled back in his seat.

"That he's been drooling over her like a dimwitted animal pretty much since they got back," Elle said.

"And yet..."

"And yet, what?"

"Well."

"Stop dancing around," Elle said. "What, because she doesn't seem to be in love with him?"

"He's the king," Rik said.

"He's a boy."

"He's the same age as us, pretty much."

"A lot of maturing happens in those couple of years," Elle said. "You remember what it was like to be that age? Wouldn't you have put it in anything that moved?"

"Well, not anything," he said.

"Anything that was willing, though."

"No, don't be crass."

"Now imagine you were the king," she said. "You'd kind of have your choice of options."

"There would probably be a lot of potential partners throwing themselves at a bachelor king, yes," Rik said.

"Right," she said. "And yet. And yet he's not taken anyone to bed since he's been here. Nobody, not woman nor man. And he's spent nearly every waking moment hanging around her."

"She's kind of the only person he knows here."

"Oh, he wants to know her, alright," Elle said.

"Right, I'm not arguing with you there."

"I know you're not."

"Because we're in agreement."

"Sure we are. You jealous?"

"Am I jealous that the king has feelings for his Guardian?" Rik asked.

"Or maybe you're worried that he'll be the one to finally melt through that icy exterior of hers."

Rik let out a laugh. "That's not going to happen."

"You sure about that?"

"I've known her longer than almost anyone," Rik said.

"Which means you've been in lo-ove with her longer than almost anyone." Elle puckered her lips and let out a series of kissy noises.

"You are positively infuriating," he told her.

Val wasn't gone on her self-ascribed mission for long before she was escorted back to her king by his uncle.

The prince hauled her into the council room by her arm, nearly dragging her towards the monarch and his advisors.

"What the hell, man?" Joe asked.

"I told you the king was going to be pissed," Val said to Angelo.

The elder royal threw her towards his nephew.

"I caught this one snooping around the locked records," he said.

Val composed herself and straightened her still-stiff uniform. "I'm the king's Guardian, I'm allowed to look at official records."

"The royal family's locked records?" Angelo's voice sharpened. "What possible reason could you have to be digging through those?"

"The king requested certain information," Val said.

"What information?"

"I don't have to answer to you," she told him.

Angelo gestured towards the king. "What about to him?"

"Him is right here and can speak for himself," Joe said.

"Then please, ask your Guardian what she was doing looking through our family's locked files without prior authorization," said Angelo.

"You don't tell me what to do," Joe said. "Go wait outside, I'll talk to Val."

"She's working her charms on you, sire," Angelo said.

"Are you kidding me?" Joe asked. "There are lots of words I would use to describe Val. Most of them very positive. 'Charming' is not one of them."

"Hey," Val said. "I'm right here."

"Angelo, out in the hall, or outside the gates. Your

choice," said Joe.

Angelo turned, masking the burgeoning redness of his face from his youngers, and stormed out of the room. At Joe's direction, the council members followed.

Once the door slammed behind them, Joe gave Val his complete attention.

"So, what was that all about?" he asked.

"That was about your uncle being an arrogant prick who can't let go of his ego."

"I mean besides that," Joe said. "What's up with this 'locked files' business?"

"I was studying your mother's public appearances from around the time you were born."

"Oh?"

"A couple of months after you would have been born, she started regularly attending public functions again," Val said. "She was never seen pregnant after that. So, you have no younger siblings. The plan of succession doesn't account for anyone older than you being hidden off-world, so, it's pretty safe to say you don't have any other brothers or sisters out there in the galaxy."

"Okay, cool. Good to know," Joe said. "And that's what Angelo got his panties in a bunch about?"

"No, he got his... what are panties, exactly?"

"Do you guys not wear undergarments?" Joe asked. "'Cause that would totally change how I see things here."

"Yes, we wear undergarments, we just don't call them that," Val said. "But no, your uncle has his... he's upset because he can't control me, anymore. He can't control anyone or anything, really."

CHAPTER 4

Angelo waited for Joe in the hallway, though no outside observer would have described his mood as patient. Still, he waited, as was proper in deference to the king.

Joe exited the council chambers a short while later. Angelo hadn't seen Val leave; she must have taken one of the other routes, purposefully or otherwise.

"Oh. You're still here," Joe said.

"Yes. I wanted to discuss some things with you." Angelo approached him quickly. "First, I wanted to assure you that I harbor no ill will over what was said in there. I know you have to placate Val, tell her what she wants to hear."

"That's not what happened. I like Val."

"Of course you do."

"Not like that. I mean... well, it's not important. What I meant was, I like her as an advisor," Joe said. "She's smart. She knows how things run."

"Does she?"

"Yeah."

"So she's got everything set for your meeting with the ambassador from the Palan system?" Angelo asked.

"The what now?"

"The Palans are one of the many systems that Kaia maintains an alliance with," Angelo said. "Our relationship with them can be a bit tenuous at times. They don't respond well to change. You'll want to make a good first impression.

That was the other matter I wanted to discuss with you. Their ambassador will be arriving tomorrow evening..."

"Nope."

"Beg pardon?" Angelo asked.

"No. No way," Joe said. "There was a bomb planted here. The castle is on lockdown until further notice. We're definitely not letting foreign ambassadors and their entourages roam around."

"Ah, perhaps a neutral site then..."

"Lockdown, dude," Joe said. "No one in, no one out."

"I see," said Angelo. "And was this her idea?"

"Nope. I came up with this one all on my own."

"Hrm."

"You should be happy," Joe said. "This might be the only reason you get to hang around if you keep pushing me. I can't make any promises on the accommodations, though. This place has dungeons, right?"

Joe smiled and slapped Angelo on the shoulder as he walked by.

On his way past the dining hall, Joe tried to recall how many meals he'd taken since arriving on Kaia, and what they all consisted of. It had been a stressful couple of days, finding himself on another world and enduring an attempt on his life.

Glancing through the door, he noticed the queen seated at the table, nibbling on some sort of dried foodstuff.

He approached trepidatiously.

"Oh. Is it suppertime?"

"No. In all the commotion, I missed lunch," the queen said. "I used to be able to get away with skipping meals, but I was feeling a bit lightheaded."

"Okay, cool. I guess I'll leave you alone, then."

Joe started away.

"Have you dealt with Angelo?" his mother asked.

"Oh, yeah. Gave him the ol' shoulder pat. Very condescending."

"And you consider the matter settled?"

His head dropped and his arms spread. "I don't know. If you hadn't noticed, I don't really know what the hell I'm doing here."

"That's to be expected, I suppose," the queen said.

"And yet," he said, "no one will cut me any damn slack for it."

"You're a king now," she replied. She delicately raised her cup to her thin lips. "You don't get 'slack.'"

"Well, you know what, I didn't ask for this."

"No one does."

"Well, you kind of did," he said. "You married into it."

"I'm not sure I appreciate your tone, young man." She set the cup down on its saucer.

"No," he said firmly. "Uh-uh. If I don't get any slack, neither do you. If I have the expectations of a king on my shoulders, then I get the privileges, too."

"More than the queen regent, I am still your mother, and you will keep a civil tongue when addressing me."

"How about someone try addressing me with civility?" His hands made a slap at his chest before spreading wide. "Huh? Because ever since I got here, even before I got here, Val was talking to me like I'm an idiot, you keep getting on my case, Trainer acted like I was a child, Angelo thinks he can manipulate me..."

"No one thinks you're an idiot."

"Bull."

"But you are unrefined," the queen said.

"And that's my fault?"

"No, but..."

"Then why am I the one suffering for it?" he asked.

"We're trying to help you," she said.

"No," he said again. "You're trying to make me into whatever it is you think I need to be."

"If you don't want to be treated as a child then maybe you oughtn't to conduct yourself as one," she dryly suggested.

"I am doing my goddamn best here," he said. All the while, she held to her cup, pinky finger out. "But I wasn't raised knowing how to be royalty. I was raised to go to school and get a decent job, and, holy crap, my parents are probably going to be paying off my student loan debts for forever."

"You're concerned… about your adoptive parents' finances?" the queen asked.

"If I don't pay, they might have to. Do you know what college costs in America?" he asked. "And yeah, I'm concerned, because those people raised me. I'm having the hardest damn time wrapping my head around being a space king, but worrying about debt, or what to do this weekend, or about the girl I like not knowing I exist, those are things I know."

"You're the king. You could have very nearly any woman in the empire."

"I don't want it like that. I want a woman who's going to…" He tightened up. "No, you know what, this isn't a conversation I can have with someone who's almost a total stranger to me."

"I'm your mother."

"My mother lives in Milwaukee and works for an accounting firm," Joe said. "She can't eat tomatoes, and she likes crappy rom-coms, and she never listens to the radio. That's my mom. I don't know the first thing about you."

With that, he thundered out of the dining hall.

The queen raised her cup once again.

"If you don't wish to be treated as a child…" she muttered.

At the sound of a heavy rap, the second council vizier pulled on his robe and rushed for the door to his chambers. They were perhaps not as exquisite, or well lit, as other rooms in the castle, but they were still nothing short of luxurious.

"Coming," he called, cinching up his coat just in time to avoid exposing himself to the man waiting at the door.

"Oh, my prince." He bowed to Angelo. "How can I be of service?"

"Earlier, when you said you supported me more than I know, what did you mean?" Angelo asked.

"I take it relations between you and the new king have not warmed?"

"The new king has all but dismissed me," Angelo said. "Worse, he's taken it into his head to offend the Palan ambassador. He should be looking to marry one of her children, not shun her."

"The ambassador's children?"

"Well, they're all certainly attractive enough," Angelo said.

"Huh. Palans aren't really known for their aesthetic beauty."

"Probably why they send their best out as ambassadors," said Angelo.

"I suppose." The vizier shrugged. "Though perhaps he ought to aspire higher. Court one of the royals."

"It won't matter if our idiot child of a king refuses to give them an audience," Angelo said. "He's not just offending me and half the castle staff…"

"Only half? Are you sure?"

"But he's risking alliances," Angelo said, "all on the word of a rank operative."

"Val is his Guardian," the vizier said. "And he is king. The order of succession must be observed. There's nothing we can do about that."

"You keep saying things like that. What are you playing at?"

"I'm not playing at anything," the vizier said. His voice was overly calm, bordering on patronizing. "Merely hypothesizing aloud. Tell me, who would take the Crown if something were to happen to Joseph?"

"You already know the answer to that."

"Who?"

"Andor had no other children. The order of succession would fall to his next eldest sibling," Angelo said.

"And that would be you."

"And what would you have me do?" asked Angelo. "Hm? You're talking regicide. Treason."

"Not necessarily," the vizier said. "Monarchs are allowed to abdicate if they so choose."

"Yes," said Angelo. "They're also allowed to name their own successor if they do."

"Theoretically, yes. But it's not like he knows anyone else here of royal blood," said the vizier. "He undoubtedly misses the planet where he was raised. I hear he's not taking well to palace life at all. It may not take much persuasion to convince him to return there."

"But suppose my sister-in-law convinced him to hand over rule to one of my cousins or some such. There's too much room for error there."

"I suppose there's only one thing left to consider, then."

"And what's that?" asked Angelo.

"My prince, all due respect, but you yourself have already indicated that tradition is being disrupted by King Joseph," said the vizier.

"So what's your suggestion?"

"Take the Crown for yourself. By force, if you have to."

"And how would I do that?" the prince asked. "Joseph has an army..."

"The army is outside the castle walls," said the vizier. "Only the royal guard remains. A guard which, until two days ago, was under your command."

"There's still no way I could just take the Crown."

"The queen would resist, but with her husband gone, her legal influence has lagged..."

"No, I mean, physically," Angelo said.

"There may be a way, sire."

After her late meal, the queen retired to her sitting room, located on one of the taller towers of the palace. What had it previously been? She tried to recall. An armory? A storage room?

The spouses of monarchs on Kaia had always been afforded spaces of their own, but, during their courtship, she had mentioned to her future husband how much she admired the view from this window. She loved the sight of the front courtyard and being able to see the city beyond the outer walls. After they were married, he'd had the official sitting room moved from its previous position in the lower east tower.

It was that view that she found herself lost in again, all these decades hence.

"You asked to see me, queen mother?" Val asked. The doorway she stood in had not been closed. It hadn't been for some time, really. "The investigation is still ongoing. I'm... doing the best I can."

The queen smiled.

"Do you know what one of the worst feelings in the world is for a parent?" she asked.

"I wouldn't, no," Val said.

"It's when your children are right."

"Really?"

"Oh, there are worse things, I know," she said softly. "Losing a child. But you're... not prepared, but you're aware that losing a child will hurt. And it does. Every day. But you're not prepared for your offspring to show wisdom that you lack."

"Um... okay."

"The king... Joe. He was right," she said. "I haven't gotten to know him. I'm so used to having people fritter in and out of my life, and I've been so... since Andor and Thoome died...

The one and only positive to come from all of this is that my youngest child, who I thought was lost to me forever, has been returned. And I can't even..."

"I'm sorry, my queen. I wish there were something I could do."

The queen sniffled and dabbed her eyes.

"You've done more than enough. More than anyone would expect from someone in your position," she said. "I've tried to be strong for you, but, I suppose that's not my job. Not anymore."

CHAPTER 5

T he staircase before them seemed to wind on to an incredible depth, more than seemed reasonable for the castle, given that their journey had started at the ground level. By torchlight, the vizier led Angelo ever downwards.

"Where the hell are we?" the prince asked. "I've spent most of my life in the castle; I've never been here before."

"We're in the catacombs beneath the original foundations," the vizier explained. Making his way around the stairs, he seemed even more hunched than before.

"How would anyone not have noticed these?" Angelo asked.

"Their existence has been obscured from view by ancient magics."

"That seems implausible."

"It's far from the most fantastic thing you'll experience today."

As they descended, the surroundings aged visibly, becoming grimier and dirtier with each step.

Their bottomward journey came to an end at a crude antechamber. It was possible that it was once an attractive, or at least functional, bit of stonework. Now, it was barely distinguishable from a natural cave.

The space that it opened to was gigantic. The pillars and etchings along the wall, those visible by torchlight, those not lost to the erasure of time, suggested that the room had once been a chapel, or part of one.

Five hooded figures stood around a circular emblem near the center of the room. Their cloaks may not have actually been black, but they might as well have been in the darkness. The figures inhabiting them were difficult to identify, though Angelo recognized one of them as the other vizier from the earlier meeting.

"And what is this now?" Angelo asked.

"These are the Mages of Kaia," the vizier said proudly. "Descended from the group that originally forged the Crown of the Five Point Star."

"The Order of Meridian forged the Crown," Angelo said.

"There was a bit of a falling out among the Order some time after the Crown was completed," the vizier said. "Some members sought to erase all knowledge of how the Crown was made from the universe."

"Trainer said that knowledge was lost millennia ago."

"I hope it doesn't upset you to find he was mistaken."

"Upset? No. Surprise? Of course. You spend your whole life being told one thing..." Angelo's grumblings trailed off. "So, your people here can, what, create another Crown?"

"Not exactly, no. The mainline Meridians destroyed enough of the Crown's secrets that it can't be replicated; however, the Mages retained an understanding of how to harness the power of a star in the same way the Crown was fashioned."

"And what good will that do us?" asked Angelo.

"The power could be harnessed into a living body," the vizier said.

"You mean me?"

"I can think of no one more deserving. You would be given the strength of a star." There was an almost childlike sense of wonder in the old vizier's voice. "For a short time."

"How short a time?"

"We're not entirely sure," the vizier admitted. "The

Kaian body wasn't exactly designed to house such power. You would risk burning out rather quickly, I'm afraid. But, until that happened, you would have powers even the Crown doesn't grant its bearer."

"But I'd be committing suicide," said Angelo.

"The only way to prevent yourself from dying would be to claim the Crown. It could absorb the excess energy and return your body to its normal state."

Angelo stroked his beard. "That's a hell of a gamble."

"Only you can determine if it's a risk you're willing to take."

Angelo turned away. His chin dropped, causing his face to be swallowed up in shadow.

"Do it."

Preparations didn't take long. The mages had anticipated Angelo's agreement.

He positioned himself at the center of the chamber, atop the foreign emblem. The five robed figures formed a sort of circle around him.

Despite his usually confident demeanor, the mages could sense his shuddering nerves.

Their complete silence didn't help set him at ease.

Angelo looked to the man who'd brought him here, the only member of the order not holding their hands over him. Instead, the vizier was as far away as he could be without leaving the chamber. Another thing not soothing to Angelo's disposition.

"Shouldn't they be chanting or something?" the prince asked.

"Why?" the vizier asked. "You think the sun will listen? They're harnessing psychic energy for what comes next."

The hooded figures each raised a hand upwards.

Beyond the castle, beyond Kaia's atmosphere, the sun stirred.

Tendrils of energy lashed their way from its mass, streaking towards the planet.

They poured from the sky, caring not a whit for the clouds, ground, or castle masonry in their path.

When the searing illumination subsided, Angelo found himself in a sunlit chamber. He hadn't been moved, yet the daylight shone through the freshly scorched tunnel cut by the energy's path.

The mages each now crackled with energy, their arms surrounded by lightning made of sunlight. They grappled with the energy, as though it were a living thing seeking to break their grasp. It took all the effort they could muster to divert that power into the man at the center of their grouping.

Angelo grunted at first, mildly distressed by the sudden influx of unnatural might. The slight discomfort lasted only a moment.

Then the pain began.

Angelo struggled to remain upright against its force. Still, he would not give in. He would not quit. He would not scream.

But there was only so long he could keep upright under the crushing weight of it all. He allowed himself to drop to a knee and braced himself against the scorching stone floor. He would not be defeated.

As they poured the power of the sun into Angelo, the mages found their own bodies rapidly deteriorating. They burned away not in layers, but in ripples. By the time the ritual was complete, the five of them had vanished.

And it was done.

The chamber was alight. The greatest of it came not from the torches, nor the newly open channel to the surface, but from Angelo himself. His entire person now glowed with the power of the sun.

The only remaining vizier inched his way towards Angelo's unmoving form.

"My prince. Are you alright?"

Angelo slowly lifted his head.

"I'm alive," he said. His eyes darted around the empty floor where the five mages once stood. "The others..."

"Knew exactly what they were doing. They were giving you the chance to stabilize our kingdom. I beg of you, sire, don't waste it."

Up in the courtyard, armed soldiers surrounded the freshly burned pit, their weapons at the ready. None of them were quite sure what they expected to do, training guns on a hole in the dirt created by a beam from the sky, but nevertheless, they advanced on it.

A flash of clean, blazing light sent most of them skidding across the ground. Many of them were able to see clearly enough within a few seconds, though what they saw didn't necessarily make sense to them. The prince of Kaia, their dead king's brother, floating towards them, light emanating from every inch of him.

He landed steadily on the grass. Some of the soldiers took aim. What else would they do?

The general in charge of this unit was among the last to reorientate himself. He got a look at the caped figure marching towards them and pushed through to the front of the battalion.

"Wait!" he cried.

Angelo smiled.

"Good man."

CHAPTER 6

The queen and the Guardian had just finished their conversation when they heard the commotion from outside.

On instinct, the queen rushed to the window for a look. It was Val's own instinct that led her to tackle the regent to the floor as the scalding light poured in.

"My queen, down!"

Val placed her hands on the queen, searching her elderly form for any sign of injuries. "Are you alright? Are you hurt?"

"Yes," the queen assured her. Val helped her back to her feet. She looked towards the window, still filled with an impenetrable haze of illumination. "What..."

"I'll find out." Val rushed to the door, where she was met by an incoming member of the guard. "What's going on out there?"

"The castle's been breached, Guardian."

The queen was quickly upon them.

"How?" she asked. "By whom?"

The guardsman looked sheepish.

"They're saying it was the sun, your highness."

Angelo marched through the halls of the castle with a newfound purpose, a newfound confidence. For a man with his self-image, that was saying something.

He was flanked and followed by loyal members of the palace guard, but none walked in front of him. A king, after all, would not lead from behind.

Another group of guardsmen, either disloyal to Angelo or ignorant of the developing situation, filed into the hall in front of them. In either circumstance, they were an obstacle.

They took aim and opened fire.

Angelo's loyalists returned in kind. The hail of oncoming bullets cut through their line, downing a few of them.

This would not stand. Angelo reached himself out, creating a shield for those who stood with him.

When a break in the firing came, he lashed his energies forward, blasting their opponents from their path.

Angelo and his troops pressed on, heading for a walkway that would lead them across the main courtyard.

Once the glare subsided, the queen perched herself at the window, scanning for an origin of the disturbance. It didn't take long for her to spot one: her brother-in-law exiting the archway at one end of an elevated bridge.

Another squadron of guards appeared at the other end of the path and loosed their rifles. Bullets seemed to spark off the prince's body.

The queen rushed away from the window.

"Where is the king?" she asked.

"I think in his chambers?" the guard said.

"Don't think. Find out. Val, with me."

The guardsman took off in one direction down the hall while Val and the queen headed in the other.

"What did you see out there?" Val asked.

"Nothing good."

Angelo's soldiers continued their slow advancement. Several of the obstructionists already lay dead at their feet.

Gunfire tore into one of Angelo's troops. It was only his shoulder, but the impact threw him off balance, twisting off the walkway's edge, into the depths below.

Several more shots impacted Angelo.

"Enough."

His fingers curled. Somehow, the stone beneath his enemies splintered and crumbled. The guards who had stood there were dropped into the abyss beneath.

Angelo relaxed.

His general lowered his weapon and stepped out towards what remained of the bridge.

"That's all well and good, sir, but how do we reach the inner halls now?"

"Take your soldiers, go around the southern side. I'll find my own way."

Angelo spreads his arms and lifted into the air.

"What's going on?" Joe asked. He rushed up the hallway towards his mother and Guardian.

"We're not sure yet," Val said.

"Never mind that," the queen said, "where's the Crown?"

"I've got it." Joe held it for her to see.

The queen looked to Val.

"Valentina, make haste."

"What can I do?"

The three of them quickly shuffled up the hall, towards the throne room.

Once inside, the queen hurried towards the empty Crown display case.

"It is time you understood your role in all of this," she said to Val.

"I know my role," Val said. "I fulfilled my role. I brought

the new king here. I've kept him alive despite himself."

"No." The queen sighed with a subtle shake of her head.

"Yes, I did."

"True story," Joe said.

"See. He's right there."

"But that is not all of it," the queen told them. "Every generation a Guardian is selected to protect the future king or queen and guide them as they learn their path. You are that Guardian."

"Yeah, I get that."

"The Guardian must also be ready to take up the Crown at a moment's notice, should their charge fall."

"What?" Val asked. "That doesn't make sense. I'm not…"

"Valentina, I'm sorry that royal tradition forced me to keep the truth from you. But now, I need for my only daughter to protect her younger…"

Val vomited.

"Oh." Joe gasped. "Oh, God…"

"Shut up!" Val screamed.

"Oh, my God."

"I said shut up!"

"Ugh." Joe clutched his stomach. "We almost did so much stuff."

"We did not. And we will never speak of it again."

The queen's fingers traced the underside of the display plate molding until coming upon a switch. The pillar split and a smaller crown, with a single point, rose up.

"By all rights, this is yours," the queen said.

"What is that?" asked Val.

"The Crown of the Single Pointed Star." The queen lifted it and handed it to Val. "I wish I could give you more."

The three of them heard a deep crack as the doors to the chamber bulged inward. They did so once more before splintering off their hinges, collapsing to the floor. Accompanying them were a pair of palace guards, their skeletal frames now the color of charcoal. The stench of burning flesh instantly fogged the room.

"Go." The queen pushed Val away.

"But…"

The queen nodded towards Joe.

"Get him out of here."

"He's not ready," said Val.

"He'll have to be." The queen placed a hand on Val's shoulder. "You both will."

She knelt beside the remains of one of the guards and scooped up his rifle. The metal was still hot, but not enough to loosen her grip or her resolve.

"Come on." Val grabbed Joe's hand and dragged him, up the throne platform and around behind the gilded seat. There she opened a short doorway that had, until her shoving, blended perfectly with the surrounding masonry. The pair of them squeezed through.

The queen glanced back over her shoulder, giving the last shadows of her children a forlorn look before redirecting her attention to the doors.

Angelo stomped his way in, the fallen wooden slabs crushing beneath his feet. His body seemed to be growing heavier.

"My God, Angelo. What have you done to yourself?"

"What was necessary."

He strode towards her.

The queen pulled a slide on the side of the rifle, throwing up an energy shield around herself just as Angelo began tossing bolts of lightning across the room.

Her finger squeezed the trigger, letting off a spray of bullets.

Angelo's hand went to his face, instinctively shielding his eyes from the gunfire. He didn't know if he could take a bullet to one and wasn't keen to find out.

He let out a grunt, trying to continue his assault from a defensive position.

The queen had one more trick up her sleeve. While the

guards' rifles weren't energy weapons, the matter replicator within them could be set to overload. The result would be a powerful photonic stream, though the effect would be short-lived before the entire weapon shorted out and detonated.

She made the necessary adjustment and, with a deep scream, squeezed the trigger once more.

Angelo pushed forward, trying to use his power to both create a barricade and attack.

A brilliant shockwave blew through the room as the weapon's destructive energy connected with the prince's.

The hallway that Val and Joe felt their way through was narrow, dark, and dirty, and grew only more so as they pressed on. It was only wide enough for them to move in single file, and so Val took the lead.

"What do you think is happening back there?" Joe asked.

"I don't."

"What?"

"I'm not thinking about it," Val said.

"Why not?"

"Because the shooting stopped a couple minutes ago and the queen hasn't contacted me," she said. She never once looked back.

"You mean mom?"

"Don't."

"Seriously, this is messed up," said Joe.

"Okay, so I'm the older sibling, which means you shut up and do what I say. Got it?"

"Yes," Joe said. "I will come with you if I want to live."

"What?"

"Nothing. It's a... never mind."

Val slowed, forcing Joe to follow suit. Her fingers brushed along the wall in front of her.

No, it should be lower, she thought.

"What're you doing?" Joe asked.

"There should be a loose brick around here that triggers a doorway," she said.

"Seriously?"

"I used to play in these tunnels when I was a kid. It's here somewhere."

Joe inspected their surroundings as best he could in the darkness.

"Sure," he said. "A tunnel with no lights that looks like it's pretty much made of tetanus. Great place for a kid."

Val's hands probed lower still. How tall had she been when she'd last come through here?

At last, she found the switch. Depressing it caused a panel to slide away from the wall in front of them. She pushed Joe back into the shadows and peeked around the corner.

"It looks clear," she whispered. "Alright, from here, it's about fifty meters down the hallway to the hangar. It's the last doorway on the left if we get separated."

"Why would we get separated?"

"Because people are trying to kill us, and they might succeed," she said. "Ready?"

"Ready?" he echoed. "Yeah, yeah, I'm ready. Sure. Ready."

"I really wish I had a weapon on me," she said.

She jumped a bit as Joe reached from the darkness to grab her wrist and hold up the hand that grasped the Crown of the Single Pointed Star.

"I think you do," he said.

"Well, okay," she said. "But since I've never used it before, hopefully I won't need to."

"Sure. Right."

"Okay, let's go."

The pair burst through the secret doorway, sprinting down the metallic tunnel.

The lit panels and ancillary doors whizzed past. Their race was going well and its end was nearly there.

Until one of those other doorways opened and Angelo

stepped directly into their path.

"Don't stop," Val instructed.

"What?" Joe asked.

His sister charged directly at Angelo. She leaped into the air, driving her knees into Angelo's face while narrowly avoiding being blasted by his energy beams.

Angelo staggered back slightly but was otherwise unmoved.

Before she could even land from her maneuver, Angelo grabbed her out of the air and threw her over his shoulder.

It was only then that he noticed that Val's gambit had paid off. Joe made it past him and to the end of the hall.

Angelo charged up his fist and slammed it to the ground. The floor paneling rippled, the jagged energy coming through in a wave. Within meters of reaching his escape, Joe was thrown off his feet.

It wasn't just a physical blow that Joe felt. The shock left him completely disoriented. His ears rang and his vision swirled. The damage the shockwave caused to the lighting in the hallway didn't help matters. It didn't take too long for his senses to return, but by the time they did, Angelo was almost upon him.

"I'm going to need that crown, boy," Angelo said.

Joe placed the crown on his forehead and pushed down. Any remaining trace of dizziness or debilitation was washed away as the armor came over him.

"Come get it."

His palms pressed against the floor and he pushed up. He found his feet under him, carrying him towards his uncle.

The unstable energy swirled its way around Angelo's arm. He balled up his hand and swung it at Joe. The younger man was thrown back into the wall.

He didn't stay there for long. Joe pushed off and threw himself at Angelo, tackling him into the far side of the hallway. Joe's fist struck Angelo just below the ribs. Again. And again. Keep the wind out of him, Joe thought. Put him down.

Angelo got his arms up to block the barrage. He then swung them out, shoving Joe back, allowing Angelo to stomp him in the chest with a powered kick.

Val finally began to get her breath back. Her vision cleared in time for her to see Joe pinned against a wall in a deluge of Angelo's energy beams.

When Angelo momentarily let up, Joe crumpled to his knees.

"No!" Val cried out. Her own voice sounded tinny in her ears; her hearing hadn't yet fully recovered, but there wasn't time to worry about that.

She slid the Crown of the Single Pointed Star onto her head. A suit of armor, lighter and slimmer than Joe's, encased her body as she scrambled up and bounded towards Angelo again.

She hit him squarely center mass, dragging him away from her younger brother. No matter the strength she now felt, she couldn't seem to get Angelo off his feet.

The older man shrugged her off. By the time he'd turned to face her, she was already coming at him once again, striking at him with a rapid series of punches and kicks. He was able to deflect most of them, but not all.

Joe rushed in, hitting Angelo from the left while Val took the right.

For at least this moment, the siblings worked in tangent, a single machine intent on a synchronized goal.

Angelo, backed against the wall, gathered his energy again. Rather than punching into the floor, he let out a burst into the air, blasting both Val and Joe back.

The machine was broken, again two individual warriors against one.

Val tried to rise again, but a swift boot from Angelo punted her down the hall, further from escape and from her brother.

She held her ribs and wheezed, desperately trying to get enough air back in her lungs to reenter the fight.

Angelo grabbed onto Joe's collar and picked him up off the ground. Joe's fist came hard across his uncle's face, but Angelo barely flinched.

The glow in his eyes had become unstable. The lighting had become a series of rupturing bubbles. His blackening skin was starting to crack and peel.

Angelo's arm charged for a moment before he forced it through his nephew's chest.

Val's hearing began to return just in time to make out the sound of Joe gurgling. Blood dripped out from the bottom of his helmet.

"I didn't want it to be this way," Angelo told him. "Truly. You forced my hand. And now, well."

Angelo pulled his fist back. Still coated in blood and viscera, it grasped the Crown and ripped it from Joe's head.

He dropped Joe to the ground like so much discarded flotsam.

Not a moment too soon, Angelo pushed the Crown to his own shaking forehead. The armor enveloped his body, snuffing out the lethal buildup of the sun's power within him. Only his cape dangled free from beneath the metallic plating that now covered him.

What little of the sun's power remained made its way out of his fingertips in harmless swirls of glistening smoke.

Angelo allowed himself a moment to admire the armor surrounding him and feel its strength.

That moment would cost him.

Without warning, Val slammed into him.

"No!" she screamed.

She swung a haymaker directly at him. With the speed and power of the Crown, Angelo was able to deflect the punch and counter with a palm to her chest. She was thrown against the far wall but remained standing.

She came at him again. A left hook, a right uppercut. A right jab. A flying knee. A roundhouse kick.

All blocked, or their impact minimal.

On the last kick, Angelo grabbed Val's leg and swung her around, again tossing her down the hall.

She pulled herself up but found that Angelo was already upon her. He swung a single punch at her, flinging her down the hall some more, further away from the hangar, and from Joe's lifeless body.

By the time she rolled to a stop, Angelo was on her again, grabbing her by the throat and hoisting her off the ground. He held her aloft, her feet dangling, feebly trying to kick away from him.

His head cocked to one side and tapped the Crown on her face.

"Huh. I've never seen this one before," he said.

He reached up and wrapped his fingers around the Crown of the Single Pointed Star.

He started to pull.

Val screamed. It was like he was trying to pry one of her limbs away from her body.

It was frustratingly secured in place. She wasn't sure how long it could remain there with the force he was applying.

Before he was able to get it loose, however, he was caught in a barrage of gunfire.

He deftly slid back into a nearby doorway, dragging her along by the grip he held on her face, shielded from most of the gunfire by the doorframe. She was still unable to free herself from his grasp.

A group of soldiers was at the far end of the hall, just outside the hangar door, their weapons trained on his position. His head poked out to get a look and was immediately bombarded with bullets.

He withdrew again.

He focused his energy and stepped back out into the hall, into the expected volley of bullets. His hand went out, as he'd done numerous times in his journey through the castle.

Nothing happened.

He looked at his unlit hand, no longer channeling the

power of the system's star.

"Oh, right," he grumbled.

Instead, he hurled Val down the hallway at the enemy combatants, toppling them like toy blocks.

Lying among her fellow soldiers, Val looked up at Rik, leading the battalion, then back down the hallway to see Angelo advancing.

"Oh, hell," she said. "Fall back to the hangar."

Rik paused.

"Val?" he asked.

She pointed towards the hangar doors.

"Go, goddammit!"

She shoved him towards the entryway. He and his troops dashed through.

Val was the last one in. Once on the other side, she punched the control panel. The door slowly began to slide shut.

Not willing to wait for the mechanism, Val gripped the emerging door and pulled. It slammed shut, with only minimal bending where she'd grabbed it.

She turned to see Rik's group of commandoes running towards the open rear hatch of a ship. Val ripped the door controls away from the frame and started to follow.

The ship her compatriots had chosen sat off to one side of the sprawling underground complex, an area usually reserved for repair on vintage craft.

The hangar door dented inward with an ear-ringing clang. Val ran for the ship.

"Get that thing in the air!" she called.

From inside the ship's rear compartment, Rik motioned for her.

"Come on!" he urged.

Val waved him away.

"Just take off!" she said. "I'll catch up!"

"You'll do what?" he asked.

The hangar door popped out of its frame and fell inward.

Angelo leaped through to see Val tearing after the escaping transport ship. From their end of the runway, it was nearly a kilometer to open air.

He took off running for her.

Val could hear Angelo's thundering footsteps catching up her, and see the daylight at the end of the enclosed airstrip growing larger.

Aboard the transport, Rik looked on helplessly as they left the hangar behind. He could no longer see his friend gaining on them.

Suddenly, she threw herself out of the runway door, barely evading Angelo's grasp on her ankle.

She landed hard on the still-open rear ramp of the craft and rolled inside. Rik slammed the lever for the hatch, sealing it shut as they turned upward.

Once in, she looked up and found herself surrounded by a squadron of confused royal soldiers.

"Hey," she said.

"Hey," Rik replied.

"What's up?" she asked.

"Not much. You?"

"I just found out I'm kind of a princess and I think my evil uncle just murdered his way onto the throne," she said.

"That sucks."

"Yeah."

Rik offered a hand. She took it and he pulled.

"Holy crap," he said. "You weigh a ton."

"Gee, thanks."

She pulled the Crown off of her head and stepped towards the front of the craft.

"Activate the fold-drive," she ordered.

"To where?" the pilot asked.

"It doesn't matter," she said. "Anywhere that isn't here."

The craft shook. It had just broken out of Kaia's atmosphere. Ahead of it, space warped, but the fold was still a ways off. Plenty of space to be intercepted, plenty of time for their trip to end before it had really begun.

Several Kaian fighter craft shot from the clouds: sleeker, faster, and better armed than the small carrier ship that Val and her allies had stolen. Their weapons fire rocked the transport.

"Royal fighters are closing in," their pilot announced.

"Just get us into the fold," Val said.

Another round of fire skidded across their underbelly. Burning gas began venting from one of the engines. The ship listed awkwardly, their momentum just enough to carry them to the safety of the fold.

The fighters flew through open space. Their pursuit was ended.

"We're in." The pilot of the royal craft exhaled. "Just barely."

"Just barely's good enough," Rik said.

The rest of the soldiers dispersed to other parts of the ship, leaving Rik and Val in relative privacy.

"So, a princess, huh?"

Val shrugged.

"I guess," she said. "Apparently I never knew. Not sure why."

"The royal family has some weird rules. Who knows?" He nodded towards the Crown in her hands. "What's that thing?"

She looked down at it. This was the first moment since it had come into her possession that she really had a chance to inspect it. It was smaller than the Five Point Crown, of course, but also thinner, more rounded.

"It's called the Crown of the Single Pointed Star," she said. "I don't know if it's, like, a backup to the Five Point one, or what."

She slumped down on a bench and set the Crown next to her.

"So, you can use that to take on Angelo, right?" Rik asked. "I mean, you're a lot better trained. Younger. In the prime of your life. He's some middle-aged dude."

Val shook her head.

"I don't think so. You saw what happened to me back there."

Rik winced. "The tail end of it."

"He got the same training I did. It doesn't seem like the Single Pointed Crown is anywhere near as powerful as the Five Point."

"You just weren't ready for him," said Rik. "You never used it before. You'll figure it out, and…"

"No, Rik," she stated. "The Crown grants a certain level of understanding. I could tell. I was outgunned. Big time. The Single Pointed Crown isn't going to be enough to take on… my uncle."

"It's all we have."

Val looked away. Her eyes betrayed a weariness she didn't mean to show.

She looked down at the Crown.

"No. I don't think it is."

"What do you mean?" Rik asked.

"The queen - my mother. God, how could she not have told me?"

"The royal family always has multiple redundancies in place," Rik said. "But, what about your mother?"

"She said she wished she could have given me more. I think - I think she was being literal. There's a Crown of Five Points and one of a Single Points. Point. There are three more. Two Points, Three, Four."

"They're just names, Val. That doesn't mean…"

"I know. But, somehow, I know." They both fixed their gaze on the Crown of the Single Pointed Star. "We have to find the other three."

"And together, they'll be powerful enough to stop Angelo?" Rik asked.

Val shook her head.

"No. But they're the best chance we've got. So that's what

we're going to do."

Rik stood up and backed away.

"Yes. My queen."

He bowed and headed for the cockpit. She ignored it and allowed her head to fall to the backrest behind her. Wearing the Crown, even briefly, was a weight. Let something else support her for as long as she could.

CHAPTER 7

It was several hours before the throne room was put back together enough for Angelo to convene any kind of gathering. The throne had to be returned to its place. As much scorching was scrubbed from the walls as could be. Curtains and tapestries were rehung. Other damage was more structural and would have to be seen to in the days and weeks to come.

The royal guard assembled; forming a pair of opposing lines, they created a pathway along the length of crimson carpeting that had been rolled out from the door to the throne platform.

They stood there, each man and woman staring into the eyes of one of their comrades. Blinking seemed rare. Spittle hung in their throats.

No fanfare was played, no proclamation declared.

Angelo appeared in the ruined doorway in full armor, his weighty cape swaying and dragging behind him. He silently marched out of the shadows and through the rows of soldiers.

At the far end of the room, he ascended the stairs, to where the vizier awaited him, beaming with pride.

Angelo removed the Crown and set it on the end of one of the throne's arms.

He turned, sat, and picked up the royal scepter. He looked it over for a brief, triumphant moment, then out at his

assembled followers.
    "Let's begin."

BOOK 3: THE SOURCE

CHAPTER 1

The edges of her vision were dark, and she moved unnaturally slowly.

King Joseph of Kaia – Joe – was only a few meters from her, engaged in brutal combat with his – their - uncle, Prince Angelo. Joe was not a trained warrior, not a soldier. He'd received maybe two days of combat instruction and an ancient Crown possessing supernatural abilities. Angelo had received… something that was making his skin glow and burn, as well as a lifetime of military instruction.

Val herself had a similar experience, though her lifetime was less than half of his.

As she watched, Angelo pulled his arm back, his fist glowing, and thrust it forward, through Joe's chest. A wave of blood painted the wall behind him. It gushed to the floor.

Angelo threw back his head and laughed. The sound echoed off the metallic walls of the hallway, burned and ashen from battle. Some parts were collapsing completely. Lighting panels flicked and sputtered; some shot sparks or flames.

Another spray of liquid doused the hall as Angelo tore the Crown of the Five Point Star away from Joe's face.

He jubilantly held the Crown aloft. She seemed to be completely invisible to him. Or maybe just insignificant. And in her current state, she still wasn't close to reaching him. All she could do was watch as blood pooled around her brother's twisted body.

◆ ◆ ◆

"Should we wake her up?"

Elle stood over Val's sleeping form, curled on the bench in the rear of their transport ship.

"How long's she been asleep?" asked Rik. They were the only two people in the rear cabin apart from the slumbering young queen. Val faced away from them, clutching the Crown of the Single Pointed Star tightly to her.

"I dunno? About an hour?"

"Great," Rik said. "The first time she's slept in days and we're waking her up after an hour."

"I know," Elle said, "but, we're here, and we need to keep moving."

"I know." He sighed and gently shook Val's shoulder. "Hey, Val?"

Val groaned. She rolled onto her back and looked up at him. Her hair was a mess and her face tightened up in a snarl.

"What?" Her voice was a hoarse creak.

"We're here," Rik said.

"Alright, whatever." She slowly sat herself up.

"We debated on waking you up," Rik said, "but…"

"It's fine. I wasn't having a good dream anyway."

"That's too bad," he said.

"Yeah, well, that's where we're at." She got up and headed towards the cockpit, still holding tight to the Crown. Rik and Elle followed.

The pilot, Metch, noticed Val's shadow on the forward viewport as she entered.

"We exited the fold a few minutes ago," he said. "Approaching Chak Clondor now, your highness."

"You don't have to call me that," Val said.

"If I want to remember why we're doing this, I kind of feel like I have to," he said.

"Your sunny personality is an inspiration to us all," Rik

said to Val.

She sneered and wiped a bit of gunk from her eye.

"You sure this is a good idea?" Elle asked. "Not to question our queen, but flying a military ship into a place like this might turn some heads."

"We should be fine. Stolen military hardware ends up in civilian hands more often than you'd like to think. And they have a habit of turning up on planets like this especially." Val looked them over. "And, it's not uncommon to see defected soldiers who went AWOL with nothing but the clothes on their back."

"We've all peeled the insignias off our uniforms." Rik showed her his sleeve, with the un-faded spots and torn stitching at the shoulders. "A palace guard, though..."

"Then give me one of your uniforms," Val said.

"We don't have any extras," Rik informed her.

"Seriously?"

"We didn't exactly pack for this trip," he said. "So, unless you want to make Elle walk around naked..."

"Please don't make me walk around naked."

"If you ordered her to give you her uniform, she'd have to comply," Rik told Val.

"Or what?" Val asked. "Face a court-martial?"

Rik rummaged around in a storage bin and produced a dull-colored blanket.

"You could wear this?" he suggested.

"Ugh. Fine."

She wrapped the blanket around herself, forming it into a sort of hooded poncho.

The trio headed back to the hold.

Once the ship touched down on a platform and landing procedures were complete, the rear hatch was opened and the ramp extended. Val led their small group out.

Palace security escorted King Angelo down the steps into the palace ballroom. He gave the area a once-over and located the vizier near the center, in discussions with caterers and fixture arrangers.

All but the vizier were dismissed as he approached.

"Ah, my king." The vizier greeted him with a warm smile. "I'm happy to report that plans for your coronation proceed well."

"Fine, fine."

"The Palans have contacted us, however, and informed us that their ambassador will not be attending," said the vizier.

"What?" Angelo asked. "After all this…"

"Instead, the royal family themselves will be in attendance."

"I know you think you're clever…"

"Yes, I was trying for a bit of misdirection."

"Don't."

"Very well." The vizier dipped his head. "My apologies."

"The Palan royal family, though?" Angelo dragged his fingers through the dense, wiry hairs on his chin.

"Yes. They felt it appropriate, as this will be both your coronation and a memorial service for King Andor and Prince Thoome."

"And King Joseph," Angelo said.

The vizier's mouth hung for a moment. "I didn't think you'd…"

"He may have been in the wrong, but he was still our blood. He just put his faith in the wrong people."

"Of course," said the vizier. "I'll have him added to the itinerary."

"There's one other thing I need from you."

"Anything my king desires."

"I need information."

"Anything you need, I can get," the vizier assured him. "You simply have but to say the word."

"I want all the information on the creation of the Crown

of the Five Point Star," Angelo said.

"Uh… please say a different word."

"Beg pardon?"

"The information about the Crown is considered forbidden knowledge," the vizier said.

"I am king. There is no information forbidden to me."

"I understand, and that's generally true," the vizier agreed. "The creation of the Crown, however, is the sole exception of which I am aware."

"There are no exceptions," Angelo said. "You swore an oath, and I'm giving you an order."

"I swore an oath to the Mages of Kaia first."

"And does that oath supersede the one you swore to uphold the true king?" Angelo asked.

"Not at all. Quite the opposite, actually," the vizier said. "I do what I do now to protect you. Information about the Crown's creation is dangerous."

"No, what's dangerous is that some… my niece is running around somewhere in the cosmos with another Crown that I didn't even know existed."

"I can assure you that the Crown of the Single Pointed Star is no threat to one who wears the Five Point."

"That's not what I asked," said Angelo.

"I know. And I am sorry. Truly, I am. I wish I could help," said the vizier. "Now, if I may have your leave, sire? I have final preparations to attend to. I want everything to be perfect for this afternoon."

Angelo waved him away. The vizier bowed and backed off, the smile on his face somewhat less sincere than it had previously been.

Alone, Angelo stood stewing in the middle of the floor. Workers rushed all about him.

It was his big day, after all.

CHAPTER 2

"This thing stinks."

Val sniffed at her makeshift poncho as she and her travel companions pushed through the crowded marketplace.

"Everything on the ship stinks at this point," Rik said. "They weren't meant for any kind of long-term use. No extra wardrobes, no showers, no laundry facilities."

"Okay, so, I don't know if it's my place to ask this," Elle said, "but, what exactly are we doing here? If we needed supplies or... anything... there would seem to be lots better places to get them."

Val caught sight of a young girl walking with her mother. It distracted her only for a moment before her focus returned to the task at hand.

"Unfortunately, we're after information," she said.

"I have informants all around the system," Elle said.

"None like what we're here for. We're here to see a mage I know."

"You know a mage?" Rik asked.

"I encountered him on assignment," Val said. "He's fairly harmless, and given the situation, he's our best place to start."

"Start what, exactly?" Elle asked.

"We need information. About this." Val held open her bag just enough to give them a glimpse at the Crown of the Single Pointed Star. "Right now, it's our only weapon against

Angelo. I need to know more about it."

"Did you add embroidery to your bag?" Rik asked.

"It's a warning," Val said. "That I will murder the shit out of anybody who tries to touch it."

"So," Rik said, "if a little ten-year-old tries to snatch your bag..."

"Can't say I didn't warn 'em."

At the feast after the coronation ceremony, Angelo was proud to wear the Crown of the Five Point Star for all to see. It sat upon his forehead, inactive, but still, it was a symbol of a status he thought he'd never have.

As was his duty, he spent much of the evening mingling with foreign dignitaries and the like. He made sure to enjoy himself, too, eating his fill from the exquisite banquet and sharing a few dances with some of the more attractive guests.

Following a particularly rousing waltz, he headed back to his table to freshen his drink. He was met there by a polite group of state representatives. Each, of course, had an agenda they were trying to push.

Angelo caught sight of the vizier approaching from across the room with an elegant, stately-looking couple in tow. He excused his other guests.

"My lord, King Angelo of Kaia," said the vizier, "may I present to you King Stelleco and Queen Daphna of Palan."

Angelo smiled.

"We've met," he said. "When my brother was king."

"Yes." Queen Daphna forced a somber smile. "We were so sorry to hear of your loss."

"Thank you." Angelo took her hand and kissed it. "My lady. Always a pleasure." He then extended a hand towards Stelleco. "And you, good sir."

Stelleco scoffed.

"Come," the rounder man said. "Let us embrace, as

fellow monarchs."

His giant arms encircled Angelo, threatening to carry him off his feet.

"Whoop." Angelo tried not to wheeze too audibly. "Alright then."

Eventually, Stelleco relinquished his hold.

"I must admit, though, I hadn't heard you announced." Angelo smoothed his coat. His usual dark crimson with golden trim. "Am I losing my hearing?"

"We weren't." Stelleco clapped Angelo on the shoulder. "This is your day, Angelo. Not just some regular meeting of royals."

"I suppose so. I guess I'd forgotten what my brother's coronation was like," said Angelo. "And Thoome and Joseph never got theirs."

"We're sure your thoughts are with them often," Daphna said.

"Yes, quite often, actually."

"Andor was a good friend to Palan," said Stelleco. "I'm sure you'll be an even better one."

"I can only hope to live up to the examples set by him and all my predecessors."

"Please. Enough of this false modesty." Stelleco hoisted a chalice and shouted loud enough for the whole gathering to hear. In such a large and crowded room, that was a feat. "To King Angelo! Long may he reign!"

All those in attendance paused and lifted their glasses.

"To King Angelo!"

They almost immediately returned to their previous business.

"Well, thank you, Stelleco," Angelo said. "That was certainly festive."

"Now, It's my understanding that you're unmarried, sir," the elder monarch said.

Angelo glanced down at his drink.

"Well, uh, sadly, yes, that's true. In my previous life,

I'd dedicated myself to advancing my brother's goals. I never really took the time to develop a proper personal life."

"Would that not leave Kaia without a direct heir?" Stelleco asked.

"For the moment being, yes," Angelo said. "There's still a whole chain of succession, should the worst come to pass. Though I'm hoping there'll be a good bit of time to rectify things between now and then."

"The reason I ask is that our youngest daughter is also unmarried," Stelleco said.

He motioned across the room.

A beautiful young woman hurried to his side. She was, at the oldest, in her late teens, though she projected an air of innocence and naiveté that marked her as even younger. It was most likely the eyes, slightly large for her features. Her mouth naturally curled upwards just a bit at each side, making her seem as though she had a permanent smile gently brushed across her slender face.

"King Angelo of Kaia," Stelleco beamed with pride, "may I present to you the lovely Princess Kavana of Palan."

Angelo took her hand and brought it to his lips.

"Charmed," he said.

Kavana smiled.

Her father shooed her away.

"So, what do you think?" he asked once his daughter was out of earshot.

"She's certainly beautiful," Angelo said.

"She is that," Stelleco agreed. "Must take after her mother."

"But," Angelo winced, "do you not have any elder children?"

"None unmarried."

"I see." Angelo considered that. "It's just, the difference in age is striking."

Stelleco gave Angelo's back a good slap.

"My good man, we are royalty." He laughed. "Propriety

is given a wide berth around us. If I can be at ease with the thought of you pumping an heir into my daughter, I think you can come 'round to doing it."

The house on Chak Clondor was cramped and piled with knickknacks and memorabilia. Piled everywhere, with only the slightest low points creating a sort of trail that would be difficult for anyone not familiar with the layout, and how it came to be over the years, to maneuver through.

The extremely poor lighting didn't help. It mostly originated from a few failing overhead bulbs, as the windows were obscured with boxes and shelving.

There was a knock on the door.

The house's lone inhabitant, an older man, slowly rose from one of the garbage piles and meandered towards the entrance. He grunted and groaned along the way, trying to stretch his aching back.

There was another knock.

"Alright, I'm coming," he grumbled. His dingy coverings were oversized even for his gangly frame. Time and a lack of proper care had stained them an indistinct color, a trait shared by the scraggly hair, both atop his head and spun from his chin, as well as his skin, teeth, even his eyes.

He opened the door, though he was only able to get it about halfway before it jammed on a pile of his belongings. Val, Elle, and Rik stood on his porch.

"Huh." He grunted. "The agency sent over two girls? And… a dude? Whatever, a party's a party."

He stepped aside and beckoned them in, looking each of them up and down as they entered.

"I'm not paying extra, though." He closed the door. "You can tell Weasel that, and if he's got a problem, he can come find me. No way did I ask for three of you, and I don't pay for stuff I didn't ask for. I honestly don't even remember calling this time."

"We're not here about that, Yost," Val said.

He squinted at her.

"Val?" he asked. "Jeez, you went from a palace guard to... this?"

Val pulled back her hood.

"Whatever you think is going on, you're probably wrong," she said.

"So, it's not definite."

"We're looking for information," she said.

"Well, I can give you Weasel's contact info, but I'm not sure he'd have what you're looking for."

"Not about... whatever the hell this Weasel guy does," she said. "We're looking for information only a mage can provide."

"Well, I wouldn't know anything about that, as unauthorized sorcery is clearly and strictly forbidden by law." He drew himself as upright as he was able. Something in his back clicked in a way it shouldn't.

"Cut the crap," Val said. "Remember the last time we met?"

"I honestly do not."

"Jeez," Val said. "Look, I'm not with the palace anymore. We're kind of having some serious disagreements with the new regime."

"Aw, dang," Yost said. "Did something happen to King Andor?"

"Yes," Rik said. "What... where have you been?"

Yost pointed to the pile of garbage on the floor.

"Over there."

"This is seriously somebody we're relying on?" Rik asked. "Potentially with our lives?"

"Well, every other mage I know is bonded and licensed by the state," she said, "which means they'd be obligated to report us."

"Don't you know any corrupt mages?" Rik asked.

Everyone present gave him a quizzical look.

"What?" he asked. "There's corruption in every field."

"Well, if there are, I don't know any. So, this is what we're working with." She turned to Yost. "No offense."

"For what?" he asked.

"Holy crap," Elle said.

"We'd like for you to take a look at this." Val drew the Crown from her bag.

"Well, would you look at that?" Yost marveled. He put on a pair of magnifying spectacles, took the Crown from Val, and paced around his cramped den, looking it over from every angle.

"You recognize it?" Val asked.

"No," he said, "but I know power when I see it."

He then tripped over a pile of trash and fell into another.

"Goddammit!" He ripped off his spectacles and threw them across the room. "I can't see anything else with these things on."

When Rik and Elle helped him up, they realized his hands were now empty.

"Where's the Crown?" Val asked.

"Well, it's around here somewhere." Yost glanced about beneath him.

Val dropped to her knees and frantically dug through the trash.

"But where is it?" she cried. "I can't let it out of my sight."

"Quite attached to it, isn't she?" Yost asked Rik.

"Dude. Clean your house."

Val stood back up, relieved to be clutching the Crown again.

"I got it," she announced. "It's sticky now, but I've got it."

"Now, if I may..." Yost reached for the Crown.

Val yanked it away. "Uh-uh. You can see it from where you're at."

"Alright, fine," Yost said. "Just set it on the table in the middle of the room."

Val, Rik, and Elle looked towards the center of the place. None of them could clearly see a table.

Rik kicked a pile of trash; it toppled over and part of a tabletop could be made out. He and Elle cleared away the rest of the garbage that buried it.

"Careful," Yost said. "Just coming into someone's house and kicking around his stuff."

Once space was made, Val set the Crown on the table.

"Have a seat," Yost offered. "No, there aren't chairs."

Elle looked down.

"I'm not sure if the floor is grosser than the trash," she muttered.

"The answer may surprise you," Yost said.

"I'm sitting on my poncho," Val said. "You see how gross this thing is, and I'm choosing to sit on it."

"Coming here was your idea," Rik said.

"I know. I'm just hoping it ends up being worthwhile," she said.

Yost held his hands out over the table. They began glowing. He lowered them towards the Crown.

"You're not going to hurt it, are you?" Val asked.

"Would it be worth much to you if I could?" Yost asked.

"I suppose not."

"Now, just place your hand on the Crown," he said.

She gently touched a fingertip to the point of the Crown.

Reality bent around her, creating a field of distortion that reached out and swallowed her up.

When the room returned to normal, she was gone.

Rik and Elle sprang to their feet.

"What the hell, man?" Rik asked.

"Where is she?" asked Elle.

Yost just smiled at them.

"Where she wanted to go."

CHAPTER 3

An endless void swirled all around her as Val fell.

No. No, it couldn't be a void if she could tell she was falling. Or that it was swirling.

What she absolutely couldn't tell was where she was. Inside of a nebula of some sort? Was her vision just blurred beyond recognition? And if so, was that a result of disorientation, or because of the speed at which she traveled? It didn't feel like she was falling fast, but if those were cosmic phenomena whizzing past her eyes, she had to be.

Her journey came to an abrupt end on a slab of stone. Val could tell she hit with a lot of force, yet somehow she was mostly unhurt.

Dragging herself to her feet, she found herself standing atop a mountain plateau. It looked like a scene out of one of the storybooks she'd read as a child, but as she'd lost interest in those at a very young age, she couldn't recall which one.

Back at Yost's house, Rik calmly asked his host for an explanation of the events that had just occurred.

"Okay, seriously, where the hell is she?" Some of Rik's spittle landed on Yost's face, though he made no effort to brush it away. "No spiritual mumbo-jumbo."

"That opening looked like a space-fold," Elle said.

"Do you see a space-fold generator around here?" Rik asked. "They're hard to miss."

Yost couldn't help but tighten his lips into a nasty grin.

"What are you smiling at?" Elle asked him.

"Answer her," Rik said.

Elle's shoulders slumped.

"He's the damn space-fold generator," she said.

"What?" Rik asked. "That doesn't make sense."

"He's a mage," Elle said.

"And not a very good one, really," Yost admitted.

"Then how the hell'd you do whatever the hell it is you did?" Rik asked.

"It's that." He pointed to the Crown. "Whatever it is, and hey, if you don't want to tell me, none of my business, but whatever it is, it's powerful. And Val's got a strong link to it. Whatever she wanted it to do, it did it. I just gave it a little nudge to get it going."

"Okay." Rik took a step back. "Damn. I don't know about any of this."

"Any of what?" Elle asked.

"Mages," he said. "Living space-folds. Those things aren't even installed on most ships. Coming here was not my idea."

"Then whose idea was it?" Yost asked.

"It was Val's," Elle said.

"Then isn't she responsible for her own self now?" he asked.

"He's kind of right." Elle shrugged.

"Okay, first of all, don't ever say that," Rik said. "Second, it doesn't matter if he's right or not. We've got a... whatever it is we're doing. A rebellion or a coup or whatever."

"Technically Angelo already staged the coup," Elle said.

"Then we've got another coup. Or a, whatever. A counter-coup? Reverse coup?"

"And Val's responsible for it, whatever it is," Elle said.

"And if she's gone, then what?" Rik asked. "Who's in charge now?"

"You, I guess," said Elle.

"Exactly. So, we've got the crazy magic hobo folding our queen into someplace that he doesn't even know where..."

"I don't even know if it's a place," Yost said.

"Okay, that doesn't make any sense to me, but neither has anything that's happened since we got here."

"So, while Val's away, assuming she's even coming back," Yost picked up the Crown. "what do we do with this?"

The next moment, Rik had his pistol out and pointed directly at the old wizard.

"I swear to God, I will shoot you right in the face."

Yost dropped the Crown.

"Don't!" Elle dove for it. She wasn't able to grab it before it hit the floor, though it didn't get too far before she was able to scoop it back up. "Aw. It's all sticky again."

Rik cringed.

Most people still in the ballroom at such a late hour were, by then, stuffed full and at least partly drunk.

The vizier pushed his way through the stagnant, swaying crowd. He himself was too disciplined to overindulge, but he expected such things at these sorts of events.

He could not find his own monarch but did come upon King Stelleco, engaged in meaningless prattle with a few other lords and ladies.

"Your highness, is King Angelo not with you?" the vizier asked.

"No," Stelleco said. "And I was hoping to ingratiate my daughter upon him a bit further before the end of the night."

"Your daughter is lovely, my liege," said the vizier.

"Yes, she is. I hope you'll impart that upon your king."

"At the next available opportunity," the vizier swore.

"But first, I must locate him. By your leave."

Stelleco nodded dismissively.

Weaving his way further through the room, the vizier began stopping random guests.

"I'm sorry, did you see where King Angelo went?"

Finally, one was able to point him towards a particular exit.

"Thank you."

Before Val, standing in a circle, were five cloaked mages. Their manner of dress was not the ornate, showy style she'd expect. The colors were earthy, drab and muted. Their coverings were synched loosely with simple cords.

Their activity, however, was quite luminous. Tendrils of energy spun down from the dark, cloudless sky, into their waiting clutches.

She had to throw her own hands up to her face until her eyes could adjust to the light.

Once they had, she was able to make out a larger ring of robed people, seated outside the circle formed by the five.

The underground chamber where the dark ritual that granted Angelo the power of a star had been performed had remained untouched since then. It was possible that whatever magic had kept it hidden for centuries was still at work, and Angelo wasn't interested in having others snoop around, so he'd declared that area of the castle to be off-limits.

Off-limits to everyone but himself.

On the far walls, there were burned five humanoid shadows, emanating from the circle at the room's center.

Angelo paced the perimeter of the place, running his hands over the scorched stone.

Hearing footsteps on the damaged stairwell, he took a

defensive position just inside the doorway of the antechamber.

His body clenched and fists tightened. He considered pulling down the Crown, but he could only hear one set of footfalls and was confident he could take on any single opponent without it.

Hearing hesitancy and a momentary wobble in the gait, Angelo threw himself around the doorframe...

To find the vizier making his way down the last few steps, one by one, leaning on the wall for support.

"Ah, these old stairs are a treachery now, aren't they?" the vizier said with a dry laugh.

He looked around at the area his king had been surveying, paying special attention to the fresh hole in the ceiling that led up to the castle courtyard.

"Amazing, isn't it? This place stood virtually untouched for hundreds if not thousands of years, and look what we managed to do to it."

"What are you doing here?" Angelo asked.

"I could ask you the same thing."

"I believe you know."

"I'm afraid I do."

"And?"

The vizier shrugged. "What would you like me to say?"

"I would like you to tell me what I want to know," Angelo said.

"I've already made plain that I can't do that. I can apologize again and again, and will if it so pleases you..."

"It does not please me."

"But it doesn't change the fact of the situation," the vizier said. "I cannot give you what you want."

"Can't, or won't?" Angelo asked. "You seemed plenty knowledgeable just the other day. Now you've decided to be less than helpful."

"I adore you, as did the others of my order. But that is the exact reason why I won't give you what you seek."

"And what else don't I know? Hm?" Angelo took a step

closer. It wasn't that he was trying to menace the smaller man, per se, but the difference in height and build, the deep shadows of the underground chamber, and his general demeanor made it hard not to give that impression. "What other knowledge have you taken it upon yourself to decide I don't need to have?"

"What I do, my king, I do for your own protection."

"So you say."

"You don't believe me?"

"I have no cause to."

"Sire, you wound me. Was it not I who introduced you to the Mages of Kaia? Was it not I who orchestrated the means of your ascension to the throne? I do now what I did then. I look out for your best interests and the interests of the people of Kaia by extension. But be careful on those stairs on the way back up. They're dangerous enough. I'd hate to have them charged with regicide."

The vizier chuckled at his own joke.

Angelo was unmoved.

"Recall that you nearly died gaining the power to take the Crown in the first place." The vizier gestured at the open wound in the ceiling. "You decided the gamble was worth the risk. There is no reward here. There's nothing more to be gained."

"I don't seek more power," Angelo said. "I seek knowledge."

"You assume that's any less dangerous?"

With a smile, the vizier headed back up the stairs.

CHAPTER 4

The number of other qualified pilots onboard being virtually zero, Metch had been pulling more and longer shifts behind the sticks than would generally be recommended. It had taken its toll.

Val was probably the next most qualified pilot. Elle had a little experience. Neither were available at the moment, and neither one had likely flown one of these older models. The newer ones all had assisted handling. Flying with that feature was like a dance with the controls; flying without it was more akin to sparring with them.

As he sat in the cockpit, reading an article off of a datapad, he struggled to maintain focus. Hell, at times, he struggled to keep his eyes open. But he didn't feel he could take a break since there weren't too many more people familiar with the communications equipment than there were who knew any other part of the craft. Maybe Hune? But if anything happened, and they needed to get in the air in a hurry, he'd need to be there anyway.

So he sat, or slouched, in the pilot's seat, his eyes drifting over the words on the screen.

The text seemed, for a moment, to be getting brighter. It took him a second to realize that wasn't the case. It wasn't that the screen had brightened; it was that the rest of the cockpit had darkened.

Massive shadows passed overhead, swallowing the

daylight.

They were gone nearly as quickly as they came.

Metch hunched forward, craning his neck at an awkward angle.

"The hell?"

Several Kaian troop transports drifted overhead. Sextengines, seventy meters long, dual decks, the outsides emblazoned with the Kaian crest. These were the big boys, not any of the little guys like the one he'd helped steal, and newer in design by decades.

The Kaian ships landed and opened their bay doors on every side. Armed troops spilled out onto the tarmac.

"Ah, crap."

Metch grabbed a mic from overhead and pulled it towards his face.

"Commander Rik, Commander Elle, come in." He released the button for a moment. Tension made him depress it again almost as fast. "Please, for the love of all that is holy, come in."

The communications system crackled.

"Uh, is this line secure?" came Rik's voice.

"I... am... unsure," Metch said.

Rik sighed. "Then, go ahead, I guess, but maybe don't use our real names."

"Right, sorry," said Metch. "We just had several royal troop transports land. Very nearby."

He watched out the forward viewport as the Kaian soldiers rushed in formation towards his ship. "And they are coming this way."

"Crap," was Rik's response. "Alright, get out of there. We'll try to be in touch as soon as we figure out where, uh, our special lady is."

"Who?"

"We're not using her name."

"Got it. I'll try to be reachable." He slotted the microphone back up and started flipping switches on the control panel.

The engines lit up and lifted the craft skyward.

Soldiers on the ground took aim and began firing, pelting the ship with small ordinance. Not enough to do any real damage to a vessel of that class.

The gunner turrets on the Kaian transports were another matter. They were brought into position. The operators would only need a few seconds to ensure a target lock before unleashing on the fleeing vessel.

Metch gave the throttle a shove, hurtling his ship into the sky and away from the landing pad. Strafing fire came for him, but a few quick pivots brought him clear. There would be no way the Kaian transports could get airborne in time to pursue before he was lost among the clouds.

"Hells yeah!" Metch yelled out. He grabbed the mic again. "Commander, we got away clean."

"Nothing about that ship is clean," Rik replied.

"Compared to where we are now?" Elle said in the background.

"Look, let's not argue over whether we'd rather be sitting in a box of dung or a box of puke, alright?" Rik said.

"Alright, now, did I hear you say earlier that you'd lost the queen?" Metch asked.

"Dude."

"What? It's not her name."

"And how many queens do you think there are on this planet?" Rik asked him.

"I actually know this bar on the southern continent…"

"Now is not the time," Rik said.

Metch checked his scopes. "Alright, well, they don't seem to be pursuing us. Or if they are, they're doing a really bad job of it."

"Or a really good job of it," Elle said.

"Could be," said Metch. "I think it's more likely they'll be coming after you all."

"Probably," Rik agreed. "But we can't go anywhere until

we find our lady. So, for now, just keep out of sight. We'll let you know when we need a pickup."

"Sure thing." He docked the mic again. "I mean, jeez, how do you lose a queen?"

The Crown of the Five Point Star began forming in the center of the five mages, hovering just off the ground. The sun's power was poured in, condensed by the conjurors into molten hunks of glowing energy that flew towards the middle of the ring, building the Crown up one fragment at a time.

Every few seconds, there was a burst of excess energy flung out of the circle. That energy was caught by the outer mages, siphoned off and used to form four other Crowns. They started with the Single Pointed crown and increased the number of spikes with each successive piece.

Val wasn't sure what to do, if anything. She was witnessing history, maybe one of the most important moments.

She stepped back.

For as large a staff as manned the palace, there were still plenty of places where someone could remain out of sight if they knew their way around. The shadow-laden hallway where Angelo stood was one such place.

A woman in an army uniform made her way up the hall. She was not as familiar with the castle as her sovereign but knew how to operate in the dark.

"My king," she said.

Angelo stepped from the wall and embraced her.

"Hello, Clerak," he said. "It's good to see you."

"I was expecting to see you at the ceremony," she said. Angelo broke his hold, but the traces of a smile she could make out beneath his beard didn't fade.

"And what?" he asked. "The view was inadequate from your seats?"

Her lips tightened.

"That's not what I meant, and you know it."

Angelo looked over her head.

"I need you to do something for me," he said.

"Name it."

"I need you to follow the vizier. See where he goes, where he might be hiding any sort of intelligence in his possession."

"Is he suspected of something?" Clerak asked.

"Not as such," Angelo said. "But he may have access to ancient knowledge about the workings of the Crown of the Five Point Star. Knowledge he's keeping from us. He says for our protection, but..."

"Whatever he knows, you will soon know," she said. "Is that all you need me for?"

"Can you think of anything else?"

"There are rumors," Clerak said. "That after the... incident... with Joseph, a small party of royal guards were seen fleeing the palace."

"And who's spreading these rumors?"

"No one you need to worry about," she said. "So they're true?"

Angelo huffed.

"A few soldiers and my predecessor's Guardian took exception to my claim on the throne," Angelo said. "They were attempting to steal the young king away. I've already dispatched forces throughout the empire to search for them, and to every friendly or neutral system."

"Joseph's Guardian?" Clerak asked. "Valentina?"

"Yes."

"And is that all she is to you? A former underling, the former king's Guardian, a rogue operative?"

Angelo's eyes narrowed.

He chortled.

"You came to me for a reason," Clerak said. "You know I

could have them here in a week."

"Perhaps." Angelo's eyes swept the surrounding area. "It may be a bit presumptuous for you to assume the two issues are unrelated. This is where I need you."

"Understood."

He nodded.

They each walked off in opposite directions.

Val slowly traced the outer edge of the clearing, trying to get a better look at what the mages were doing. Not the five in the center, but the ones that formed the surrounding circle. That's where her chances laid if she had any. For some reason, she was having trouble seeing them. The glare of the energy they worked with assaulted her eyes, and yet they remained singularly focused without so much as squinting.

One of them suddenly looked up at her.

"You shouldn't be here," the mage said.

Val stopped in her tracks.

"What... you can see me?" she asked.

The mage furiously returned to his work.

"Please. I need to know more about..." She reached for her bag and found it empty. "Crap. I left it back at Yost's."

"Do not speak here." The sound that came from him was as close to a hiss as it was a voice. "You're an invader. Our work is too important for you to disrupt."

A second mage took notice.

"She has touched the power. And made it back here."

"She seeks to interfere," the first mage said, his concentration remaining intently on his work.

"She seeks knowledge," the second mage said.

"Yes. I do," Val said. "I – there's a lot we don't know about the Crown."

"As it should be," the first mage said. "Knowledge of it is not your concern. Use of it is alone."

"It's not that simple," Val said.

"It is if you let it be," said the second mage.

"I come from a time – in my world, no one knows about the extra Crowns. Just the Five Point."

"Shh," the first mage implored.

"Did – did you just shush me?" Val looked around at the proceedings. "Wait. Those five guys in the middle, do they even know you're here?"

The two mages looked away.

"You're maybe two meters behind them, and there are ten of you," Val said. "How do they not know you're here?"

"Their work requires a great deal of focus," the first mage said. "So does ours."

Val watched as the ten surrounding mages pounded the Five Point Crown's castoffs into the additional Crowns: Single Pointed, Two Point, Three, and Four.

"Please. My... okay, I didn't even know I was part of the bloodline until a few days ago. My uncle, who I didn't even know was my uncle, killed my brother, who – I need to take back the throne. Or, take the throne, since I never really had it."

"That's not our concern," the first mage said.

"Not your concern?" Val asked. "You made the Crowns to protect Kaia. How is it not your concern?"

"Will your uncle not protect Kaia?" the second mage asked.

"That's not the point," Val said.

"Isn't it?"

"We did what was asked of us," the first mage said. "We forged the Crowns. We can't be held responsible for what the royal family did with them after that."

"I need help," Val said. "Angelo has the Crown of the Five Point Star. I only have the Single Pointed one, and I know that's not going to be enough to beat him."

"No," the second mage agreed. "It's not."

Val pointed to the craftwork of the other secondary mages.

"But these others. Where are they now?" she asked.

"Bound to the bloodline," the second mage answered.

"I know that," Val said. "That's not a location."

"Seek the blood, find the Crowns."

"Okay, and how do I do that?"

"Once you've touched the power, you'll know."

"But you said I already touched the power." She looked at the crackles of energy that birthed the Crowns. "Or do you mean...?"

The mages again returned to their work.

Val took a step towards the flailing energy stream.

She reached towards it. She stopped just short of contact.

"Wait," Val said, "I'm not going to interfere with anything important, am I?"

"How can you?" the second mage asked. "You're not even really here."

The stream lashed out, smacking into Val's outstretched hand.

CHAPTER 5

Outside the hovel that Yost called home, Kaian soldiers filled up the streets. Dozens of armed men and women pounded on doors, questioning whoever came to answer. If no one did, the door would be kicked in and the homes searched.

A handful of soldiers finally made their way to Yost's house.

One of them thumped on the door.

"Royal army! Open up!"

Yost did as they requested.

"What?" he asked.

"This dwelling is to be searched by order of the Royal Kaian Army."

"Do we even have an army on Chak Clondor?" Yost asked.

The soldiers pushed their way in. Yost was forced to back away to let them pass.

Rik and Elle remained uneasily seated.

"There have been reports of a stolen army vessel landing on Chak Clondor," the battalion leader said. "We were dispatched from Kaia to investigate."

"From Kaia?" Rik asked. "You guys made good time."

"Really," Elle said.

The soldiers looked over their clothing.

"Deserters?"

"Uh..." Rik groaned.

"C'mon, you start arresting every deserter on the planet, you'll have to take half the population back with you," Yost said. "Heck, I might've even served. I don't really remember."

"Maybe if you tell us what you're looking for?" Elle suggested.

"Unless you came here to bust a couple of deserters and a guy who's clearly on some kind of illegal substance," Rik said.

Yost shrugged.

"The transport that was reported matches the description of one that fled Kaia just days ago," the battalion leader said. "The people on board were responsible for an attempted coup, as well as an attempt on the life of King Angelo. One woman in particular was the former king's Guardian."

"Who's King Angelo?" Yost asked.

"What?" the battalion leader glared at him. "He's king of Kaia. How can you not know that? He is your king."

"I thought Andor was king of Kaia," Yost said.

"No, King Andor passed away weeks ago. His brother Angelo took the throne," the battalion leader said.

"What about Andor's son?" Yost asked. "What was his name?"

"Thoome," said Elle.

"Yeah, Thoome," Rik said.

"Yeah. What about him?" Yost asked.

"He died in the same accident that killed his father," the soldier said.

"Aw. That's sad," Yost said.

The soldier took a step towards Yost.

"Are you alright?" he asked, peering into the old mage's eyes. They didn't react as he bobbed and weaved his head.

"I don't think he is," Rik said.

The soldier held up a finger to Rik.

"I didn't ask you." He looked back at Yost. "You seem like you're stalling. What would you be stalling for?"

"I'm not sure he is," said Rik.

Rik's hands flew up as the soldier pointed a gun towards his head.

"Do not speak unless spoken to. Do I make myself clear, deserter?"

"Hey, whoa, easy," Rik said. "I just meant, I think he really might be that detached from reality."

"And this woman you want? She was King Andor's Guardian?" Yost asked.

"No, she was King Joseph's Guardian," the soldier said.

"Who's King Joseph?" asked Yost. "How does he fit into this?"

The soldier violently swung his gun back towards Yost's face.

Rik leaped up to get between them.

"Hey. Hey! C'mon, man, that's uncalled for," Rik said.

"I should listen to you?" the soldier asked. "You don't even seem to know him that well. What're you doing here?"

Rik looked to Elle for support. She just shrugged.

"Just, look." Rik turned back to the soldiers. "Do you see anybody like that here? The woman you're looking for? Anywhere? Look around. This isn't a big place. And it's kind of full of a lot of crap."

"Uh, valuable collectibles," Yost said.

"Really not the time." Rik stayed focused on the armed men. "But, see, you can tell there's nobody else here. It's just us, and none of us are..."

Directly behind him, space violently warped. Val quickly materialized and the air settled.

"Goddammit," Rik said.

He and Elle drew their guns. Val snatched the Crown off the table and slung it on.

She grabbed the lead soldier's arm and twisted it around. His finger still squeezed at his gun's trigger, forcing him to shoot two of his own troops. She then kicked his legs out from under him, grabbed the back of his head, and slammed his face into Yost's table.

A fourth she kicked square in the chest, hearing a sickening cracking sound followed by shattering glass as he sprawled through the window.

In the time it took her to accomplish all of this, Rik and Elle each shot one of the remaining two soldiers. The distraction of Val tearing through their comrades no doubt provided a distraction.

Rik turned to Val.

"So, how'd it go?"

She shook her head and moved for the door.

Rik nodded towards her.

"I think we should…"

"Yeah," Elle said.

Clutching their sidearms, they followed Val out.

By the time they made it outside, they found that Val was already a ways up the block, pushing her way through oncoming waves of Kaian soldiers. Some were punched, some kicked. One was grabbed and flung into the air. He landed on Yost's porch, between her two comrades and the house's owner.

The man groaned and rolled to his side.

Yost waved to Rik and Elle as they cautiously made their way off his porch and across his yard towards the open street. Once they made it past his fence, they'd be completely exposed.

"Well, it was good seeing you," Yost said.

"He's coming with us," Val called back.

"What, me?" Yost pointed to himself.

"It's not safe here anymore," Val shouted.

Rik flared his eyebrows and sighed. "Queen's orders." He grabbed Yost by the arm and pulled him towards the road.

"Wait, she's the queen?" Yost asked. "What happened to Andor?"

The cockpit radio buzzed to life.

"Hey, it's the commander." Rik's voice was intelligible enough amongst the static. "You there?"

"Yeah." Metch pulled the mic. "And we've had nothing but clear skies."

"Thank heaven for small favors. Come..." The air was filled with the sound of a massive, wet explosion. "Oh, God!"

"Commander?!" Metch asked frantically. "Commander, are you there?"

"Yeah, that wasn't me," Rik said. "But damn do I wish those ships had showers. Home in on my signal. We'll be about thirty stories higher in the next few minutes."

"Roger that. See you in a few."

CHAPTER 6

T he group of insurgents had, surprisingly, made it back to their ship without much further incident. Metch picked them up from atop a tall structure. They'd thought it was some sort of office building, but there had also been ample parking. A combination office building and parking structure? That would certainly be convenient for the people working on the higher floors.

Val slumped on a bench in the rear hold.

Rik approached from an adjacent passage.

"Hey," he said.

"Hey."

He took a seat near her.

"I was hoping we could find a more private place to talk," he said, "but..."

"Yeah," she said softly. "We really need to think about getting some roomier ships."

"Hey, if you know anybody who can get us a good deal."

"What?" she asked. "No. We're totally going to steal them."

"Okay, that works, too." He took a pause. "So, did you find what you were looking for?"

"I think so, actually. Weirdly."

"Good," he said. "I'm glad we got something out of all of this, because..."

Yost stumbled through the compartment, not even

acknowledging their presence before disappearing into a different corridor.

Val chuckled.

"Why did we bring him, again?" Rik asked.

"Because he might be useful," Val said. "And because we kind of would have left him with a target on his head otherwise, which would not be very noble of us."

"Well, what do we know about nobility?"

She furrowed her brow at him, the corners of her lips squiggling.

"Oh, right," he said. "Because you're technically a queen."

"Yeah. Technically," she said. "Look, I was talking to Elle..."

"About me?"

"Yes, about you."

"Really?" he asked. "I was joking. What'd you say?"

"No, look, she was telling me what you were saying, about not understanding any of the magical stuff going on."

"Do you?"

"No," she said. "I'm not insulting you. That's my point though. I don't have any idea what this sort of stuff really is, either. And I'm supposed to be the one using it, plus I'm supposed to be queen on top of that."

"That's not really your fault, though," he said. "We had the same kind of upbringing and the same training. Nobody could be expected to get all of this."

"Well, I'm kind of expected to," she said. "And I'm kind of going to have to if we ever think we're really going to beat Angelo."

"And we do think we're going to beat him?"

"We have to," she said. "A lot's riding on us. I guess we'll both just have to learn as we go. Because I was definitely not prepared for any of this."

"Right. So, we'll figure it out. Together. Or whatever."

"Yeah," said Val. "That's why I want to name you as my Guardian."

"Whoa. Wait, what? Really?"

"Yeah. I need someone I can trust. You might not get all this. Neither do I. But we can figure it out."

He leaned back.

"Wow. The queen's Guardian. I never even considered that."

"Well, I never really thought about being a princess."

"Really? Never?"

"Nope."

"Not even as a wee little girl child?"

She smirked and shook her head.

"Come on," said Rik. "Even I imagined being a princess."

Her eyebrow rose towards him.

"What?" He relaxed and slid down on the bench. His hands folded behind his head. "I'd have made an awesome princess."

CHAPTER 7

For a man his age, Angelo was in remarkable shape. The result of a lifetime of disciplined military service and physical training, no doubt. As he'd aged, he'd bulked up a bit, more beefy than lean now. Still, the sight of him shirtless, as he was, was both impressive and alluring.

A knock came upon his chamber door.

He growled as he sat up, swinging his legs off the side of the bed.

"Enter."

The door opened and the vizier made his way into the room.

Angelo was quickly on his feet. He didn't bother to dress himself any further.

"What do you want?" he asked.

"I came to speak with you, sire." The vizier was his usual demure self in the presence of his king. "And, as always, to see to your interests."

"You know where my interests lie, you stubborn little man."

"I hope so," the vizier answered. "I live to serve."

"And how long do you suppose you'll go on living if you continue to disobey me?" Angelo asked. "Hm?"

"I'm sorry, my king, but you have nothing to threaten me with. My order is all but extinct. There's no other source for the information you're after. Having me tortured or killed would serve you no purpose."

"It might make me feel better."

The vizier held up a single finger.

"I have something else for that."

He leaned out the door and made a beckoning motion.

A servant entered, gently pushing Princess Kavana into the room. The evening gown she'd worn earlier had been replaced with one of a sheer material that left little to the imagination.

"Oh?" Angelo peeped.

"After all, one in your position cannot properly make such an investment without sampling the goods." The vizier bowed and backed away. "I'll leave you to your duties."

He and the servant shuffled their way out of the room.

Kavana smiled up at Angelo.

The door closed.

BOOK 4: THE SECOND

CHAPTER 1

The planet she now stood upon, as far as she was aware, did not have a name. It surely had some sort of designation in the scientific archives, named for the star it orbited and its position in the solar system.

Those sorts of titles were generally meaningless, only ascribed to essentially worthless hunks of rock in space. After all, no one would actually name their world something like "Volligar 3" or "Zazhar 5."

Still, Val wished this planet had a name, if for no other reason than so she could curse it to the heavens.

The snow she trod through was higher than her knees.

The fierce winds whipped at her poncho. In truth, the woolen wrap provided little protection against the sub-freezing temperatures. It was only the power of the Crown of the Single Pointed Star that allowed her to survive in such a merciless climate.

She made her way across the world's southernmost continent, though none of the planet's weather was more hospitable. It just sat a bit too far away from the system's sun.

And, unfortunately, her progress couldn't be tracked well from orbit.

Rik and Elle stood just behind the pilot's seat in the cockpit of their ship. As usual, Metch sat at the controls and monitored communications.

Every few seconds, Rik would flex his arms, though they

remained crossed against his chest. All the while, he bounced on the balls of his feet.

Finally, he leaned over Metch and grabbed for the radio.

"Val, how's it going down there?" he asked to no response.

"You know she can't hear you," Elle said.

"We knew she probably wouldn't be able to hear us," Rik said. "That doesn't mean for sure."

"Yeah, but you should probably plan for the most likely thing," she said.

"Not trying to take sides here," said Metch, "but we barely made it off the planet after we dropped her. No way a radio signal's getting through. We just have to sit and wait for the flares."

He took the mic from Rik and hung it back up.

"I really don't like this," said Rik.

"I am shocked by that news," said Elle.

"She shouldn't be down there alone," Rik said.

"Nobody else can survive in that climate," Elle said.

"Well, clearly somebody can, or else the thing she's after wouldn't be there," he said.

"She said it's down there," Elle said. "She couldn't tell us if anyone's there with it. It might have just been left there. And who knows how long ago? She might have to dig it out of a glacier that wasn't there when it was hidden."

"I'm having fun," Metch said. "Is everybody else having fun?"

"I'm having fun," Yost called from the rear compartment.

"Yeah, but the other people back there with you aren't," Rik shot back.

Elle leaned out the cockpit door. She pulled herself back in quickly, her face having lost a good bit of color.

"You might be right," she said. "Going down to the ice ball where nothing can live may have been preferable."

"Yeah," Rik said, "We seriously need to steal some bigger

ships."

CHAPTER 2

King Angelo crawled out of bed and gave himself a stretch. He paused for a moment as he walked past a mirror and tapped his fuzzy stomach. For a man his age, it was pretty solid. Very little paunch.

A pair of pants and a dressing gown were retrieved from the wardrobe. As he pulled them on, he looked over at the bed, where Princess Kavana of Palan slept still. She wore not a stitch below the collar and the silken sheets did little to obscure the rest.

He turned and left.

It was slightly easier going once Val reached a higher elevation. Rather than trudging through snow nearly half her own height, she could shimmy along a hillside made of solid ice. It came with its own perils and required deliberate movement.

Peering around a corner, she found a heavy metal door embedded in the base of one of the hills.

"Huh."

The old, weighty door creaked loudly as Val slowly pulled it open. Even with the strength the Crown gave her, it was heavy.

She dragged the door shut, cutting off the billowing snow that followed her, as well as any light trailing in. A bit further ahead, where the cave branched off, she could see a dim glow. It may have been obvious, but it seemed as good of a direction to go as any.

Upon reaching the source of the light, Val found an open cavern.

A large, burly man, wrapped in layers of furs, huddled over a glowing plate. It looked to be made of the same material as the door Val had passed through moments earlier.

From what she could see of him, there was nearly as much hair on him as there was on the pelts strapped to his body.

She peeled back the hood of her poncho as she stepped forward.

"Um... hello?"

"Come on in." He didn't even look at her.

Val paced her steps as she moved closer.

"You won't need that here," he said.

"What?" She pointed to the Crown on her head. "This?"

"Mm-hm."

"Okay." She lifted the Crown up to her forehead. The armor retracted. The air that hit her face stung, but not as badly as she'd expected. "So, I'm not freezing to death. That's cool. Uh, no pun intended."

"None taken."

"I'm Val, by the way."

"Bontu."

"And you... live here?" She took in the sight of the sparsely furnished hole in the ice. Crude cubbies and shelves were dug straight into the walls, though she couldn't readily identify the contents. A few other metal plates were strewn about, along with the rotted frames of some chairs.

"Yeah," Bontu said. "Sorry, I don't have much to offer you. I didn't really expect you to be here today. I didn't expect anyone to be here ever."

"Yeah, I don't suppose you get a lot of visitors."

"No," he said. "None. I haven't seen another person for most of my life."

"I wasn't sure if I'd see anyone here, either," Val said. "Our sensors couldn't pick up any life signs, but with all the interference from the storm, we couldn't be sure if there was anyone here or not."

"So, you must be my, what, fortieth cousin sixty times removed?" Bontu asked.

"I'm not even going to try to figure out how we're related," Val said. "If we can both wear the Crowns, then we're both descended from the first Kaian king to have worn one."

The few soldiers who'd escaped Kaia with Val spent most of their days mulling about their purloined transport. There wasn't much purpose to most of what they did to pass the time.

Elle meandered into the rear compartment to find Rik seated on one of the benches, looking over his weapon.

"You think your ammo clip has changed since you last checked it?" she asked.

"Just trying to keep busy," he said. "Which isn't easy. On a cramped ship with a handful of really tense soldiers who don't have a mission."

"Uh-huh."

"I should be doing something," he said. "Something more than just sitting around waiting to find out if she's okay."

"We already established, there's physically nothing any of the rest of us can do about it."

"I know that," he said. He holstered his gun.

"Intellectually, I know that. But, okay, I don't know how many people she's told, but she made me her Guardian."

"Yeah, I know," Elle told him. "She asked me to be a member of her honor guard."

"Wait, when was this?"

"Right before we arrived at Chak Clondor," she said.

"Huh."

"She didn't ask you until after, did she?" asked Elle.

"Maybe."

"And you're jealous that she came to me first."

"No. I'm the Guardian; you're just a member of her honor guard," he said. "That means I'm in charge of you."

"You were already my commanding officer."

Angelo strolled out onto the balcony, a steaming mug clutched in his hand. He closed his eyes for a moment, breathing in the morning air, enjoying the sun pouring over him.

"You couldn't have picked a more secluded spot?" Clerak approached. She did not arrive through the archway, nor was she there when he walked out.

"This is the royal balcony," Angelo said. "Access is highly restricted."

"And yet, here I am."

"How does the new day find you, general?" Angelo asked.

"Busy as ever. How did you enjoy your evening?"

"It was satisfactory," he said.

"Will Kaia be celebrating its new queen soon?"

"Let's not get ahead of ourselves," he said. "Besides, I asked you to gather information on the vizier, not on me."

"Gathering intelligence on someone in his position opens one up to all sorts of secrets about the goings-on in the castle," she said. "Besides, he did hand-deliver her to your chambers last night."

"Oh, that's right. I guess I'd pushed his squirmy little face out of my head."

"I can't say as I blame you," she said. "I'd never want to picture him during intimate times, either. Even if you were trying to last longer, having his visage dancing in your head would probably drain someone of all virility."

"And what have you found on him?"

"As of yet, nothing that suggests he's kept records of anything," she said. "His chambers are coated in opulence, but there are no books, no datapads, no file storage. He keeps nothing on him save his clothes and jewelry, none of which contain any hidden compartments."

"You are thorough."

"That's why you came to me."

"I came to you because I trust you."

"More than the Palan girl?" Clerak asked.

"Are you jealous?"

"Of her?" Clerak scoffed. "No. She's far more suited to be queen than I ever would be. She's young, pretty, and in all likelihood healthier for bearing you an heir."

Angelo turned to her.

"You are a gorgeous woman, Clerak."

"Perhaps once."

He gently lifted her chin towards him.

"Always," he said. "I admired you all our years of service together, and not just for your skills as a soldier."

"You should have said something then."

"I was the king's Guardian," he said with a touch of wistfulness. "Honor and law dictated that my life be devoted to him."

"And now?"

"Now I am the king. I can have everything I ever wanted."

"A king with an informal agreement with another king to wed his daughter," she said.

"Kavana is a fine thing. She's young and nubile and

willing. But she is not experienced nor particularly skilled." His hands grasped at Clerak's waist. "There can be only one queen, and as you've said, logically, she is the prime choice. But law does provide for the king or queen to have more than one husband or wife."

"And what would your first bride think of that?"

"I don't care."

"And what would her father think of it?"

"I care even less."

He pulled her closer, bringing their lips together.

Just inside the doorway, the vizier looked on; the darkness cast by the rising sunlight against the support pillars obscured the sharpening of his features.

CHAPTER 3

Rik found Elle lounging in one of the ship's smaller compartments, reading from a datapad.

"Hey." His head whipped around the corner. "You got any money on you?"

"What for?"

"Just, do you have any money?" he asked again.

"No, I don't have any money," she said. "I was on duty when we had to leave. What would I have been carrying money for?"

"I don't know. Sometimes people have a little on them just because."

"And what do you need money for, anyway?"

"I'm going around asking everyone," he said. "I was trying to get a budget going. You know, for our insurgency."

"And how'd that work out?"

"I got about three and a half coins."

"Oh, well that's fantastic," she said. "You could buy a meal at a moderately priced restaurant."

"Yeah."

"If you ordered off the children's menu."

"I know."

"What are you even trying to budget for?" she asked.

"Because, look around," he said. "The entirety of our rebellion is in this ship. And eventually, we're going to run out of rations. We need supplies. Ships. Soldiers. Food. Changes of clothes."

"You can't buy soldiers."

"You can hire mercenaries."

"You want to raise an army of mercenaries?"

"No. Angelo could just pay them more to switch over to his side," he said. "But we're going to need… something. We definitely need more ships. This place is smelling ripe and everyone is seriously on edge. We need space. Sleeping quarters. Hopefully showering facilities. Val's got to be the brokest queen in history."

He put his hands on his hips and let out a huff.

"I wonder…"

"What?" Elle asked.

"On Chak Clondor, Val was talking about how older military ships sometimes end up in private hands," he said.

"Right. But that's because people pay for them."

"Yeah, but if we win this, Val becomes Queen of Kaia," he said. "And anybody who helps her out now, they'll know they're sitting pretty when that happens."

"Okay, but you just said 'if we win this,'" she said. "If even you're not sure we will, no ship dealer is going to give you a line of credit on the off chance that maybe our underfunded insurgency is gonna work out and then they'll get paid."

"Do you have a better idea?"

"No, I don't. Which is why I've kept my mouth shut. Because no way is anyone selling us a ship on blind faith."

"Well, hopefully, it would be more than one ship," he said.

"Yeah, okay. Let me know how that works out for you." She went back to reading.

Val and Bontu still sat around the glowing plate. Neither had moved.

"So," Val spoke. "What do you do for fun around here?"

"I masturbate. A lot."

"Oh, God."

"Yeah, it's pretty lonely," he said.

"How long have you been alone here?" she asked.

"I've kind of lost track of time," he said. "But, I was definitely a child when we got here."

"Who's we?" Val asked. "Were there other people with you?"

"There were. My mom and my dad. They're gone now. I had to bury them in the snow, because, you know, there's nothing else to bury them in here. They're probably a hundred feet deep by now."

"And... how did they die?" she asked.

"I didn't kill them if that's what you were thinking."

"That is exactly what I was thinking."

"Well, I didn't."

"And why on Kaia would they have come to this place?" she asked.

"My branch of the family made a pact about a half a century ago. They wanted to let the bloodline die out, and the secret of the Crown die with it."

"That doesn't make any sense," Val said. "They were sworn to protect the Crown."

"They were tired," Bontu said. "They'd been in hiding, they'd been scared, for so long. They just wanted it to be over. So, they all swore to never have children, to let them be the end of it. Dozens of aunts and uncles and cousins, all decided to let their family lines die."

"That sounds messed up."

"Who am I to judge? I came to an ice planet to die."

"So what happened?"

"My father didn't stick to the pact."

"Well, obviously."

"My dad loaded my mom into a ship and took off," Bontu said. "He didn't want to face his family with what he'd done. My mom had me in orbit around some gas giant in the Brurray system. We stopped occasionally for fuel and supplies, but mostly, we lived our entire lives in that ship."

"And then?"

"Then mom got sick. Then dad got sick. I'm not a doctor, so I don't know what with, but they passed within hours of each other. I took the ship down to the nearest breathable planet, which was this one, but it was too late. I was too damn stupid, I guess, to think to look for one that wasn't covered in a never-ending ice storm."

"You were a child." She tried to be assuring.

"A stupid child."

"A child who was losing his entire family," she said. "I might not have been a child at the time, but I know what that part's like."

"The Crown was supposed to give me some kind of wisdom." He poked at the glowing plate with a stick. "I don't think bringing your ship down on an uninhabitable iceberg qualifies itself as wisdom. It's kind of funny, though."

"What is?"

"Without even meaning to, I've kept my dad's end of that pact."

"I don't think that qualifies as funny."

"I've been alone for a very long time."

Val mouthed the word, "wow."

"What about you?" Bontu asked.

"Me?"

"Yeah. What about your family?"

"I don't really have one," she said.

"How does that work?"

"I grew up thinking I was an orphan. I only found out I'm royalty a couple of weeks ago. My father - still weird to think of him like that - my father the king and my older brother, the crown prince, were killed in an accident. My other brother, the younger one, was brought in to take the throne, but then he was killed, too. By my uncle, who my brother would call a feminine hygiene product."

"What's that?"

"You probably don't need to know," she said. "But my uncle killed my second brother, and my mother gave her life to let the two of us escape."

Bontu burst out laughing. Val's face screwed up, her mouth hanging slightly.

"I get it," Bontu said. "Because your mom died so the two of you could escape, but only one of you did."

"No, that's not funny either."

Included in Angelo's rounds that day was a march through the palace's Hall of Honor. The life-sized visages of every previous monarch to rule the empire looked back at him as he moved deliberately from portrait to portrait. He'd seen them all before.

The only ones that interested him now were those being installed at the very end of the line. One of Andor and Thoome, another of Joseph.

Either the workers hanging the paintings took no notice of him, too engrossed in their task, or, more likely, they nervously avoided eye contact with the king in their midst.

Angelo stood and stared, taking in the sight of his brother and nephews emblazoned on the walls. The inhabitants of the hall had long been more of an abstract concept to him. Even his own father, a man he had no recollection of. The presence of those so close to him suddenly made the entire place more real, more a tomb than a history lesson.

He turned sharply and walked quickly from the room, his boot-falls echoing through the now crypt-like stone chamber.

Rik next encountered Elle in the rear hold of the

transport, still fixated on her pad.

He hadn't actually been looking for her, and so paid her little attention as he passed through, a duffel bag slung over one shoulder, striding with purpose towards the rear hatch.

"And where do you think you're going?" Elle asked.

"As Guardian, I'm not required to answer that."

"And as my friend?"

He stopped and turned to her.

"I'm going to secure more ships and supplies," he said.

"Really?"

"What? Don't give me that."

"I'm not trying to be pessimistic, but how are you really planning on doing that?" she asked.

"I have some contacts still. People I trust." He shifted the bag. "Some of them are rendezvousing with us any second. They're going to take me to a market world in neutral space where I should be able to bargain for some help."

"With your three and a half coins?"

"Yes, Elle, with my three and a half coins."

"That'll be impressive to see," she said.

"Well, prepare to be impressed, then."

"Oh, I'll prepare alright." She returned to her article.

A loud thud rang through the hull plating.

"That'll be my ride docking." Rik made for the hatch.

"Hey, what kind of memorial service do you want?" Elle didn't look up from her pad. "Presuming we can't recover the body."

Rik waved over his head. "Love you, too, Elle."

"So what is it I can do for you?" Bontu asked.

"Wha..."

"You didn't come here just to see me," he said. "No one ever has. You must want something."

"I was drawn to the power of the Crown," Val said. "It

called to mine. My uncle has the Crown of the Five Point Star. No one on Kaia, except the queen, seemed to even know the others existed. And the Five Point Crown is a lot stronger than mine. It's stronger than yours."

"How do you know?"

"I just know," she said. "The Crown gave me insight. None of the other Crowns are enough to oppose him. But, all of the Crowns together..."

Bontu reached down towards the glowing plate. He grasped it by one edge and heaved. It only went a couple of feet into the air, but it was enough for him to slide his thick arm under and pull out the Crown of the Two Point Star.

He dropped the plate back down. Its glowing had ceased.

He gave the Crown in his hand a forlorn look.

"But, if you take the Crown, I'll pretty much die here," he said.

"I'm not going to take your Crown. Not if you don't want me to," she said. "But, you could come with me."

He pulled his head away slightly, looking at her out of the corner of his eye.

"Think about it," she said. "The Crowns only speak to people with royal blood. Who else is going to wear it?"

"I don't... I mean, I've never..."

"Hey. I know it's a lot to take in." She placed a reassuring hand on his arm. "You haven't seen another person in years. You haven't left this planet since you were a kid. But this is important. Angelo can't be allowed to stay on the throne."

"Why not?"

"Beg pardon?"

"I mean, sure, he killed your brother..."

"And you need more reason than that?" she asked.

"But how do you know he's a bad king?"

"No one who murders his own family to get to the throne can possibly be a good king," she said firmly.

"I don't know," Bontu said. "I think there's some moral gray area here. I haven't heard his side of the story."

"You don't need... you're stalling, aren't you?"

"No," he said. "Well, yes. Maybe. But you have to admit, I made a good point."

"No. Trust me, I know Angelo. I knew Joe, and Andor, and Thoome."

"Well, I don't know you," he said. "Why should I trust you?"

"Put the Crown on," she suggested. "Let it tell you if I'm right or not."

"Oh, jerky?" he asked.

"What? You had better not be suggesting..."

Bontu reached for one of the cubbies in the wall. He returned with a large, worn cloth sack.

"There's not much moisture in the air here, so it was pretty easy to slap together a makeshift dehydrator." He held it out towards her. "Want some?"

Val rolled her eyes.

"Fine." She took a piece of dried meat from the bag and nibbled at it. "This is actually pretty good."

She took another bite.

"Wait." She paused. "Where'd you get the meat?"

They heard a sound like a low growl in the distance.

Val snapped around, her eyes locking on the entrance tunnel.

"What was that?" Val asked.

Another sound came, like metal being rent.

Bontu sprung up.

"You closed the door you came through, right?" he asked.

"I thought I did," Val said. "I'm pretty sure I did."

Bontu ran. Val hoisted herself up and sprinted after him.

"The cold warps the metal," he breathlessly explained. "Sometimes it doesn't shut all the way."

"Well, how was I supposed to know that?" Val asked.

They slowed their run and approached the door cautiously. The door, easily a foot thick of solid, reentry-grade alloy, was badly bent inwards.

The pair stared at it.

"What does this mean?" Val asked.

Bontu took off running back down the tunnel.

"Hey," Val called after him. "What does this mean? What's out there?"

By the time she reached his cavern again, he was frantically gathering up an armful of crude, simple tools from his cubbies.

"Talk to me," Val said. "What's going on?"

"What's going on is I've got to get that door fixed or else."

More sounds of twisting metal, more snarls and growling, came from the cave.

"I've been living here for decades because I've made sure they couldn't get me," Bontu said hysterically, "but now..."

He gestured at her.

"Look, I'm sorry," she said, "I'm sorry about the door, but it's sounding like we're past the point of repairing it."

"Well what the hell am I supposed to do?" he asked, nearly in tears. One of the largest, strongest men Val had ever laid eyes on was suddenly a lost little boy.

She picked up the Crown of the Two Pointed Star and held it out towards him.

"Put this on. With both of us, we can fight it."

Bontu took the Crown from her.

"It's not it," he said. "It's them."

"What does that mean?"

More snarling and growling, a deep metallic clang, a dry crack of breaking and falling ice.

"Bontu, we can do this."

He took a beat, looked at the Crown in his hands.

"I haven't worn this in a very long time," he said quietly.

"I'd never worn the Crown at all until a couple weeks ago."

"Uh-huh. Very reassuring. And how'd that work out?"

"I made it, didn't I?"

"And how'd it work out for the guy who was with you?" he asked.

CHAPTER 4

Val and Bontu approached the broken metal door, a renewed confidence in their steps.

Val grasped her Crown.

"You ready?" she asked.

"No."

"Alright, let's do this."

Val slid the Crown down her face; her armor materialized beneath her poncho.

Bontu put his Crown on and pulled it down, manifesting his own protective bodysuit that wove its way through the hides he wore. Like hers, it was thinner and less intricate than the one the Kaian monarchs wore, but, given his size, he was a virtual tank in comparison.

Val took off in a dead run, leading the charge out into the blizzard. Bontu followed close behind her.

She stopped less than ten meters from the cave entrance.

She tried to survey her surroundings, but the enhanced vision that the Crown provided was almost completely negated by the swirling snowstorm.

"Can you see anything?" she shouted to Bontu.

"No," he replied. "But that probably means they're out here."

"What? That doesn't make any sense."

"How does that not make sense?" he asked.

"If you could see them that would mean they're here. If

you can't see them, that also means they're here?"

"I guess I hadn't thought about…"

They spun around at the snapping sound of a falling ice shelf, just in time to see frozen sheets sliding from the side of the glacier, burying the entrance to Bontu's home.

"Aw, dang," he groaned.

"I'll help you dig your stuff out after this is all over," Val said.

"It's not my stuff I'm worried about," he said. "Okay, I'm a little worried about my stuff. But right now I'm mostly worried about them."

He pointed off into the distance. Several humanoid forms, riding on the backs of giant white bears, galloped towards them.

Several more riders and mounts descended from the top of the glacier.

The pair was quickly surrounded.

"Okay, this is bad," said Bontu.

"Is it? Is it really?"

"Yes. I've spent most of my adult life avoiding them for a reason."

"How are they even here? You told me you hadn't seen another person."

"They're not people anymore."

"Nothing's supposed to be able to survive on this planet," Val said.

"They've adapted."

"They're riding giant bears!"

"The bears are the worst part."

One of the riders drew back a spear and hurled it towards them. Even with their heightened speed and reflexes, Val and Bontu were barely able to dodge.

"But the riders are still pretty bad," Bontu said.

Taking the initiative, Val ran straight at one of the bears. It reacted with unreal swiftness, batting her away with a swipe of its colossal paw before she could even start her strike.

She flew a good fifteen meters out into the wasteland before coming down sideways into the drifting snow.

She hadn't been able to rise back up when one of the bears was on her, snarling in her face.

Bontu dove in, throwing her out of the way just before the bear could close its jaws around her head.

"Come on," Bontu said. "We've got to go."

Val scrambled to her feet.

"Go where?" she asked.

"Away from here."

"That's sensible."

They took off running across the frozen landscape.

"How do you usually take on these things?" Val asked.

"I don't."

"Well, not all at once, but…"

"No, not at all," he said.

"You strongly implied that's where you got the meat for the jerky."

"Not from the adult ones," he said.

"You killed baby bears?"

"Well you've seen how the adult ones are. No way could I take one of them, much less six."

"Well, we're going to need to figure out how," Val said.

"No way. It can't be done."

"If we're going to live, we have to."

"Are you not listening?" he asked. "Can't. Be. Done."

"You have a better idea?"

"You have a way out of here, don't you?" he asked. "Off the planet, I mean."

"I have signal flares my ship can detect."

"Great. Use those. Get us out of here."

"Oh, sure, now you're in a hurry to leave," she said.

"There are bears now!"

"I can't, anyway," she said. "Not on the run. They need to be able to home in on my exact position, which means I have to stay still for a few minutes after I set one-off."

"Okay, so, this is how I die," Bontu said. "It's not really a surprise, I guess."

"We're not going to die, Bontu."

"Pretty sure we are."

"We're going to fight."

Still moving at top speed, Val reached down, snatching up a piece of ice. Her armor charged it with energy as she leaped into the air and spun, hurling the crackling projectile towards the closest of the pursuing animals.

The ice chunk slashed through the bear's cheek. It slowed only for a moment and let out the most horrifying scream.

"What was that?" Val asked.

"I think you made it angry," Bontu said.

Val balked. "It wasn't angry before?"

"I've never actually seen one angry. And I've eaten their children."

"Guy."

"I don't know what happens now," Bontu said.

Angelo sat sprawled out on a recumbent chair in his chambers, once again in a state of partial undress, when the door was knocked upon.

"Enter!"

The door cracked open just far enough for Clerak to slip in, then it was shut again.

"How did you know it was me?" she asked.

"I didn't." Angelo lifted his scepter off the nightstand and looked at the round, heavy head of it. "If it was someone I didn't like, I'd have dealt with them appropriately."

Angelo set the scepter aside and sat on the bed. He patted the space next to him.

"Come."

Clerak rocked on her feet.

"I'm not here for that, sire."

"Sire?" Angelo smiled. "Ooh, this is tense. Then what are you here for, general?"

"It's about my investigation," she said.

"And your discovery is so important it overrides your desires for the pleasures of the flesh?" Angelo asked. "What have you found about our mutual friend?"

"I'm not certain it's about him."

Angelo rose off of the bed.

"Well, out with it."

"I'm not certain it's not, either," she said. "It pertains to Andor's death."

"What?"

"I don't have the files to give you," she said. "I didn't want to risk creating a trail. But there are inconsistencies in the official reports. His ship was badly burned…"

"Of course it was. It went through a planet's atmosphere after the explosion."

"But the explosion didn't originate in the generator room," she said. "And the accelerant definitely wasn't the liquid fuel onboard."

"And you think this means, what, sabotage?"

"Or neglect," she said. "But the propulsion systems on royal vessels are rigorously maintained…"

"I know that," he said. "This was all discussed in the official inquiry."

"Believe me or not, but something on that ship caused the fatal damage. Either a deliberate explosion or someone onboard was smuggling something highly volatile."

"What makes you suspect smuggling?" he asked.

"Because there's nothing in the official manifest that could do what was done to Andor's ship."

Angelo took a step back from her.

"It could be any number of things," he said. "Andor could have been transporting something privileged, something no one was supposed to know about."

"What could Andor have been transporting that would have caused... this?" Clerak asked.

"I don't know," he said. "The royal family's always had secrets, even from each other. Until a few weeks ago, I had no idea there was more than one Crown. Which I still need information on, by the by."

"And I'm working on that. But this came to my attention, and I thought you should know about it."

"If this came to your attention, why wasn't it brought to mine?" he asked. "Through official channels?"

"That I couldn't tell you. You'd have to ask your Guardian. If you'd selected one yet, that is."

"It's hard to know who I can trust anymore."

"You can trust me," she reminded him. "You said so yourself."

"And a few days ago I thought I could trust the vizier. And until minutes ago I trusted the official cause of my brother and nephew's deaths."

Her hips swayed slightly as she moved closer to him.

"Have I not proven myself in a lifetime of service?" she asked. "Did I not prove myself on the balcony earlier?"

"I won't besmirch you," he said, "but a physical act of passion can be used for many reasons."

"That sounds a bit besmirching to me."

"I tried to be as delicate as I could."

"Angelo, you're the king now. I know it's hard, but you have a kingdom to run. That requires trusting someone to carry out your orders."

"I just need some help."

Clerak moved closer still.

"That's what I'm saying," she whispered.

"Not now. Dammit. As pleasant as it would be, I've thought of something else I must do first."

He maneuvered past her and out the door.

Once he was gone down the hall, the vizier emerged from the nearby shadows. His face remained inscrutable.

◆ ◆ ◆

The giant bears circled tightly around Val and Bontu. Rather than attack, they bent their forepaws.

They were bowing.

The one that Val had injured nudged closest.

Val petted it on the nose.

"So, I'm pretty sure I just established dominance," she said.

Bontu muttered, "Huh."

Under the bear's fur, Val could make out traces of scarring. The lines were too clean to have come from another wild animal.

The riders, frustrated and a bit frightened of the animals that were no longer responding to commands, slowly dismounted. Once on the ground, they ran off into the distance.

"What are we going to do about them?" Bontu pointed to the fleeing hunters.

"I don't really know them, and I don't know their story," Val said.

"They've spent years trying to murder me."

"That's your side of it," she retorted.

"Seriously? I – oh, I see what you did there."

"And," Val added, "my babies've gotta eat."

Val pointed after them. The bear she was petting snorted.

The pack rose and charged after their former masters.

Metch sat in the pilot's seat, his feet up, reading from a datapad, only occasionally glancing over at the panels.

Finally, after many hours of this, he saw a signal light up.

His pad was dropped as he hoisted himself to an upright position. He went for the mic.

"We got the signal."

The ship adjusted its pitch and dove towards the planet.

Pure white covered the viewports for several minutes. Metch was forced to fly on instrument readings alone.

Even once they'd broken through the clouds, the snow reduced visibility to an absurd degree. Elle joined Metch, hunkered in the copilot's seat, to help scan the ground visually.

"There she is." Elle pointed towards the horizon.

The high winds jostled the ship, rocking it back and forth even once it had completed its landing.

Once the secondary landing clamps were down, the rear hatch was dropped.

Most of the ship's complement, bundled as best they could be, stood at the top of the ramp. Elle was at the fore.

They looked out to see Val lounging atop a pile of full and sleepy bears.

"I made some friends," she said.

CHAPTER 5

That evening, Angelo sat in the royal dining hall, alone at the head of the table.

The vizier entered from behind him and slunk to his side.

"My king," he said. "May I join you?"

His mouth full, Angelo hesitated but gestured at an empty chair.

The servants rushed to provide the new arrival with a meal.

"Thank you," the vizier said, both to Angelo and the servers. They smiled, nodded, and walked away. He picked up his glass and watched them go before partaking. "Not very talkative, are they?"

"Who?" Angelo asked. "The servants?"

"Yes."

"Perhaps they've just learned the value of silence."

"Indeed."

"So, was there a reason you wished to dine with me tonight?" Angelo asked. "The food at any of the palace venues is just as fine, and the cost to you is the same."

The vizier laughed.

Angelo glared at him.

"But the company is nowhere near as pleasant," the vizier said.

"Is that so?"

The aged little man smiled and nodded gracefully.

"There is one subject about which I'd like to hear you speak," Angelo said.

"Oh. I see." The vizier started to get up. "Perhaps my coming here was a mistake."

"Sit."

The vizier froze momentarily before doing as he was told.

"Eat," Angelo insisted. "Enjoy."

"Thank you, my liege."

"I'm curious, vizier, about this knowledge you've decided is forbidden from me," Angelo said.

"Your highness…"

"Oh, I know you're not going to share it," the king said. "But I'm curious about the knowledge itself. If it's forbidden, how did you come to possess it?"

"It was passed down to me."

"How? By whom?"

"By my order, the Mages of Kaia."

"Yes, but how were you selected?" Angelo asked. "Is it hereditary?"

The vizier chuckled.

"No, there's no nepotism in the Mages," he said. "Unlike the royalty, there's nothing special about our bloodlines. It's all about the knowledge, the proper mindset to absorb the teachings."

"So you were, before the mages took notice of you…?"

"An average student in an average city living an average life," the vizier said. "There was nothing outwardly extraordinary about me."

"And the knowledge of the mages, what were they, sacred texts?"

"Oh, no," the vizier said. "No, they can't be seen to leave a trail. That knowledge can't simply be left lying around in someone's bedchambers for a maid or housekeeper or some such to stumble across. The Mages' knowledge is passed down orally."

"Huh." Angelo paused to consider that. "It doesn't seem that would be a particularly effective way of maintaining the integrity of the teachings. Bits could get lost or added or changed in the retelling."

"The Mages are very rigorous," the vizier said. "Fidelity to all of the stories is strictly enforced, sometimes physically, if need be. None of the lessons are altered in any way. Everything is passed, word for word, from one generation to the next. Unlike, say, the Order of Meridian, who clearly have lost the knowledge their forbearers once possessed."

"And yet the Meridians have maintained their place above ground, in the good graces of the royal family, for generations."

The vizier raised his glass.

"And all due credit to them," he said. "But tell me, where are they now? Hm? The Mages taught us that there is a special circle of hell for traitors, spies, and those who fail the royal family. I will keep that vow to my last."

Angelo raised his glass as well.

"Let's hope," he said.

CHAPTER 6

The insurgent crew huddled in the read hold, digging into the sack set in the middle. Slab after slab of dried meat was pulled and shoved into hungry mouths.

"You know that's baby bear, right?" Val asked. She stood off to one side.

"It's the first thing we've eaten in weeks that wasn't vacuum-packed into a little foil pouch before any of us even entered the service," Elle said. "Let us have this."

Val paced around to the other side of the circle, trying not to focus on the sound her crew's gnawing made.

"So, you all just let Rik do what now?" she asked.

"Nobody let Rik do anything," said Elle. "He's a grown man, and he's our superior officer. And your Guardian, if I can remind you."

"Well how's he gonna guard me if he's off... where did he say he was going exactly?"

"He didn't, exactly. Just that he was going to a 'neutral planet.'"

"Great," Val said. "That narrows it down to about eight hundred known worlds. Did he say how we were supposed to find him once he was ready to be picked up?"

"I have literally given you all of the information I have," Elle said.

"Great," Val said again. "This just keeps getting better. Okay, well, without knowing anything about that, I guess we just have to keep going. I'll go consult with Metch about our next course."

She left the passenger compartment.

"So you say this is baby bear?" Elle asked Bontu.

"Mm-Hm. The baby ones are easier to kill."

CHAPTER 7

At such an hour, Angelo would have thought he was through with visitors for the evening. Yet, here he was, well after sundown, well after dinner, with someone pounding at his door.

He pulled it open. A royal guard stood at attention just outside.

"Pardon the intrusion, sire," the guard said, "but there's been an incident."

"An incident?"

The guard leaned in close.

"A murder, sire."

"In the castle," Angelo said.

"Yes."

"Who was it?" the king asked. "A service member? Former?"

"One of the viziers."

"I believe you'll find that he's the only remaining vizier," Angelo said. "Or was, I suppose."

"For your own safety, we've put the entire place on lockdown and have posted extra security 'round the clock."

Angelo patted her on the shoulder.

"Excellent work," he said. "I'll limit my movements and await further development."

"Yes, your highness." The guard gave a nod, spun on her heel, and left, shutting the door behind her.

Angelo headed over to his bed and spread himself out on his back.

A sound of running water came from an adjoining room. Kavana appeared in that doorway.

She strolled towards him, biting her lip.

"There's been a murder in the castle," Angelo said. If he felt any emotion at the news he did not betray it. "One of my most trusted advisors is dead. Probably better that you stay with me until this is resolved. It's the safest place in the palace right now."

The princess smiled and climbed into bed with him.

He expected her to immediately cuddle up close, but instead, she reached behind her back, under her top, and produced a small object wrapped in cloth.

Angelo sat up.

"What's that?" he asked.

"A gift."

She undid the rag. Sat within was a small bloodstained dagger.

BOOK 5: FOUR

CHAPTER 1

Val stood atop a building, looking out over the rundown urban environment below. She wasn't too high up, only four floors, but there were plenty of ventilation pipes, stairwell accesses, and other obstructions to hide her from view.

The quality of the local air didn't help. The whole place was covered in a greasy mist and smelled dirty.

"It's close," she said. "I can sense it."

She watched people mull about the streets below her. A young child pointed to something in a shop. Her father knelt down beside her. He pulled a small purse from his pack and counted out some coins. He counted again. Two of the coins went back in the purse. The rest were handed to the shopkeeper. The shopkeeper handed the girl her treat. She hugged her father, took his hand, and they strolled off together, smiles all around.

Even on Val.

"Try not to worry so much," Metch's voice came over her earpiece. "It ages you."

Val turned from the edge of the building, the hem of her poncho cutting through the air.

"Ages me?"

"I meant, more like, you know, the generic 'you,'" said Metch.

"Uh-huh," Val said. "I should be down there."

"And I should be back in the ship if we need to make a speedy getaway."

"Well, without Rik here, we're a man short," Val said.

"What are you talking about?" Metch asked. "You've got Bontu and Yost here now."

"I said what I said." Val knelt down behind a vent.

Metch, flanked by Elle, navigated his way through the market. Street vendors stood in front of carts parked in front of shops, pushing most every type of ware. Food, clothing, electronics, toys, and certain items unfit for the younger patrons.

"You know, that's a great idea," said Elle. "You should be down here with us. No one would notice the queen of Kaia in their home."

"You realize that very few people actually recognize me as queen, right?"

"Right. And those who don't, recognize you as a domestic terrorist." Metch said.

"You know, by that measure, you're a domestic terrorist, too, right?" Val asked.

"Yeah, but nobody knows who I am," Metch said.

"I can guarantee you my uncle knows," Val said.

"I meant the general public," Metch said. "You're the face of this whole movement. The rest of us are pretty anonymous."

"Oh, I'm the face now?" Val asked.

"And such a lovely face," Metch said with a grin.

"Uh-huh. What happened to worry aging me?"

"Sorry," Metch said, "I think you're breaking up. I didn't catch that last bit."

"I'm sure," Val said.

"We've got this, okay? Elle out."

Having reached the outskirts of the marketplace, she and Metch approached a small, timeworn house. It wasn't much to look at, though none of the surrounding dwellings were. A smoggy atmosphere and strong sun had their way with the neighborhood for too many years, tinting every structure a dull sandy gray.

Standing on the covered porch, they found no sign of a buzzer, so Elle gave the door a few good knocks.

A few seconds later, it opened just a bit. Just enough so that a glowing slit could be seen in the opening, at about eye level.

The door quickly slammed shut.

"Okay, uh, what was that?" Metch asked.

"Was that a robot?" Elle asked.

"A robot? A door-answering robot?"

"It just looked like a robot, okay?" she said. "Or at least the optical sensor of one."

"Why would someone who lives in an area like this have a robot built just to not answer their front door?"

"If they're descended from royalty, they might have money to burn." Elle knocked again. "Hello? Whoever's in there? We just need to talk to you."

"No," came a voice from inside, "you need to get off my property."

"That sounded like a person, not a robot," Metch said.

"So, at least we know he's in there."

"Dammit," the voice groaned.

"Seriously, guy," Elle said, "we just want to talk."

"It's Gyu!" the voice shouted.

"What?" asked Metch.

The door opened slightly again. A sliver of a man's face could be seen, grimy and unshaven, lower down than the glowing slit had been.

"My name is Gyu, not Guy," he said.

"That's not really what I..."

Elle threw her shoulder into the door.

Gyu stumbled, not very sure on his feet. By the time he could regain his balance, Elle and Metch were in his home, the door shut behind them.

"Whoa, easy," Metch said. "We don't want any trouble."

"You just broke into my house."

"Technically you let us in," said Elle.

"No I didn't."

"Well, you opened the door," she said, "so…"

"We just need to check something," Metch said. "Is there anyone else in the house right now?"

"No," said Gyu. "I live alone. It's just me and my robot."

Metch moved towards the back of the entryway, to the kitchen door, and had a peak around the corner.

"Is that a Syman?" he asked Gyu.

"A what?" Elle asked.

"Yeah," Gyu said.

"What the hell's a Syman?" asked Elle.

"It's a household robot," Gyu said.

"Humanoid," Metch added.

"Humanoid?" Elle asked. "What for?"

"They used to make them that way," Metch said. "I guess some people found it comforting. I thought it was creepy as hell."

"It sounds creepy," said Elle.

"It's not creepy," Gyu said. "It's versatile…"

"And it sounds really inefficient," Elle said.

"It was," Metch said. "That's why they don't make them that way anymore."

"Well, all the newer robots are specialized," Gyu said. He had a tendency to make too many hand gestures as he spoke. "A Syman can do anything a person can do. It can cook, vacuum, help with projects and stuff. I don't get around so good anymore. I don't know what I'd do without it."

"I dunno." Metch grimaced. "Find an actual wife?"

"Oh, gee thanks. Because I never thought of that."

"Did you, bud?" Metch asked. "Because I can't figure you'd keep a Syman around if you did."

"Talk to me." Val came back on the earpiece. "What do you see?"

"I see a guy," said Metch, "and get this: he's got a Syman."

"A Syman? What the hell?"

"Right?"

"So has everybody heard of these things but me?" Elle pulled a device off of her belt, just a bit larger than her palm, flat, with a screen and a few buttons on one face. There was a silver sphere embedded in one of the shorter ends. "Okay, can we just do this?"

"Do what?" Gyu asked. "I didn't agree to let you do anything. This is my house."

"Uh-huh. Sure." Elle looked to Metch. "Hold him."

"Me?" Metch asked.

"Yes."

"Why should I hold him?"

"Because I have the scanner and I told you to," Elle said.

"I'm not actually sure you can tell me what to do," Metch said.

"Chain of command is mission-specific," said Elle.

"She's right," Val interjected. "This is her op. You follow her orders."

Metch groused but did as he was told. He took a grip on Gyu's arm and pulled up the sleeve.

"Hey," Gyu said. "You can't do that."

"Look, it's no big deal, alright?" Elle showed him the device. "I'm just gonna put this up against your arm, unless you have a preference for another part of your body that isn't weird, it'll go boop, and then we'll have what we need to make a decision."

"A decision about what?" Gyu asked.

"I will explain everything after the 'boop.'" Elle assured him.

The spheroid at the device's end was placed against Gyu's skin.

The device went "boop."

Elle looked at it.

"Huh."

"'Huh?'" Metch echoed.

"'Huh?'" Val asked. "What's 'huh?' What's happening

189

down there?"

"You're not going to like this." Elle's lips splayed out; her teeth held firmly together

"Don't worry about what I like. Tell me what's going on."

"The scan came back negative," Elle said. "It's not him."

"What? That can't be right."

"We don't know if we're looking for one of your relatives," Elle said.

"Who are you talking to?" Gyu asked.

"Shut up," Elle said.

"The Crowns were handed out to branches of the royal family," Val said. "No way would they let them out of their hands. They knew how important they were."

"Well, I don't know what to tell you," Elle said. "The scan says it's a no-go. You said you could sense the Crown, right? Can't you, I don't know, hone in better?"

"Unless the Crown's being worn, I only get a vague sense of where it is," Val said.

"Well, that doesn't help. So, how about we..." Elle's voice was drowned out by a clatter from the kitchen. "Now what the hell is that?"

She drew her weapon and pushed Gyu aside, moving cautiously but swiftly towards the back of the house.

A dark shape shot past the kitchen door. By the time Elle and Metch reached the kitchen, the source of the silhouette was gone.

The rear window flapped open, gently pushed by the breeze from outside.

Metch leaned out, then back in, tapping his earpiece.

"It's the Syman," he said. "It's the goddamn Syman."

Val stood and looked over the edge of the building, into the alleyway behind the house, in time to catch a glimpse of the robot running through.

"Well. Damn."

CHAPTER 2

The back door to Gyu's house burst open. Elle held her sidearm at the ready as she and Metch ran down the narrow alley.

Reaching the end, they were forced to reduce their speed to a brisk walk as they made their way through the crowd. Elle held her gun down, hopefully out of sight of too many passersby, but didn't want to holster it completely.

"Which way did it go?" she asked.

Metch sucked for air and pointed to the right. "I think he went that way."

"Are you already out of breath?" Elle asked. She again took the lead in their pursuit.

"I'm a pilot," Metch said. He managed to work himself back up to a slow jog, barely keeping up with Elle's steps.

"Basic physical fitness is still supposed to be part of your routine."

"Yeah, this seems like the right time for that sort of conversation."

It took several tense moments of them pushing their way through the mass of people before they spotted the Syman partially hiding behind a cart and shop awning.

"There!" Metch shouted.

"I see him."

They took off running.

The robot broke out in a sprint. With its superior speed

and strength, it was able to simply toss bystanders aside as it went and was far too fast for Elle and Metch to possibly hope to keep up with.

They continued their chase anyway.

Long out of sight of its pursuers, the Syman grabbed onto the brick corner of a building, swinging itself around and into another alleyway. The brick crumpled easily in the robot's trio of long, flat fingers.

The alley was mostly empty; only a few people milled about near the entrance. None took notice.

No one was ahead of the Syman as it charged through the narrow space between the buildings.

It glanced back over its shoulder, making sure the pair of strangers weren't still behind it.

When it turned back it found a cloaked woman in enchanted armor standing before it.

The robot yelped and skidded to a halt.

It was several tense moments before Metch and Elle finally caught up. Once they'd reached the robot's location, Metch doubled over, gasping for air.

"I am never going on a field op ever again," he wheezed.

"Agreed," said Elle.

"Yeah," said Val.

"This is one of the reasons I signed up to be a pilot."

It was at that point that Val realized the robot had its optics fixed on her. It had since it stopped running.

"You," it said. It had no mouth; the sound projected from a vocal processor somewhere near the bottom of the mostly-featureless panel at the front of its long, narrow head.

"Me. Yeah." Val nodded. "What about me?"

"They said you would come."

"Who did?" Val asked.

"All these years," the robot muttered.

"Could you please answer the questions?"

"Ah, this thing's got some bad programming, or loose wiring, or something," Elle said. "It's probably just cheap junk."

Val stepped towards the robot and looked it up and down.

"No," she said. "It's not cheap. Just... old."

"How old?" Elle asked. She finally stored her weapon.

"Really, really old." Val looked to the robot. "How old are you?"

"I actually don't know," it said. "My internal chronometer only has two digits for the year."

"Goddamn," Elle said. "But I have to buy a new sky-flyer every five years."

"What's your name?" Val asked the robot.

"I am called... Four."

In the castle morgue, Angelo and Kavana stood over a cold table, across which was laid the pale corpse of the king's former vizier.

Even in his death, something about the man transfixed their gaze.

"Not that I can't appreciate what you did or why," said Angelo, "but you do realize that without him, the information I sought is lost forever."

"Did he tell you that?" Kavana asked. Her manner of dress seemed a bit meager for the chilled air.

"Yes, though I've had it independently verified."

"By whom?" she asked.

"Someone I trust."

"They must be a very special person indeed," she said.

"Hm. Well, we're still faced with this little problem." He gestured at the man's hollowing form.

"Who do you think you're marrying?" she asked coyly.

"I don't believe I've made any such overtures."

"Palan is not without mages of its own," she said. "As the daughter of the king, I have them at my beck and call. Especially this one young one. I believe he quite fancies me.

He'll do anything I ask."

"And how will that help me?"

"Memories are just energy engraved in the soft matter held within the skull," she said. "They can be retrieved. Doing so by technological means can be unreliable, especially after death. But with magic…"

"Even using magic, time is of the essence," Angelo said. "How soon can you have your mage here?"

She leaned against him, wrapped herself around his burly frame.

"My dear king," she said softly, "you think I would travel without him?"

On its inside, the trade center was a cavernous marketplace: clean, white, and bright. Brilliantly-dressed men and women casually mingled in and around the common spaces, moving in and out of various shops. The center of it all was occupied by a series of decorative pools, the contents of which changed in color as they waved across the smoothed, shallow basins.

Rik and his contact rode a propelled stairway down from one of the upper floors. The contact was as respectably adorned as the rest of the crowd. Rik had cleaned himself up a bit, and somehow even managed to get his clothes washed, but still looked a bit shabby in comparison. He was trying his hardest not to appear overwhelmed by the scope of everything around him.

"You know, when I picture the black market, this is really not what I had in mind," he said. "I feel a little underdressed."

His companion gave him a quick glance over.

"You are."

They stepped off at the lowest level and made their way across the main courtyard.

"If all you're looking to do is hire a few guys with guns

to guard a thing or take a thing from people who are guarding it, then, yeah, you can make a deal in some shady backroom of a bar," the man said. "You want to hire an army, like you're talking about doing, you have to deal with a higher class of people." He gave Rik another look and shook his head. "And they only deal with a higher class of clientele. If I hadn't vouched for you, no way would they be taking any meetings with someone like you."

"Yeah, well, you know who I'm here representing."

"You don't have to sell me on it, bud," he said. "I'm not the one with the army for sale. I'm just a middle man."

"Still, I appreciate what you're doing."

"I'll take your appreciation in a more practical manner if you don't mind."

"Hey, you don't get a finder's fee until the deal actually goes through," Rik said.

"Thank you, I'm aware of how my job works."

The man led him into one of the storefronts. Even the guards at the entrance were nicely attired. Their suits were well-tailored to show off their hefty physiques without leaving any concealed weapons visible.

Rik's contact gave the woman behind the counter an up-nod, which she returned.

She was almost unbelievably attractive, so much so that Rik was momentarily distracted as he followed his friend behind the counter and through a doorway, into a formal conference room.

Seated at the ornamental table within was a man somehow dressed even finer than average for the building. The lieutenants flanking him were garbed to match. It was almost unnerving how closely their personal style mirrored their employer's.

The arms dealer stood and embraced Rik's friend.

"Sco," the man behind the table said warmly.

"Nak," Rik's contact replied.

"What've you got for me today?" Nak asked.

Sco gestured at Rik.

"This is my boy Rik," Sco said.

Nak's eyes moved slowly over Rik.

"Your boy?" He chuckled. "You mean your errand boy? How're you bringing something this shabby into my establishment?"

Rik scowled a bit.

"Hey, me and Rik go way back," Sco said. "I said I'd get him an audience with some nice people. I'm fulfilling my end of the bargain."

Nak nodded.

"Alright." He took a seat. "Let's hear what he's got to say."

"You know I'm right here, right?" Rik asked. "You can just talk directly to me."

"And you're very lucky for that," Nak said. He gestured for Rik and Sco took a seat. "You come into my place dressed like that. That's very nearly just plain disrespect."

"Looks can be deceiving," said Rik.

Nak's head shook at an odd angle.

"But they're usually not. I'm sure Sco's told you what it is I do here." He placed a palm on the table. A holographic projection was activated, cycling through a series of schematics for warships, weapons, and body armor. "This isn't bargain basement junk that you can get anywhere. These are current generation ships and tech. This is the same ordinance that the Kaians, the Palans, and the Artondy use. All factory direct, no second-hand jobs, plus people to train your people how to use it all. And people to be your people, if you need that. We can provide you troops by the hundreds or the thousands. Whatever you need, and whatever you can pay for."

Nak shut off the display and leaned forward.

"Which brings me to a very practical order of business. How much are you looking to spend? Or should I ask, how much are you able to spend?"

Rik pointed to where the display had been.

"How do I know this stuff's any good?" he asked. "Until

a few weeks ago, I was in the Kaian army, and that didn't look like the stuff we use."

Nak rocked back, scoffing incredulously.

"I have a reputation to maintain. My merchandise is good. But you don't have a reputation. I still don't think I've ever heard of you."

"I'm Rik. I think Sco used my name when we came in."

"Your name?" Nak asked. "'Rik?'"

"Your name's 'Nak,'" Rik stated. "How is that any different?"

"Because people know, Nak's got a knack for delivering."

"Wow that's corny."

"You still haven't answered my question," Nak said. "That usually means trouble. Trouble I don't need."

"You'll get your money when I've confirmed the merchandise."

"When you've confirmed? Nah, that isn't how this works. You place an order, you pay, I deliver. I didn't work all those years building up a business so some sloppy-ass punk like you could come in and tell me how it's gonna run."

"Do you know who this sloppy-ass punk is?" Sco asked.

"C'mon, man," Rik whined.

"This is the Guardian of the Queen of Kaia," Sco said.

Nak tried for a brief second to keep a straight face, but couldn't stop himself from bursting out in laughter. His lieutenants followed suit.

"Kaia's got a king, not a queen," Nak said.

"The king died months ago..." Rik told him.

"And was replaced by another king," Nak said. "I keep up with the news, boy. You can't hustle me."

"That motherlover on the throne right now is not the rightful king," Rik said. His finger stamped down on the table for emphasis, an action that Nak clearly didn't appreciate. "I serve Queen Valentina, daughter of King Andor, and the rightful heir to the throne."

"Uh-huh. And does Queen Valentina have access to the

royal treasury?"

Rik hesitated. "Not at current, no. But..."

"There's no 'buts' here. Your girl can call herself the Lord High Empress of All Comets for all I care, but if she doesn't have the coins to back it up, she's not my empress of comets. And her errand boy coming up in here in rags doesn't impress me."

"Okay, I've had enough comments about how I look," Rik said.

"And smell," Nak added.

"I took a shower this morning."

"You need another one," Nak said. "And a tailor. I'd recommend someone, but we've already established you can't afford jack."

"Valentina's claim to the throne is legitimate," Rik said.

"I don't care."

Rik turned to Sco.

"Fine. Sco, who else can we talk to? I'm sure one of his competitors will be more open to a royal payday."

Sco recoiled a bit.

"Nak was your best shot, really."

"Really?"

"I've got a bit of a reputation as a softy," Nak said.

"Really?"

"I help the hard-luck cases no one else will. But I've still got a business to run here. Look, Sco, I know this is your boy. You wanted to help him out. I get that. Me and you are still cool. But he's wasting my time. Time is money. Not only can't he pay me, but he's taking time away from other legitimate clientele I could be attending to."

"There wasn't exactly a line out front," Rik said.

"Now, you're just being disrespectful," Nak said.

His lieutenants started around the table towards Rik.

Sco backed away, his hands in the air.

CHAPTER 3

Four had returned to its master's house, along with the trio of Kaian insurgents. Gyu seemed more receptive to their presence now, offering them refreshments as they sat and conversed.

Four tilted its head at the sight of Gyu handing out beverages.

"Here you go," Gyu said to Val, the last to receive her cup.

"Thanks."

"And who are you again?" Gyu asked.

"Someone you're better off not having seen." She looked to the robot. "But I'm interested in you, Four. We've been looking for..."

"I know what you've been looking for," it said. "It's better not to say in front of those not of our lineage."

"Lineage?" Metch asked. Four cocked its head at him. "You're a robot. How do you have lineage? Unless you're talking about previous production models?"

"Lineage isn't just defined by blood," Val said. "You were entrusted with one, weren't you?"

Four nodded. "Yes."

"How?" Val asked. "By whom?"

"I only have scattered memories of my early years. The power of the item you seek sustains me, but the sentience that it granted me came slowly. I wasn't fully aware of what was happening for... I don't know. Decades? Centuries?"

"But you must have some memories from before you were, you know, sentient, or whatever," said Metch. "Right?"

Four shook its head.

"My original storage banks were rather limited in capacity. I suppose it wasn't considered necessary for my functions, whatever they were. Like my self-awareness, my ability to retain information, memories, greatly increased with exposure to the item you seek. I have memories of previous owners, other worlds I've worked on, but my original purpose and masters have been forgotten, save for one instruction they left etched into my hard memory: protect it and myself at all costs. Someday, someone might need it. If they do, the fate of everything could be at stake."

"Unfortunately, that last part's come true," Val said. "We need it, and we need someone to wield it. You have no idea who your original, and I hate to say this, who your original 'owners' were?"

Four shook its head.

"No. But I have to assume that if they entrusted the object to me, it meant they were no longer capable of safeguarding it themselves. The likeliest reason for that would be that they were all killed."

"And you... can you access its power?" she asked.

"No. Not in the way that you're thinking, anyway. It sustains me long past when my parts should all have given out, it gives me sapience beyond anything an artificial being should possess, but it seems to interact differently with artificial creatures than organic ones."

"Well, that's unfortunate," Elle said. "Who else could we give it to?"

"What?" Val asked.

"You must have cousins or something like that who'd be willing to help," Elle said.

"Are you not understanding what's going on here? Four's self-awareness, its identity, its life, all comes from having the Crown..." She turned to Four. "Where?"

Four's metal fingers gently tapped its chest, eliciting a tinny echo.

"We take away the..." Val said.

"You already said 'Crown' out loud," Metch said.

"...and you take away everything that Four is."

"Okay, I don't know who Four is," Elle said. "I know who Angelo is. I know what we've already sacrificed to try to beat him, and I know what's at stake if we don't win."

"Uh-huh. There's a real simple solution here," Val said. "Four comes with us."

"No, you can't take Four from me," Gyu said.

"I didn't say I would," Val said. "Four is sentient, as far as I'm concerned. It's its choice if it wants to come or not."

The group all fixed their eyes on Four.

"I... no one's ever asked me what I wanted before," it said.

"That can't be true," Gyu said. "I... um... well, I didn't know you were alive."

Four stood. Its partly-skeletal frame brought it up over two meters in height.

"I exist only because of the artifact in my chest. I've known no other purpose than to safeguard it and await the one who needs it. I cannot have waited this long to not fulfill that purpose."

"You can't go," Gyu said.

"You can stay here if you want, or not, but Four is coming with us," Val said.

"No, you don't understand," Gyu said. "You can't take Four from me because it's not technically mine."

"What?" Val's voice was a croak.

"I actually lease it..."

"I'm on a lease?" Four asked.

"You pay monthly for this thing?" Elle was indignant.

"Well, semi-annually," Gyu said.

"Okay, if you don't own Four, who does it belong to?" Val asked.

"The, um, the pit boss, actually?"

"Oh, for heaven's sakes," Four groaned.

"Who's the pit boss?" Val asked.

"He runs the local fighting ring," Four said. "And when I say local, I mean for this solar system."

"Okay, well, does this really change our plans?" Elle asked. "We were going to just take Four from this guy, no offense, guy. Why can't we still just take him?"

"Because Four is tagged," Gyu said. "No way it gets off-planet without being noticed. Or, remotely detonated."

"Well... crap," Val grunted. "Who do we have that's good with tech?"

Elle thought on it. "Ah... pshh... maybe Hune? She's probably the best technician we've got."

"Yeah, no way are we getting this tag off," Hune said.

She lay on the floor beneath Four. Even if she were standing, she came up noticeably short on the others, with darker features.

The others stood around her expectantly. She poked a set of tools inside an open flap on Four's lower leg.

"Seriously?" Val asked.

"Not with the tools we have here," Hune said. "It's synced to the power system. Remove it, it blows. Remove the limb it's in, it blows. Try to deactivate it without the proper code, it blows. I'm actually going to move away from it now, because, yeah, pretty much doing anything with it could cause it to blow."

She gently shut the leg panel and then quickly got up off the ground.

"And I've been walking around with that in my leg for decades," Four said.

"It's a wonder you're still walking around and not, you know, exploded," Hune said.

"I wonder if that's some effect of the Crown?" Val said.

"Do we really have time to get philosophical right now?" Elle asked.

"You thought that was philosophical?" Val asked.

"So, what are we doing?" asked Elle.

"You could buy Four from him," Gyu suggested. "He'll sell his own mother for the right price."

"The pit boss's mother died several years ago," Four said.

"Uh-huh. And?"

"Well, as our dearly departed comrade Rik reminded us before leaving, we have no money," Elle said.

"That would be a problem for you guys," said Gyu.

"And any money we would have would be in Kaian coins, not the local currency." Val turned to Gyu. "What about you? Do you have any money around?"

"Not enough to buy Four. That's why I've been leasing it."

"What about a trade?" asked Elle. "Anything we can barter with?"

"I doubt he'd be interested in anything you have," Gyu said. "Except that fancy crown."

"That's not happening," said Val.

"And sometimes, uh, if you can't make your payments, he'll accept other forms of, you know, payment."

"That's definitely not happening," Val said.

"I could..." Elle began.

"No," Val said quickly.

"You're my queen," said Elle. "If you asked me..."

"As your queen, I'm telling you not to do that."

"Okay. Just saying, it's not off the table."

"I appreciate the loyalty, I think, but we'll find another way," Val said.

"Okay, but, the only other thing I can think of is, he's always looking for fighters for his pits," Gyu said. "I mean, he keeps those things going almost around the clock. It's basically the only form of entertainment on the planet."

"Fighting isn't entertainment," Val said.

"Where'd you hear that?" he asked.

"The military," Val said with a sigh. "Where I learned the skills that it sounds like I'm going to have to use to fight for entertainment."

CHAPTER 4

The exterior of the market center belied the extravagance within. Outside, it was as grungy and dilapidated as anyone would expect, appearing much like a disused warehouse or sports stadium. The outward appearance that Rik had been so heavily criticized for would have only stood out for being too formal in the place the building's shell suggested.

A set of doors opened into an empty street; Rik was sent tumbling out. No one but the clientele inside would be around this area this time of night.

Rik scrambled to his feet as Nak's lieutenants filed out of the building, moving to surround him.

"You know I could take any of you one-on-one, right?" he asked as he took a fighting stance.

"That's why we're not fighting you one-on-one," one of them said.

"Okay, as long as we all acknowledge that."

Rik took a swing at one, clocking him across the jaw. Another grabbed him from behind. Rik threw an elbow into her stomach, breaking her grip, but not before a third slugged him in the gut.

Winded, but not dismayed, Rik kicked the first man, pushing him back a good bit. Rik hoped that would give him a little breathing room. That hoped was dashed when the woman behind him knocked him across the back of the head.

He stumbled, trying to get through the space between two of them, but the gap was quickly closed and he was set upon by all three. He delivered a haymaker to the first lieutenant, putting him to the ground and out of the fight, at least for the time being.

The other two overwhelmed him, punching and kicking him furiously. He got his arms up, tried to protect himself as best he could, but was grabbed from behind by the woman again. The second man went to work on his stomach and ribs.

His vision reddened and blurred.

Though he couldn't see what was happening, he found himself unexpectedly freed from the lieutenant's grasp. With the beating he'd taken, and without her physical support, he dropped to his knees. He took a few more blows to the head before the pounding stopped entirely.

Rik was hacking and wheezing, but nothing felt broken and none of the coughs produced any blood, so that was good. He figured he should probably at least try to focus on the world around him, since he didn't know what had stopped the attack and if it might resume.

He looked up to see a massive man tossing the last of the goons aside.

"Trainer?" he asked.

He managed to get up to his feet, even if his first few steps towards his old mentor were a bit shaky.

Trainer looked down at the pile of people on the ground.

"That took more effort than it should have," he said. "I guess I'm a bit out of form."

"I would think so." Rik wiped at his nose. Still no blood. "You got blown up a few weeks ago."

"A good soldier wouldn't let something like getting blown up slow them down." Trainer folded his arms and exhaled deeply.

"That's legitimately one of the dumbest things I've ever heard anyone say, but I'm glad you're alive."

The door on the side of the building was shoved open

again. At least ten more guards rushed out.

"Dammit." Rik groaned. "Come on."

"You all need to leave us alone," Trainer told them. Just the calm in his voice was a little unsettling. "Don't make us destroy you."

The head of this goon squad started to laugh.

"You and what army?"

The pit boss of the planet was also a large man, but not at all in the same way as Trainer. He spent much of his days seated behind an old desk in a dusty office; he looked like a low-rent gangster, a big fish in a little pond with delusions of grandeur. His jaw was wideset. The sleeveless jacket he wore, one which very obviously had started its life with sleeves, strained against his bulk. A worn hat sat low on his brow.

Val, Elle, Gyu, and Four stood barely inside the doorway. There was just something about the man that made them not want to get too close.

"You want to fight for ownership of a Syman?" the pit boss asked.

"I don't want to, but we're pretty much out of other ideas," Val said.

The pit boss squinted at Four.

"You know this thing's a piece of crap, right?"

"Hey," Four said.

"You want a decent robot, I can get you a lease."

"We don't have any money," Val said. "That's why we're reducing ourselves to this. And we don't want a decent robot, we want this one."

"Hey!" Four said.

"Sorry," she said.

"Don't apologize to the Syman," the pit boss said.

"I'll speak to my Syman however I please," Val said.

"It ain't yours."

"It will be."

"We haven't come to any terms yet."

"Name them."

The pit boss leaned back in his squeaky chair, considering his options.

"Alright, you seem like you're in a hurry," he said. "Normally, to earn enough to pay off a robot, even a crap one like this, you'd have to work your way up to at least a quarter-finalist. But we've got a big dusk show tonight."

"Dusk shows are always popular," Four said.

"Shut your mouth, robot," the pit boss said.

"I don't have a mouth," Four said.

The pit boss went into his desk and pulled out a remote control. He held it out towards them.

"What is that?" Val asked. "I don't get what's going on. Is that supposed to be intimidating?"

"That's the remote to the tag in my leg," said Four. "He's threatening to detonate me."

"Oh, jeez, don't do that," Val said. "Not even as a joke. My tech lady says that thing could go off if you look at it funny."

The pit boss set the remote down.

Everyone at the door held their breath, silently wishing he'd be a bit gentler with the device.

"Anyway," he said, "before I was so rudely interrupted..."

"I wasn't being rude," said Four. "I was agreeing with you."

Val glared at Four. It recoiled a bit and lowered its head.

"The more fights we get at the show, the better. A lot of our fighters are kinda busted up right now. And always. Point is, your guy gives us a good mid-card show and comes out on top, you can have this piece of crap." He went into another drawer and pulled out a datapad. "Who're you putting up, anyway?"

Val and her compatriots looked at one another.

"Uh, me," Val said. "I thought that was implied."

"Outright stated, even," Four added.

The pit boss dropped his pad.

"Are you shitting me?"

"Look, just put me on the card, alright." Val turned towards the door. "I'll meet your terms, and I'll walk out of here with the robot."

CHAPTER 5

Val stood on one side of an arena as the sun descended. She'd finally managed to find a change of clothes: a tank top and culottes. Her hands and forearms, feet and legs, and, beneath her tank top, her chest were bound with tape wraps.

Four and Elle stood in her corner.

Across the ring, as it were, was a very sizeable, brutish looking man. His face and body showed the signs of years of professional underground fighting, and a decided lack of corresponding medical attention.

"Are you sure this is wise?" Four asked. "Those fighters are rather large and quite savage. Most have what would be considered, on a more civilized planet, illegal enhancements."

"Before all this started, I was a high ranking operative in the Kaian palace guard," Val said. "I can kick some serious ass. It took me longer to strap down my tits than the fight's gonna last."

The opposing fighter started towards her.

"Is he coming at me?" Val asked. "Isn't there a bell?"

"Or a referee?" asked Elle.

"There is not," Four informed them. "The fighters just decide when to start. The sooner the better, for the crowd's tastes."

With her opponent advancing, Val felt it was only proper to walk out to meet him.

He gave her a gap-toothed grin and gestured towards his face.

"C'mon, little lady. I'll give you the first shot."

"I wouldn't do that," she said. "I'm gonna mess you up real bad."

He continued egging her on as they neared one another.

When they'd gotten within striking distance, Val swung a fist up over her shoulder, swiftly catching the opposing fighter square in the nose. Blood sprayed instantly.

He stumbled back, clutching his face and screaming.

"Oh, God, I can taste bone."

Val slowly shook her head. "I told you."

"At least I think that's bone. I've never actually tasted bone before."

Val looked around.

"So, does anyone end the match, or..."

Four called to her. "The match isn't over until someone is at least unconscious."

She looked back at her stumbling opponent. "That just seems mean at this point."

"I mean, it's definitely not blood. I know what blood tastes like, and this isn't it."

Val swung her foot out, catching her opponent's leg and sending him flopping to the ground.

She got behind him and wrapped a forearm around his neck. It didn't take long for him to drop to the dirt: unconscious, but breathing. Breathing fairly awkwardly, but still breathing.

The crowd booed.

Val held her bloodied arms out in front of her.

"It's probably going to take me longer to get the blood off than the fight lasted, too." She looked around again. "Why are they booing?"

Without even taking the time to change, Val returned to the pit boss's office. Elle, Gyu, and Four hung back a bit as she approached the desk.

"I said you could fight for its freedom," the pit boss said. "That wasn't a fight."

"That's not my fault," Val said.

"It doesn't matter whose fault it is."

"It does if it's your fault," Val said. "Put me up against someone better if it makes you happy."

"I really don't have anybody better," the pit boss admitted.

"How about if you get a bunch more guys and send them all at me," Val said. "How many would it take to equal a fight, to you?"

"It's not about numbers. If you tear through a bunch of my fighters like you tore through that last guy, the people are gonna start thinking my fights aren't quality entertainment."

"Then give us Four and we'll go away," she said. "You won't have to worry about us messing up your fights anymore."

"No."

"Why not?"

"Because you've made me unhappy." He looked her over, standing there in her loose-fitting pants and baggy sleeveless shirt. "Of course, I can think of some ways I could be made happy."

Elle stepped forward.

Val gently pushed her back.

Four stepped forward next.

"I want to fight for my own freedom."

"No. Hell no. A robot can't go in the pit."

"There's no rule that says a robot can't fight for itself," Four said.

"There aren't a lot of rules in general," Val said. "This is not a well-regulated sport."

"I said no. Now get the hell out of my office."

"Then how are we supposed to win Four?" Val asked.

"You ain't. You lose. I win. That's how this works. Now get the hell out."

"You're worried about what the crowds will think if I decimate this sport?" Val leaned on the desk. "What if I tell them you don't honor your word?"

"They already know that," he said.

"I could've told you that," said Four.

"How the hell do you run a business?" she asked him.

"People around here don't have a lot of options."

"Okay, well, I'm not going anywhere until we get Four," she said. "So, if that means that I go out into that ring and beat the ever-loving crap out of every single guy..."

"And girl," the pit boss said. "There're women in there too."

"There are?" she asked. "Then why've you been acting... never mind. Point is, I could ruin this thing, exactly the way you're worried I could."

"I say who goes in the ring."

Val drew herself upright.

"Yeah, but you don't exactly guard the arenas. You really should have some kind of rules. Seriously. I could just walk in there right now and beat the crap out of both the fighters. Then your next fighters. And the next."

"Could you?" he asked.

"Are you gonna stop me?"

"I might not have a lot of security, but the ones I got are all armed. Are you bulletproof?"

Val smiled at that.

"You wanna find out?"

Before he could answer, the windows of the office went dark.

One of his goons rushed in.

"Uh, boss, I don't mean to alarm you, but we may have a slight situation here."

◆ ◆ ◆

Val made it out of the arena first, followed by Four, Elle, Gyu, and finally the pit boss, hustling his hulking frame along as fast as he could.

Val stared up in disbelief. Filling the sky were dozens of Kaian warships. A lifetime of training and experience had taught Val to prepare for the worst.

The pit boss was even more astonished. He kept swaying his head from side to side, trying to take in the full scope of the fleet that hovered over his place of business.

Elle heard a crackle in her earpiece.

"Hey, Elle."

"Rik?" she asked.

"Rik?" Val echoed her.

"Rik, is that you?" Elle asked.

"Is that you down there?" he asked. "I'm waving to you. Can you see me waving? You probably can't see me."

"No, we cannot," Elle said.

The pit boss still stared bug-eyed at the sky. "Those are your ships?"

"Looks like," Val said.

Without averting his gaze, he raised Four's remote and tapped a button.

There was a clank inside Four's leg. The casing panel on it opened and the deactivated tag fell out.

"Please leave," the pit boss said.

"I knew we could come to a reasonable agreement," said Val.

She, along with Elle and Four, started towards the descending lead ship.

Val paused for a moment, turning back to the pit boss.

"I just want to let you know, this is a garbage planet. When I become queen of Kaia, one of the first things I'm gonna do is come back here and take this whole place over."

They walked off, leaving Gyu and the pit boss still standing in shock.

Gyu leaned over towards him.

"I'm going to need a lease on a new Syman."

CHAPTER 6

Four timidly followed along as Val and Elle approached the landing vessel.

"Nice," Elle said, "but, should you've told him about the whole becoming queen thing? Won't that kind of raise some flags?"

"Unfortunately, we're past the point of that mattering," Val said, her voice fluttering just a tad.

"What do you mean?"

At the orders of the king, the throne room had been sealed off. No one but Angelo, Kavana, and her mage got in. No one questioned the contents of the long box that had been delivered there just prior to their arrival.

The three of them stood around the Crown of the Five Point Star's pedestal. On a cot nearby lay the body of the vizier, his head pointed towards the column.

"You're certain this will work?" Angelo asked.

"My king, as a military man you should know that nothing in the universe is certain," said Kavana. "However, this is the best chance you'll ever have of learning the secrets that your vizier was hiding."

Angelo looked to the younger, slenderer man, bedecked in an off-color robe and slippers.

"You believe you can do this?" Angelo asked.

"Yes, sire. Without question."

The mage's glance fell upon Kavana, just for a moment. It felt much longer to everyone there.

She gave just a hint of a return.

"Then do it," Angelo said. "Every second we waste here is a second my niece and her insurgents are out in the universe unfettered."

The mage nodded gracefully and turned to the vizier.

He stood, slowly waving his hands over the vizier's body, taking the most time over the head. The mage closed his eyes and breathed deeply; he was far too comfortable, the others thought, inhaling heavy whiffs of the decaying corpse before him.

His whole body relaxed, every muscle loosening at once.

Wisps of vaporous energy floated out of the dead man's skull, up into the mage's hands.

"He's doing it," Angelo gasped.

"Hush," Kavana whispered, her attention fixed on the ritual playing out before her.

"You don't hush me. I'm your king and future husband."

"Let him do his work," she said. "This is still tricky business."

The mage's eyes opened, giving off a cool-colored glow that matched the vapors he'd been manipulating.

"Please put on the Crown." His voice sounded deeper, hollow, and with something of a reverberation to it.

Angelo picked up the Crown and placed it on his head. He shifted it down and was covered in the armor.

"You already have the information you seek," the mage said. "It just needs to be unlocked. Allow me."

He touched his fingertips to the Crown. Energy, brighter and stronger than before, flowed from him.

The current became more forceful. Power gushed from his body. The Crown thirsted for it until he wasn't giving energy to it so much as it was being pulled from him.

His flesh began to dissolve. He screamed.

"Hush now," Kavana chided. "You'll ruin his moment."

Angelo was staggered. This felt too much like the ritual the Mages of Kaia had performed on him weeks earlier, only now it was all happening inside his head.

The mage howled as his skin, then his bones, were converted into illumination and poured into the Crown.

Once he was reduced to no more than a wisp of ash, Angelo straightened up and surveyed the scene.

"What happened to him?" Angelo asked.

"The energies he was channeling were far too much for his body to handle. Your vizier must've been a hell of a wizard to have contained all that."

"You knew this would happen?"

"I had a strong suspicion, yes."

"And you had him do it anyway?" he asked.

"Yes."

"Did he know?"

"Maybe. I'm not sure. But he went through with it anyway."

Angelo took a step back.

"What kind of sway did you have over him?"

"I have no magic if that's what you're worried about." She giggled. "None beyond the touch of a woman."

"And that was enough?"

She nodded.

"To secure his faithful service in more than this."

Angelo looked down at the scorch mark where the mage had stood.

"What a poor, wretched man," he said.

"It's not polite to speak that way about the dead. Besides, it worked, didn't it?"

Angelo touched the Crown.

"Yes. I think it did."

Sights flashed through his mind, from the creation of the Crowns through the great wars of the past to the current locations of the other Crowns. His vision finished with an image of Val leaving an arena.

As he shook off the effect, Kavana looked at Angelo with some concern.

Ignoring that, he started towards the exit, removing the Crown as he went.

He stopped short and turned back.

"Thank you, princess. Truly. If there's anything I can do to repay you..."

She moved towards him, her shoulders back, her hips swinging generously as she walked.

"I've been waiting for you to ask."

"Oh?" He smiled down on her as she reached him and loosely draped her arms over his shoulders. "And what sort of wedding present would you like?"

"What I want is simple, my king. I want my home."

BOOK 6: ROOTED

CHAPTER 1

A junior officer sped across the base's hangar bay. Meant to house several large fleets, the cavernous building was lined with rows of military vehicles and dotted with support staff going about their daily business.

Moving on foot, and not running so as to draw as little attention as possible, it took him quite a while to cross the entire space. Protocol was to maintain a walking speed at all times within the building, except in emergencies. He felt this qualified but was doubtful anyone else knew it.

Finally reaching the other end, he entered the office of General Lank and stood at attention.

"Sir."

Lank rose up from behind his desk and returned the younger man's salute.

"What is it, son?"

"We've received urgent news from the capital."

Lank gestured at the computer terminal on his desk. "Well, put it through."

"It's not a communique as such," the young officer said. "It's more of a news report? There's been a... there's been a coup, sir."

In a lifetime of military service, Lank had never received news that squeezed on his chest the way this did.

"A coup?"

◆ ◆ ◆

Lank gathered the other five base commanders in a conference room. Just the six of them: no assistants, no field commanders, no recorders or service personnel.

"The prince, Andor's brother, Angelo, has killed King Joseph and taken the Crown of the Five Point Star for himself," Lank announced.

A round of gasps and sucked air filled the room.

General Trev stood.

"What happened, exactly?"

Lank shook his head.

"Reports are still coming in. We're not even supposed to know about it yet. We only do because some of the junior officers are a little too chatty with members of the Palace Guard. It sounds like Angelo decided that Joseph wasn't Kaian enough to rule us and took matters into his own hands, figuratively and literally. All we know is that one king is dead at the hands of another."

"'King?'" asked General Farbo. The youngest of the base commanders, indeed, among the youngest of all generals in the Kaian army, Farbo looked of any of them to still be field combat-ready. "You can't be talking about Angelo."

"That's what he's calling himself," Lank said. "Until a higher power than us declares otherwise, that's the title he's earned."

"It's a title he murdered his way to," Farbo retorted.

"That's our current ruler you're talking about," said Trev. "If he stays in power, I'd watch how you're heard speaking of him."

"There's more," Lank said. "It seems that Andor left behind another heir, one of whom no one was previously made aware."

"Who?" Farbo asked.

"She's called Valentina. She was hidden as a member of

the Palace Guard. She escaped Angelo's assault on the castle. Her current whereabouts are unknown."

"What does all this mean?" Trev asked. "For us? For the military?"

"That's what I called you all here to decide," said Lank. "I imagine similar conversations are happening at nearly every military installation that Kaia has claim to. We have, by all measure, the rightful heir in Valentina. And, we have the current occupant of the throne and bearer of the Crown in Angelo. As members of the military – not just members but leaders — we've sworn a sacred oath of loyalty to the Crown. But, where does that loyalty fall in this case? With the Crown, or with the one who should be wearing it?"

"Who says that this Valentina 'should' be seated?" Trev asked. "Has she been prepared for leadership? Had Joseph? We've had neophytes making assertions to the throne of late, haven't we? And Angelo isn't without a legitimate claim."

"He murdered his predecessor," Farbo said. "His nephew. Is that a man you want to follow?"

"I swore my oath to the Crown," Trev said. "Angelo has the Crown. It speaks to him. He's of the blood."

"And had the lawful order of succession been followed, Valentina would have it," Farbo said. "Or Joseph, if Angelo hadn't murdered him. I feel as though too little emphasis is being placed on that fact."

"Time is very short," said Lank. "We're unlikely to reach a consensus among us. The chaos in the capital is still being sorted. But it will be settled soon. By then, we'll have no choice. So this is what I propose now:

"Each of you, each of us, must choose where our loyalties lie."

Lank stood at a podium on a makeshift stage set up in the hangar. Thousands of soldiers assembled, standing in rows in front of him.

"The situation we find ourselves in is unprecedented in Kaian history. To that end, anyone who does not support the currently named king, that being Angelo of Kaia, and furthermore does support the challenger to the throne, that being Valentina, daughter of the late King Andor and sister to Prince Thoome and King Joseph, will be allowed to leave this base with no resistance.

"However, you are not released from your oath to the Crown and the service. You will be expected to maintain order and the command structure, reporting to those senior officers who also sincerely hold the belief that Valentina is the rightful heir. You will be allowed to leave with an amount of equipment, ships, and provisions proportionate to the percentage of soldiers absconding.

"You will have one day's time to vacate the base. After that time has elapsed, all remaining personnel shall be considered loyal to King Angelo and be expected to conduct themselves as such. Good luck to you. Good luck to us all."

Less than a day later, hundreds of ships departed from that and other bases.

It was weeks until they'd completed the first leg of their self-ascribed mission: finding the woman they'd sworn to serve.

The large contingent of battleships used to scare off the pit boss broke away from the planet's atmosphere and rejoined the fleet.

Kaian warships filled space in every direction.

General Farbo stood in the command position of the lead ship. Rik and Trainer waited nearby. The rest of the bridge was occupied by support staff going about the business of maintaining such a vessel. Command personnel still wore full uniforms; lower ranks were allowed a more casual, utilitarian style. Short-sleeved shirts were the most popular option, paired either with uniform slacks or baggy, pocket-laden trousers tucked into the boots.

The room was spacious and sleek: efficient, but comfortable. This class of ship was designed to impress, inside and out.

The doors at the rear of the bridge slid open. Val, Elle, and Four entered, surrounded by guards.

Val had managed to put her uniform trousers and boots back on, but still wore the top from her pit fight.

"Queen on the bridge!" Farbo announced.

"Is that even a saying?" asked Val.

"I don't know," Farbo said. "I've never had a queen on my bridge before. Your majesty. You honor me."

"Glad I could help."

In her periphery, Val spotted Rik and Trainer.

Rik waved.

"Hey."

Val ignored him and approached Trainer. Tears welled up in her eyes; Trainer's own began to water.

"It's good to see you," she said.

"No crying for soldiers, young one. I taught you better than that."

"I'm the queen. I make the rules now. Speaking of, at some point, we're going to have to have a conversation about what you knew and when."

He smiled down on her. "I look forward to it."

"You shouldn't." Finally, she looked to Rik. "And you."

Rik pointed at himself with faux incredulity. He mouthed the word "me."

"We're having a talk right now," Val said.

She walked off the bridge.

"Oh, damn, she's not joking around," said Rik.

"Now!" Val's voice came from the adjacent corridor.

Trainer gave him a firm pat on the shoulder.

"Nice knowing you."

"You mean that?" asked Rik

"Sort of."

Rik took a deep breath and made for the door.

He found his queen waiting for him in an empty office. He almost wondered who it belonged to and how Val had located such a space so quickly, but the anxiety the situation filled him with overrode such curiosity.

Val leaned against the desk, her arms folded, her eyes boring straight through him.

"I kind of want to punch you right now, for dramatic effect, but that would be, you know, abuse. So I'm just going to tell you, you are this close," she held out her hand, her thumb and forefinger nearly touching, "to forcing me to name a new Guardian."

"What? What'd I do?"

"Besides leaving without telling anyone where you were going?" She chortled.

"Well, I didn't know exactly where I was going," he said. "Besides, it worked, didn't it?"

"What worked?"

"The plan." He gestured around. "The plan to get you a dang army. I went out. I came back with an army."

"I didn't ask you to do that."

"So you don't want the army?"

"And Trainer is… he's Trainer," Val said. "You don't think he would've found us sooner or later?"

"Unbelievable."

"And, your self-proclaimed mission was to go out and

buy ships and an army," she said. "How many ships did you buy? How many soldiers did you recruit? All you did was stumble into Trainer."

"You know what…"

"No, I'm the queen, and I'm not done."

"Well, some queen you are."

"That is exactly my point!" Her hands swung out to her sides.

"What?"

"Do you even know what the Guardian's job is?" she asked.

"It's, yeah, to look out for the monarch's best interests," he said. "Which is what I thought I was doing."

"No. The Guardian's first priority, and it's right there in the name, their first priority is to guard the king or queen."

"Like you need a bodyguard." He scoffed. "It sounds like you proved you can take care of yourself."

"Yeah, in a fight."

"I… I don't even know what that means."

"Forget it." She waved him off. "I'm going to go talk to the general. There's probably a lot of stuff that we need to go over."

After she'd left the room, Rik didn't move from the same spot on the floor for a long, long time.

CHAPTER 2

After spending weeks aboard the small transport ship, the long, broad corridors of the warship felt positively lavish to Val. A strange way to think of a warship, she supposed, but these were strange times.

She strode with purpose back towards the bridge.

"Valentina," she heard.

Val stopped and looked around.

"Hello?" she asked. The hallway was empty, save for some soldiers off in the distance going about their business. "Is someone there? Someone calling me by my full name?"

She pulled the Crown out of her pocket and looked at it.

She put it back, put the thought of that voice out of her head, and continued on her way.

Yost and Bontu sat in a corner of the bridge, out of the way and, at least they assumed, out of notice.

Four entered and approached them.

"Hello," it said. "I'm Four."

"Wow," Yost said. "I actually don't even know how old I am."

"What?"

The doors behind them slid open. Val entered and crossed to where Farbo, Trainer, and a few other officers gathered around a briefing table.

"Your majesty." Farbo nodded to her. "I was just saying, between all the soldiers and ships that, ah…"

"Rebelled?" Val offered. "Defected? You can say it."

"We've been trying to avoid terminology that carries too negative a connotation," Farbo said. "We're doing whatever we can to keep morale up."

"Me and my group fled Kaia in a class G, 3rd model troop transport," Val stated. "If we can keep it together, your people ought to have no troubles in luxury like this."

Rik silently entered and approached the table.

"Yes, my queen," said Farbo. "Apologies. When we broke away from Angelo's supporters, we took a full third and some of our military might with us."

"Which means Angelo still has almost two-thirds of it," Rik said.

Val gave him some side-eye.

"He's right," Trainer said. "We won't beat Angelo through sheer force. We'll need to rely on tactics more than strength, which will be a new concept for many of our people."

"I'm afraid he's right," Farbo said. "Many of our soldiers have taken it for granted for too long that their side possesses overwhelming firepower. Fighting smarter will be an adjustment that, frankly, I'm not confident they'll all be able to make."

"If we had time, perhaps, they could be taught," Trainer said.

"Well, we don't," said Val. "It's a good thing we've got the best military minds in the service with us."

"Until a matter of weeks ago, the leaders of Angelo's forces were my respected colleagues," Farbo said. "I'd place any of them against anyone we have on our side."

Val looked to Trainer. "Yeah, but we've got the guy who taught them everything they know."

"Or, at the very least, taught the people who taught them

everything they know," Trainer said. "I never thought I'd regret how thorough my lessons were."

"There's something else we're not talking about," said Val. "Angelo has the Crown of the Five Point Star."

"We're aware," Farbo said. "That may give his side all the advantage they need. But it doesn't mean we stop trying."

Val pulled out the Crown of the Single Pointed Star and set it on the table. "Well I have this."

"What is that?" Farbo asked.

"That's the Crown of the Single Pointed Star," Trainer said. He looked to Val. "Your mother gave it to you before you escaped?"

"Again, we're gonna have us a talk about all that," Val said. "But, yeah, she gave it to me. And it started speaking to me. Which is how I found those two."

She pointed back at Bontu and Four, who huddled back in the corner. Bontu looked frightened, like a trapped animal.

Four waved. "Hello."

"I was wondering what they were doing on my bridge," Farbo said. "And who are they?"

"The big guy's Bontu and the Syman is called Four," Val said.

"And the… vagrant?" Trainer asked.

Yost let off a burst of energy from his hands. Four recoiled. Bontu jumped to his feet and drew an ax from beneath his furs.

"That's Yost." Val sighed. "He's an unlicensed practitioner of sorcery. He's an old contact of mine. His head's not all there, but he can be a lifesaver. Anyway, apart from Yost, each of them has another of the Crowns."

"Other Crowns?" Farbo asked. "This needs to be explained to me."

"Right. When the Order of Meridian forged the Crown of the Five Point Star millennia ago, part of their group siphoned off some of the excess energy and made four more Crowns," said Val. "I'm not sure why they did it. Maybe as backups? I don't know. I didn't get to ask them."

Trainer cocked his head. "Get to ask them?"

"Not important," Val said. "The thing is, they did, and the other Crowns are the only things that even stand a chance against the Five Point Crown."

Rik looked at her. "You told me…"

One glance from her and his mouth was shut.

"Angelo did something just now," Val said. "He, I guess, unlocked the Five Point Crown's full knowledge. So, he's aware of the location of the other Crowns."

"And three of them are on my bridge?" Farbo asked.

"Those ones are the safest," Val said. "The Three Point Crown is still out there, and not surrounded by a third of the Kaian fleet. We need to get to it before Angelo does."

"Angelo's attentions seem to be elsewhere at the moment," said Farbo.

"What do you mean?" Val asked.

"We received word just before we arrived in this system that Angelo had moved on Palan."

"Are you freaking kidding me?" Val asked.

"He's marrying the Palan princess," said Farbo. "It seems she asked for control of her homeworld as a wedding gift."

"Oh, my God, what an ass," Val said. "He was so pissed that Joe offended the Palan ambassador, and now he's attacking their homeworld?"

"To be accurate, he's not attacking yet," Farbo said. "The fleet is still mobilizing."

"Not interested in semantics," Val said. "Just raging against the rampant hypocrisy of my douche of an uncle."

The others looked at one another.

Trainer raised a finger. "What is a…"

"It's a term Joe taught me," Val said. "It's not a compliment."

"Yes." Farbo nodded solemnly. "We honor those who've fallen by remembering their words."

"So, what're you all going to be doing?" Val asked her.

"Beg pardon?"

"While I'm gone," Val said. "Are you gonna look into the Palan situation? Let me know what you decide."

"Your majesty, we've only just found you," the general said. "We can't risk losing you."

"You also can't stop me." Val shrugged.

"Yes, your highness," Farbo said, "but I believe it would be prudent if you were to remain, as you said, surrounded by a third of the Kaian fleet. You're too valuable."

"I appreciate where you're coming from," Val said, "but Angelo can't be allowed to find the last Crown. If he does, we don't stand a chance."

"My queen." Farbo's voice was beginning to tense. "I don't know anything about magic crowns, but I know military tactics."

"That's why I'm leaving any action in the Palan system up to you," Val said. "But I do know about magic crowns, at least a little bit now, and I know Angelo can't get his hands on any more. Hell, separating him from the one he's got should be a priority, but one step at a time."

"My queen," Farbo pleaded, "I can only beg of you..."

"You're wasting your breath," Rik told her.

"You would do well to remember your place, commander." Farbo's tone was that of someone who'd spent a career keeping young people like him in check.

"Ha. Yeah." Rik let out a smug sigh. "Chain of command is situational. As the queen's Guardian, I have a lot of authority over military operations."

"There's really no equivalent promotion," Trainer said to Farbo.

"Have Metch ready the transport," Val instructed Rik.

"My queen..." Both the queen and her Guardian glared at the general. "My queen, I was just going to say, if you insist on going, we have more advanced transport ships in our hold than that one you've been flying around in the last few weeks."

Rik looked to Val.

"That thing could use a good tune-up," he said.

"And an airing out," she said. "Okay, fair enough. Let our pilot know which one to take. Give him whatever supplies he asks for."

Farbo bowed her head and backed away.

"Did she just... did she bow to you?" Rik asked.

"It did look like," Val said.

"You're going to have to get used to that sort of thing," Trainer said.

"Hey, I wanted to ask you about something," she said.

Her eyes darted to Rik. He took it as a sign to slink away.

"If this is about 'what I knew and when,'" said Trainer, "I think that can wait until we've more time."

"No, this is something else. You know the Crown, or, Crowns, better than anyone, right?"

"Better than anyone here anyway, yes," Trainer said. "Though you've got me curious about what secrets you've uncovered."

"Do the people who wear them ever hear things?" Val asked.

"What do you mean?"

"Voices."

"Have you been hearing voices?" he asked.

"I'm trying to discuss this without coming across as crazy, but, yeah, just now, I heard someone saying my name out in the hallway," she said. "And there was nobody around, and it didn't sound like a transmission."

"I see."

"Does this happen to people who wear the Crown?" she asked. "Or, am I going crazy? Or, is the Single Pointed Crown defective or something?"

"The Single Pointed Crown is not 'defective.'"

"How can you be sure of that?"

"Utilizing the Crown has often been referred to as having the Crown 'speak' to you," said Trainer. "It's mostly a metaphorical sort of speech, but it's possible that it's more literal with you. It's also possible that, how do I put this; the Crown has been known to connect its wearer to other realms, beyond our own world. It's possible you've touched another plane of existence."

"Oh. Wow. Cool," she said. "Just what I need right now."

"If the Crown is showing you that, it may be," Trainer said. "But, that's just a theory. Have you heard these voices before?"

"No, just this once."

"If you hear them again, will you let me know?" he asked.

"Sure."

"Thank you," he said graciously. "I'd like to help in whatever way I can."

Farbo approached.

"My queen, your pilot has sent word to the bridge that he is ready to disembark whenever you are."

"Wow. That was fast."

"That's what can happen when you have the resources of a full battleship's crew at your disposal," said Farbo.

"Good, good."

"I still wish you'd reconsider," the general said.

"We've all got problems."

Val left the bridge.

Farbo shook her head. "We're being ordered around by children."

"Did I not teach you to take your ego out of decisions?" Trainer asked.

"I don't remember that at all."

"Well, I'm sure I meant to."

CHAPTER 3

At last officially betrothed to the king of arguably the most powerful star empire in known space, Kavana gladly started every day with a cheerful stroll through the castle. Heading nowhere in particular, she was more than happy to give a friendly greeting to everyone she passed, from guards to advisors to servants. A large smile, perhaps the most genuine to ever grace her lips, was always on display.

Nearly finished with the morning ritual, she returned to the doorway of Angelo's quarters and the Kaian general who waited, cold and clinically, outside them.

"Good morning, Clerak," she said.

The response from the general was somewhere between a scoff and a smirk.

"Princess."

Kavana took her by the hand.

"Come," she said.

"I was waiting for King Angelo," Clerak said.

Kavana gently but firmly led Clerak into Angelo's chambers.

"And as I share his bed, I am giving you permission to enter his chambers." She released the other woman's hand and shut the door. "Though, it's my understanding that you do, as well."

"I don't know what you mean, princess," Clerak said. "He and I..."

"Don't be so literally minded," Kavana said playfully. "You may have never actually been in his bed, but you've engaged in the same activities. It's probably much more comfortable here. Or are you one of those women who enjoys that little element of danger?"

Clerak froze. Instinctively, she wanted to take a step back from this brewing conflict, but a lifetime of military training had taught her to stand her ground.

"It's alright," Kavana said. "We all have our little kinks. You're being awfully quiet. That doesn't match your reputation."

"My reputation doesn't usually extend to include my personal activities."

"Oh, is that it?" Kavana asked. "You're dominant on the battlefield, but in the bedroom, you prefer…"

"I prefer privacy, is what I prefer."

"As we're sharing a man, I think we're past the point of that," Kavana said.

"I…"

"I don't want there to be barriers between us. Do you understand my meaning?" Kavana asked. "It's my hope our relationship can be informal, even warm. So, please stop calling me 'princess' or 'your highness' or any of that, alright? You'll notice I've not addressed you as 'general,' even though that's your proper title."

"Alright," Clerak said. "I believe that I can agree to."

"Excellent." Kavana bounced with a youthful exuberance. "Nextly, I've no interest in anyone being the 'other woman,' or man, if it comes to that, in this relationship. One wife or husband shouldn't be placed above the others."

"By the nature of your royal title, that's going to happen," Clerak said.

"Publicly, surely, but in private matters, as far as I'm concerned, we should be as equals," Kavana said. "Would this be agreeable to you?"

Clerak looked down upon the smaller woman, taking in

her words and sizing up her physical stature.

"You're saying I would be your, what, co-wife?"

Kavana giggled.

"That's not quite what I'm saying, no," she said. "The idea is, you would be his wife, and I would be his wife. He would be your husband, and he would be my husband, and I would be your wife, and you would be my wife."

"Wait, what?"

Kavana moved in closer.

"An equal union," she said. "That's what I want. Is that agreeable to you?"

"I... hadn't thought about it." She had, however, spent the last few seconds contemplating how much pressure she'd need to apply to each of the younger woman's bones to snap them.

"So?" Kavana asked. "Think about it now. I'm sure we'd have much to offer one another. There should be no jealousy, no envy. More importantly, no distrust. I wouldn't see you as the other woman, you wouldn't see me as an outside threat to your beloved king. Just three happy people. Or however many we eventually choose to include."

Clerak's eyebrows arched. Her breathing quickened.

"Everything you've said sounds reasonable," she said. "Unless, of course, you're just trying to lull me into a false sense of security."

Kavana wrapped her arms over Clerak's shoulders.

"I take my commitments very seriously," Kavana said.

"Your future husband is currently organizing an attack on your own homeworld at your behest."

"I was born into that family," Kavana said. "I never made a vow to them."

Kavana lifted herself onto her tiptoes and brought her lips to Clerak's.

The general reciprocated, at least for a moment. After a few seconds, she gripped Kavana by the arms and shoved her away.

The younger woman staggered back a few steps. Her mouth hung open and her heart raced. If there was to be a fight between the two of them, she didn't stand a chance against such a fit, well-trained warrior.

Clerak advanced on her, gripping her around the waist. She hoisted Kavana off the floor and tossed her through the air, onto the bed. Kavana squealed as she flew and bounced across the mattress.

Before she had even a hope of regaining her bearings, Clerak was atop her, pinning her to the bed and shoving her tongue down her throat.

Kavana writhed but did not struggle or make any attempt to break away.

CHAPTER 4

Val, several decks down now from the bridge, made her way through an excessively lengthy corridor, towards the large double doors at its end.

Upon nearing them, she found Trainer, leaned against the wall, his arms folded. It was perhaps the most nonchalant she'd ever seen him.

"Ah, I was hoping I'd see you before you headed out," he said.

"Really?" she asked. "Shouldn't you be planning with Farbo or something?"

Trainer drew himself up straight, instantly taking on a stately and commanding presence. This was the Trainer she knew, the mentor she needed on her side right then.

He produced a long, thin object from beneath his arm, wrapped in cloth.

"There's something I wanted to give you." He handed the bundle to her.

"What's this?"

"Unwrap it and you'll find out," he said. "That's how gifts work. Has no one ever given you one before?"

"Not often," she said. "It's not like I know when my birthday is or anything like that."

"Really?"

"Do you know yours?" she asked.

"No, but I'm not royalty."

"Until a few weeks ago, neither was I." She untied the rope that bound the bundle and pulled back the cloth. Her brow furrowed as she reached in and drew a short sword.

"Do you recognize it?" Trainer asked.

She gripped it by the handle and held it out.

"It's a training sword. It's similar to the one you trained me with." He smiled at her. "No. Seriously? You kept track of which one was mine?"

"I took it out of circulation when you completed your training," he said. "I do that with the very best of my students."

"Why?"

"If they go on to do great things, they might be valuable someday," he said.

"Really?"

"A man's got to have a retirement plan."

"I'm still mad at you, but thanks," Val said.

She took up her new old sword and headed for the doors.

They parted for her and she entered the hangar. Joining her just inside were Metch, Elle, Rik, and a few of their fellow castle escapees.

The ship they'd been traveling in sat off to one side. Compared to the sleek, clean craft that filled the rest of the landing pads, it looked a bit clunky, not to mention worn.

The team gave it one last look as they passed by.

"You know, I'm almost gonna miss that old piece of crap," said Metch.

"Really?" Val asked.

"No."

"Good." She lightly punched his shoulder. "It's not the ship that's important. It's the crew."

"Remind me again why that's the one we took?" Rik asked.

"Because that's the one I was doing a maintenance check on when you came running screaming into the hangar and told me to get in the air," said Metch.

"Right." Rik nodded. "So this was all your fault."

"Sure," Metch said.

They boarded their new ship.

The bay crew cleared the area and waved them out.

The shuttle lifted into the air, flying out of the larger ship and off into the blackness.

Hours later, Val sat in the passenger cabin, huddled in her seat, arms folded, head down.

"Valentina."

Her eyes shot open.

She groaned. "Hm?"

The others looked at her, at each other.

"What?" Rik asked.

"You didn't hear anything?" she asked.

"Like what?"

Val brushed her hair back.

"Nothing," she said. "I was probably just half asleep."

"Yeah, that happens all the time," he said. "You don't know if you're awake or still dreaming. I get it."

Val let her focus wander out the window.

"Yeah."

CHAPTER 5

O nce again on solid ground, Val and her group approached a white fence at the edge of a field. She opened it and they walked up the cobblestone pathway towards the large estate house. All across the yard were servants hard at work.

The vegetation, from the grass to the fields of crops to the surrounding woods, was a brilliant shade of green, brighter than anything on Kaia. Even the clear sky reflected a bit of the emerald hue. It almost felt surreal to the travelers.

"This is a change of pace, at least." The comment from Rik didn't go over well with Val. "I'm saying, from the uninhabitable frozen wastelands and the, you know, that dump with the fighting pit where you found Four."

"You weren't at the dump with the fighting pit," Val said. "You don't get to talk about the dump with the fighting pit."

With an ear-punishing shriek, the front door to the house swung open. A well-groomed man, middle-aged, in two pieces of a suit, stepped out onto the wooden porch.

"Are you the new help?" he called to them.

"Beg pardon?" Val asked.

"I'm Colonel Lonce. I'm sure we'll be getting to know one another real well." He placed his buttocks on one edge of the porch railing. "They usually clean you up a bit more before they send you over. Well, head round the back. Clernce'll get you settled in and assigned."

"Yeah, I'm not sure what you think is going on, but this isn't that," Val said.

"If you're not the new help, then may I kindly ask what you think it is you're doing on my property?"

"Is this a Kaian planet?" asked Rik.

"Beg pardon?" Lonce asked.

Rik pointed to Val. "Because if it is, then it's technically her property."

"I'm not sure what you're babbling on about, boy, but this planet is more what you might call a protectorate of Kaia than an actual piece of the empire."

"You heard about the coup that Prince Angelo staged against King Joseph?" Val asked.

"I'm familiar with the prince," Lonce said. "I've never heard of a man called Joseph, kingly or otherwise."

"You're kidding?" Rik asked. "Everyone's been talking about it for weeks. The whole empire's divided."

"As I said, we don't quite consider ourselves to be a part of the empire here," said Lonce. "News travels slowly through these parts."

"King Andor and Prince Thoome died. The reserve heir, King Joseph, took the Crown. For about two days. Then Angelo killed him. But it turns out, Andor was also my father." She held up the Crown of the Single Pointed Star. "The queen gave me this."

"I see." Lonce puckered the lower half of his face and nodded slowly. "So you're here for the other one."

He turned and walked inside.

"So, uh, do we follow him?" Rik asked.

Val started up the stairs.

She and the others entered the old house to find Lonce standing near a fireplace, his hands jammed into his trouser pockets. Another Crown, one with three points, sat in a window box above the mantle.

"It's been in the family for generations." Lonce looked at it wistfully. "I hate to part with it. Sentimental value, you know. But, if you're here for it, I'm not in much of a spirit to put up a fight."

"Huh." Rik grunted.

"You're giving it up?" Elle asked. "Just like that?"

Lonce shrugged.

"This isn't some kind of trick, is it?" asked Rik. "That's not a fake or a decoy."

Val reached out towards the Crown of the Three Point Star.

"It's real."

"And it's all yours," Lonce said. "All I ask is that you take it and leave me in peace."

"It's not that simple," said Val.

"It's been my experience that life is as simple or complicated as you choose to make it," Lonce said.

"It sounds like your experience has been severely lacking," said Rik.

"Maybe," Lonce said. "But I've enjoyed it."

"It also looks like your experience hasn't included a day of actual work in your life," Elle said.

"Lord be blessed," Lonce said with a smile.

"You have to come with us," Val said.

"Young lady, I mustn't do a darned thing I don't wish."

"Look, I've been through this whole argument twice already, and I'm very tired," Val said. "Can you please just cooperate? You seem to be an educated man."

"I'm not so sure about that," Rik said.

"I agree," added Elle.

"Just make this easier on everyone," Val said.

Lonce folded his arms and leaned against the mantle, a flat, disinterested look on his scraggly face.

Val grabbed him by the collar and swung him around, slamming him into a wall hard enough to shake the paintings hung there.

"Listen here, you pompous ass..." She froze. Her ears perked up. "You hear that?"

"No, but I'm assuming your super senses are hearing something we don't," said Rik. His hand went to the grip of his sidearm.

Val released Lonce. He straightened his shirt and vest as the others rushed outside.

Upon reaching the creaky porch, she and her compatriots were greeted by the sight of Kaian warships breaking through the clouds overhead.

"Okay, we are out of time," said Val. She turned back towards Lonce, who casually strolled out of the house. "What kind of defenses does this place have?"

"We've got some rifles and things to fend off poachers and wild animals." He twiddled his thumbs. "Nothing with which you'd want to engage a battleship."

"Well, there goes that idea," Val said.

"So, what're we doing?" asked Rik.

"Waiting until the lead ship gets closer," she said.

The forward ship drew nearer to the manor. Though not in the same class as Farbo's command cruiser, it was still a beast of the spaceways, larger by far than the house it hovered over.

The ship dropped very low, enough so that the crew on the bridge could view what was happening on the ground and vice versa.

Val held up the Single Pointed Crown for the bridge crew to see. She placed it in her head and activated it, armoring up beneath her poncho.

Lonce stepped back at the sight of her transformation. He dipped into the house, returning a moment later, carrying the Three Point Crown.

He raised it over his head, just as Val had.

He set it down on the porch ledge and gently backed away.

"Are you serious right now?" asked Val

"As I said, I've no spirit for a fight."

"Angelo murdered his way to the throne. He's attacking

ally systems." Her tone betrayed her exhaustion, like she was running through a list of talking points rather than making an impassioned plea.

"And that's got nothing to do with me and mine."

"He killed his own blood," she said. "Your blood."

"Let's just grab the Crown and go," Elle said.

"And who's going to wear it?" Val asked.

"I'm sure you can find someone."

"I've never met the extended royal family," Val said. "I was raised as a palace guard."

Rik pointed a thumb towards Lonce.

"Well, would you really trust this guy in a fight against your uncle?"

"I don't know." Val's voice softened. "Bontu and Four came along. I thought I could convince…"

"Young lady," Lonce said, "were my wife still living, I'm sure she would tell you that my mind, once made, cannot be convinced of a thing."

"So you're a proud coward," Val said. "Got it."

"You won't be able to shame me into joining your hopeless cause," he said.

"I'm not trying to," she said. "I'm just calling you names. Because you suck and you deserve it."

"So, what's the move?" Rik asked.

The lead ship was very low, maybe ten meters off the ground.

"You guys get back to the transport," Val ordered. "Get it prepped for take-off. I'm gonna beat up that warship."

"You're gonna what?!" Rik's voice jumped at least half an octave.

Val hopped up to the roof of the house. She backed up to the other side to get a running start. After sprinting forward, she kicked off at the edge, launching herself through the air.

The ship's captain and crew stared out the forward port.

"What is that crazed witch doing?" the captain asked.

Val landed cleanly on the nose of the ship, drawing her

sword and slicing through the hull plating.

"She's breached the hull," the tactical officer announced.

"With what?" the helmsman asked.

"Get her off the damn ship!" the captain ordered.

"How?" the tactical officer asked. "Our cannons can't point that way."

"Roll the ship," his commander instructed. "Shake her loose."

Val trudged across the ship's surface, towards the bridge, slicing and hacking as she went. Her energized sword tore massive gashes through the plating.

"Inside an atmosphere?" the helmsman asked. "Artificial gravity won't keep us on the deck."

The captain took his seat and strapped himself in.

"Just do it!"

The other bridge officers raced for their chairs and buckled in.

The captain leaned over a microphone on his armrest.

"All hands, strap in or hold on!"

The ship tilted to starboard. Val held on, running up the hull. She dropped the tip of her sword, letting it gouge a deep wound in the ship's exterior casing as she ran along.

By the time the ship was perpendicular to the ground, there was enough damage done to it that it could no longer remain aloft.

Val made the near-vertical run up the ship, jumping away and rolling to safety on the house's roof as it crashed to the ground. A large section of Lonce's property was torn through, spraying earthen debris high into the sky and far across the land.

The field workers fled in every direction.

Lonce watched the collapsing ship in disbelief. Val hopped down from the roof, landing gently next to him.

"Convinced yet?" she asked.

"Of what?" He was sputtering. "That you're a psychopath?"

"I'm the psychopath?" she asked.

"You just destroyed an imperial warship," he said. "You've wrecked my property. Who knows if all my servants made it to safety?"

"I'm pretty sure they all did."

"What is wrong with you?!" he asked.

"I'm not the one who brought a warship to your farm in the first place."

"Aren't you?" he asked. "Would they be here if they weren't looking for you?"

"They weren't looking for me." She pointed to the undisturbed Three Point Crown. "They're looking for that."

"I'd have given it to them without destroying my property," he said.

"Shut the hell up about your goddamn property. There're more important things in the universe than your crappy little farm." She picked up the Three Point Crown and shoved it towards Lonce's face. "Now put the damn thing on and let's get out of here."

Lonce tried to push her away, his fingertips barely touching the Crown. It was enough to awaken something within it.

"I'm not going anywhere with you!" he said.

"There are a ton more warships here," Val said. "If you want to live…"

Energy cannon fire ripped through the area. More of his farmland was tossed into the air in chunks and clouds.

Val and Lonce were hurled from the surface of the porch.

As Val watched, Lonce's body was shredded by the plasma discharge.

The Crown left his fingertips only moments before they burst into a swirling mix of red mist and fluttering bone chunks.

Val looked on in disbelief as the Crown pivoted in the air, flinging itself towards her face.

When the blazing discharge from the cannon fire

cleared, she found herself wearing an altered suit of armor. The plating was denser and more intricate and covered a bit more of her body. Moreover, she could feel a difference in it. It felt stronger, sturdier.

The Three Point Crown sat on her face, the curves and edges having merged with the Single Pointed Crown.

"What the hell?" she asked, gasping to herself.

She took only a moment to glance over Lonce's charred remains before fleeing the area, running faster than she ever had before.

The captain of the nearest ship pointed Val out to his crew as she bolted from the wreckage of the house.

"There!" he said.

The warship started firing again as Val dashed for the tree line. Several shots impacted behind her, but she made it to the forest without a scratch.

The ship's gunner shook his head in frustration.

"Sorry, sir. She was too fast."

"Keep looking," the captain said. "She couldn't have gotten far on foot."

Val darted across a clearing to where her transport ship awaited.

Once she was up the rear ramp, Rik slammed the door controls, raising and sealing the hatch.

"Go!" Val said.

"I'm going," Metch said.

There was a burst of glowing gas from the engine vents as the ship blasted into the sky.

This craft had individual chairs for the passengers, rather than the benches of their old transport. Val slumped into one.

Rik took a seat across from her.

"Hey," he said.

"Hey."

"What's, uh..." He gestured to his face. "You've got a little something..."

"Yeah."

The lead warship remained in position over the remains of Lonce's estate and the crumpled husk of their sister ship, while the others dispersed in a search pattern across the area.

On the bridge, the captain paced the floor.

"Anything?" He'd lost count of how many times he'd asked in vain for an update in the hours since the encounter with the insurgents.

"No, sir," the scanner operator reported. "No sign of them. Nor from the other ships. I'm sorry, but if we haven't found them by now..."

"You're sorry?" the captain asked. "You're not the one who's going to have to explain this to the king."

CHAPTER 6

Angelo sat at the head of the table in the royal dining hall. A small number of advisors huddled around.

"So, the royal chapel will be available on the date," one advisor said.

"Of course it will," said Angelo. "I'm the king. This is a royal wedding we're planning. Everything will be as I decide."

"Yes, but those decisions still must be made. Down to the smallest detail. Now, when the bridal party exits, should they move to the left or right?"

"You've got to be kidding me."

"No, sire. As I said, the smallest detail."

"Do I also get to decide how many grains of dust will be on the altar," Angelo chuckled, "or how many flies will buzz about the church doors?"

"Well, ideally, there would be none."

Angelo glared at him.

"Now, as you said…"

"And where is my betrothed?" Angelo asked. "I'm threatening war on her behalf, the least she could do is join me for dinner."

"She requested dinner be brought to your chambers a short while ago," one of the servants said.

"Did she?" Angelo turned in his large, cushioned chair. "And why wasn't I informed?"

"You were busy with wedding preparations," the servant

said.

"Oh, yes, we wouldn't want to distract from all this excitement."

"Now, uh, your majesty, there is one bit of business I hesitate to address," said the advisor. "The guest list."

"I'm fairly certain I already addressed that bit of business," said Angelo.

"Yes, sire, however, we've had an unusual number of invitees respond in the negative."

"What?"

"It's mostly been members of your extended family, I'm sorry to say," the advisor said. "They've cited safety concerns."

"Safety concerns?" Angelo's brow furrowed. "At a royal wedding? It will be the most secure location in the known galaxy. What could they possibly have to fear?"

No one responded.

"What would you have me do then?" Angelo asked. "Hm? Force them here at gunpoint? No, if any of those ingrates don't want to attend, let that be their business."

A man in a red military uniform, general's stripes on the epaulets, rushed into the room.

"Ah, general." Angelo tossed down his napkin. "Please tell me you have some news to brighten these dour faces I'm surrounded with."

The general looked concerned.

He leaned in and whispered to Angelo.

Angelo pushed away from the table and stood.

"I see," he said. "Yes, that's... that's fine. That's fine."

He walked away. Out into the hall, and towards his chambers.

He paused by the door as he heard something unusual from within.

Giggling. Two female voices.

His mood shifting to one of intrigue, he opened the door.

He entered his chambers and observed the source of the commotion.

On his bed, Kavana and Clerak could be seen play-wrestling under the covers. Neither appeared to be clothed.

"Well then," said Angelo. "This is new."

They disengaged from their activity and turned towards him.

"New," Kavana said, "but not temporary."

"So, you'd better get used to it," Clerak said.

"Oh, had I?"

Try as he did, he couldn't help his mood from growing somber.

"What's wrong?" asked Clerak.

"How do you know something's wrong?" Kavana asked.

Clerak scoffed.

"Please. You must learn to read your... our future husband."

"She's right." Angelo set himself down on the edge of the bed. "There's been a, I'm not sure the right term for it, a setback? A catastrophe?"

"Oh, dear," Kavana said.

"The forces we sent to Mambja failed to recover the Three Point Crown," he said. "Valentina and her crew now have possession of all four of the secondary Crowns."

"That's still not enough for her to challenge you," said Kavana.

"No, but it is a problem," he said. "It's forced me to reconsider our current plans."

"Oh?" Kavana asked.

"Yes. I'm sorry, my dear. I see difficult choices ahead of us, and I'm not sure they'll all make sense to you." He spun the Crown on his palm before setting it down on the nightstand. "It darkens my soul that I cannot share the insight of the Crown with you. Either of you."

Clerak pouted, a look of faux-ponderance on her face.

"Well, now, if only there was some way for us to cheer you up?"

Angelo smiled. He pulled off his vest, peeled away his

shirt, and undid his belt before climbing onto the bed. Clerak rose up and kissed him, her bare body pressing against him. Kavana slipped out from under the covers and crawled towards them.

CHAPTER 7

Val's shuttle flew back towards its mothership and nuzzled itself inside the embracing shuttle bay.

Trainer, Farbo, and a small contingent of soldiers arrived to meet it.

The rear of the shuttle lowered. The crew walked out. Val still wore the armor.

Trainer's face screwed up as he stared at it.

Val finally removed the Crown as she walked towards him.

"What happened?" Trainer asked.

"Long story." Val didn't lose a step. "It's my understanding these ships have actual beds and stuff?"

"Uh, yes, your highness," Farbo said. "I can show you to your private quarters."

"Just the deck and section number is good."

"Deck six, section three-alpha."

"Cool."

She left the hangar, found a lift, took it to deck six, and went to section three-alpha.

The door to her executive quarters slid open with the tap of the keypad.

She didn't bother to turn on the lights as the doors shut behind her.

The Crown was set on a nightstand and she flopped onto the bed.

Within moments, she was falling towards a desperately needed and well-earned sleep.

"*Valentina*."

"Goddammit."

INTERLUDE

A bright young Kaian boy sat at the kitchen table in his family's home. In his small, thin hands were a trio of metallic ropes, each of a different hue. Tal was deeply transfixed in weaving the three cords together in an elaborate pattern.

His father sat opposite him, sipping a beverage and reading a news feed.

His mother approached with a plate of food. She took note of her son's project. "Ooh, that looks neat. What've you got there, Tal?"

"It's a Manheian love knot," the boy said.

"Oh."

His father peered over at his son's work. "You're doing it wrong."

"Dear!"

"What?"

"I had to come up with my own design," Tal said, "to make it with three strands instead of two."

"Oh?" his mother asked. "And why's that?"

"They represent the king and the two queens getting married."

"Oh, that," his father said gruffly.

"Oh, hush you," his wife said. "He's excited about the royal wedding."

"I don't see why. We're not invited."

"The whole kingdom's invited," Tal said.

"There, you see, the whole kingdom." She arched both her eyebrows at her husband.

"To stand in the street and maybe catch a glimpse of their coach as it goes by," the father said. "Maybe."

"Don't be such a killjoy," his wife said.

"I can't kill something I haven't seen in years."

She scoffed at him. "You know, I seem to recall your mother telling me that you waited out in the streets all night to get a spot to see Florana the day of her wedding."

"And what did I get for my troubles?" he asked. "A glimpse of the coach as it rode by."

"Your mother said Florana waved to you."

"Mothers tell their kids a lot of crap," he said.

She returned her attention to their son. "So, Tal, once you get the knot finished, what are you going to do with it?"

"I'm going to give it to the king and queens."

"How?" his father asked.

"I'm going to give it to them at their wedding."

"Are you sure that's the best idea?" his mother asked. "They're going to be awfully busy that day. Maybe you should mail it to them. You could write them a nice note wishing them well."

"Okay," Tal said.

"I know," his mother said. "Why don't you send it from your school? The palace is more likely to make sure the king and queens get it quickly if they see it came from a school. Kings and queens love children."

The father snickered.

"You wanted to say something?" his wife asked.

"No, I believe my incredulous scoff conveyed my meaning sufficiently."

"What are you doing?" Rik asked.

Val had positioned herself perpendicular to the doorframe. She pushed against it, twisting her upper body as far as it would go against her planted feet.

She didn't answer his question, instead grunting as she pushed harder against the jamb.

"You... alright?" he asked.

With a defeated gasp, she released her hold and brought herself straight.

"Yeah. I've just... my back has felt like it needs to pop all day, and I just can't get it to."

He grabbed her around the waist and hoisted her out into the hallway. The hem of her plain undershirt, the only thing that covered her upper body just then, bunched up as she was moved.

"Here."

"What are you doing?" she asked.

He pushed her towards the bulkhead.

"Press yourself against the wall," he instructed. "Put your arms up. Way up. It would help if there was a bar or something for you to grab onto."

She glanced back over her shoulder.

"Did you want to do this in the doorway?"

"No, you need to be against a hard surface for it to work."

"I'm still unclear what this even is."

He shoved her harder. "You need to be flat against the wall."

"I am flat," she told him. She felt a bit ridiculous in this position; more so because she was allowing herself to be manipulated so casually. "This is literally as flat as I can go."

"Okay."

Both of his palms pressed sharply into the bare, sweaty flesh of her lower back, eliciting an unsettlingly loud popping sound.

"Ooh." She moaned. "Oh."

Rik took a step back. She moved away from the wall and rubbed the spot he'd just pushed.

"Oh my God," she said, "that feels so much better."

"Don't mention it."

He walked away, passing their robotic companion as he went.

"What was that about?" Four asked.

"Nothing," Val said. "Don't worry about it."

Four's head tilted.

"Don't look at me like that," Val said.

"How am I looking at you?" Four asked. "My facial features, such as they are, are incapable of change. Unless... are they changing? Has the power of the Crown transmutated my body further?"

"No," Val said. "But I can tell. You're like a pet."

"You view me as a pet?"

"Not like that," Val said. "But, you know, animals don't really express emotions the way people do, but you can read them. Same thing with you."

"Have you had many pets?"

"Not really," Val said. "None, actually."

"Do you not like pets?"

"I've never been in a position where it would be practical to own one."

"Is practicality a concern?" Four asked.

"When your life could lead to a place like this at any second, yeah, it is," Val said. "This being a warship, I mean. I wouldn't want to bring a pet on a warship."

"Hm." Four tapped its chin, such as it was. "Should I get a pet? When we are done with warship-related business, of course."

"You can do whatever you want to do," she said.

"What about you? Your life will undoubtedly be very different after this is all over."

"Uh-huh."

"What will you do?" Four asked.

"I hadn't really thought that far," she said.

"Why not?"

"There doesn't seem to be a lot of point."

"Why not?"

"Because we might not win," she said. "What's the point of planning for victory that isn't certain?"

"So you presume you will fail?"

"I didn't say that, either."

Four nodded.

"Perhaps," it said, "It would be prudent to devise a plan in case of each eventuality. Then you will be prepared no matter the outcome."

"Um, except that if we don't win, I'll probably be dead."

"Oh, yes," Four said. "I hadn't thought of that."

"I find it's best not to think of it," Val said.

"Of what?"

"Death, dying, whatever."

"I see," Four said. "Why not?"

"Dammit, stop asking me that."

"Why?"

"That's not much better."

"Perhaps I am being unclear," Four said.

"Perhaps you're being annoying," Val said. "I'm sorry, I... what was it you were asking?"

"Why you don't want to think about death."

"A lot of people don't," Val said. "It's not pleasant to think about. If I focus on it, I won't be able to get anything worthwhile done."

"Are you afraid to die?"

"I... maybe." She shrugged. "I don't know. I'd have to think about it."

"Is it just your own death you fear?" Four asked. "Or others, as well?"

"What do you mean?" Val asked. "People under my command, or..."

"Anyone," Four said. "I've never had anyone I care about enough to be concerned with them dying. Have you?"

"That's probably more complicated than it should be,"

she said.

"Your parents and brothers were recently killed," Four said. "Is that what you're referring to?"

"Yeah, I guess," she said. "Because I didn't know they were my family. Keeping them alive was, I don't know how to say this, it was more of a sense of duty than real concern. Which maybe it shouldn't have been."

"Are you upset because you failed in that duty?"

"That's not it."

"Val. Maybe I call you Val?"

"Yes, of course."

"Val, have you given yourself any time to grieve?" Four asked. "At all? In the weeks since they died?"

Val gave Four's arm a squeeze. Or tried to, anyway. It was made of a very rigid alloy.

"I'll see you around, bud," she said softly as she walked away.

"Val."

She turned back only for a moment. "Yeah?"

"I am concerned as to whether or not you die."

She nodded and walked off.

Tal's mother stalked through the empty halls, approaching the principal's office.

Before she had reached the door, a man in a suit stepped out. "Ah. You're Tal's mother?"

"That's right," she said. "I heard there was a fight?"

"Yes," the elderly man confirmed. "It seems your son struck another boy."

"That doesn't sound like him at all."

"The teacher in his classroom confirmed it."

"And what did Tal say?"

"Ma'am, your son is an eight-year-old boy who's in trouble with the principal," the man said. "He'll say anything to get out of it."

She folded her arms and looked dead in his grey eyes.

"I would like to hear it from my son."

With a raise of his bushy eyebrows and a deep exhale, the principal escorted her into his office. There she found Tal sitting alone in front of an intimidating desk.

His mother took a seat beside him while the principal moved around to his chair. It squeaked horribly as he sat down. It had probably been there as long as he had.

She took hold of her son and looked him over, patting him down to feel for any wounds. Aside from some scrapes on his knuckles, there was nothing visibly wrong with him.

"Tal, are you alright?" she asked.

Tal nodded.

"Tal," the principal said, "why don't you tell us why you struck the other boy?"

"You're starting from the presumption that he did hit the other boy?" Tal's mother asked.

"I did," Tal said.

His mother's shoulders sank. "Why did you do that? You know you're not supposed to hit people."

"I brought my knot to school," he said, "to show to the class and get the teacher to mail it like you said."

"His knot?" the principal asked.

Tal lifted his shirt and pulled the love knot, still in pristine condition, from his waistband.

"He was working on it as a gift for the royals for their wedding," his mother explained.

"I see."

"Go on," Tal's mother said encouragingly.

"She didn't want to mail it," the boy said. "Then Cruvo said that Angelo shouldn't even be king."

His mother and the principal looked at one another, their eyes bulging.

"Cruvo said that?" his mother asked.

"Ma'am, the child is only eight years old, just like your

son," the principal said. His voice shook just a bit.

"Don't worry, sir, I'm not going to report a primary school child for sedition." She looked to her son. "But is that why the teacher didn't want to mail it?"

"I, ah, of course, I have no way of knowing," the principal said. "But if he'd like, we can make sure his kind gift to the royals gets into the post as soon as possible. They'll get it before their wedding, I'm sure of it."

Tal perked up. He moved to hand the braided knot to the principal.

His mother stopped him.

"No, son. You can make sure to hand-deliver it to the royals on their wedding day."

With that, she took her son by the hand and led him out of the room, staring daggers at the principal as she went.

Rik came upon Elle, breathlessly leaving what appeared to be a random room. It certainly wasn't crew quarters. He knew this wasn't the deck she was assigned to, anyway.

"Hey," Rik said to her.

"Oh, hey." Her voice was a hoarse whisper.

"You alright?" he asked.

"Yeah, fine." She nodded.

He took note of the sweat dripping from her forehead and her unusually bulky manner of dress.

"Since when do you wear turtle necks?" Rik asked. "That are clearly men's turtlenecks?"

"It's been a long day," she managed to croak out. "A long month or… two? I don't know. We all have our ways of blowing off steam."

"Whatever." He shook his head and continued up the corridor.

Tal and his mother sat in a pair of portable chairs on the side of the street. The sun barely hung in the sky. It would be many hours into the next day before the wedding procession was to pass by.

Several more early arrivals were scattered up and down the pavement. Temporary dividers separated the footpaths from the road itself.

Hours later, long after his mother had fallen asleep, Tal still sat upright, fueled with youthful enthusiasm.

The surrounding roadside was starting to fill in.

Later still, Tal's father approached, bundled against the night chill. He tapped his sleeping wife's shoulder. Once her eyes opened, he jerked his head away.

With a smile, she rose, handing her blankets, and supervisory duties, to her husband before wandering back towards home.

The man gave his son's back a pat. Even the boy's eyelids were becoming heavy.

The sidewalk had become quite crowded, but Tal and his parents maintained their place at the front of the pack.

When daylight broke, people began putting away their chairs and tents. The sidewalk was packed; standing room only.

Tal's mother returned with some warm beverages for her boys.

Though Tal would chastise himself for failing to maintain an all-night vigil, there was still time before the festivities began.

It wasn't long before the celebration kicked off. A military escort stepped in unison ahead of the royals' open-air coach. It took up nearly the width of the road and was even longer. The body of it had a pearlescent sheen, and the trim was pure gold. The members of the wedding party sat on wide cushions within.

Tal's father gave his shoulder a thump. "This is it, son."

Some other members of the crowd started to shove, tried

to force their way to a closer spot than their arrival time had earned them.

Tal's father elbowed back.

"Hey, watch it." He knelt down to his son's eye level. "I can see them coming up the road. Make sure to get close, see if you can get their attention."

He pushed the boy forward, up to the divider.

The royal coach approached slowly. They were in no hurry. There was nothing else for them, or anyone else, to attend to that day.

The three members of the bridal party waved to the crowds. Kavana was by far the most animated.

"There they are," Tal's father said.

"My king!" Tal shouted. His hands flailed frantically, one clutching tight to the handmade gift. "My queens!"

The youngest bride looked directly at him and smiled. She reached out and gave him a quick finger wave.

Tal lit up.

The father looked at his wife and smiled.

Tal held out the love knot and waved it towards the coach.

Kavana motioned for the driver to stop.

She quickly dashed out and up to Tal, gingerly taking the knot from his slender fingers.

"Thank you." She rushed back to the coach. As it pulled away, she showed the knot to her soon-to-be spouses. They didn't seem as enamored of the present, but she couldn't stop cooing over it.

Tal looked up at his parents, beaming. "She spoke to me."

He suddenly felt someone pushing against his back, pressing him into the divider rail.

The shoving continued as more of the crowd surged forward, trying to get a look at the royals.

Tal couldn't catch his breath. Moreover, he couldn't see his parents anymore.

The coach stopped in front of the chapel. Angelo was out

first, helping his brides step down and directing them up the church's stairs. Once they were inside, he looked to the head guard.

"This crowd is getting out of hand," he said. "Rein them in, by any means necessary."

Angelo turned and ascended the chapel stairs to meet with his wives.

The guard smiled. He faced the crowd and cocked his rifle.

A gunshot rang out.

Tal dropped to the ground, along with several others nearby.

People in the rear of the crowd had not yet caught on to the danger when those in the front panicked and tried to push their way back. Those unaware were still attempting to force their way forward, fighting against those who were trying to flee the gunfire. The result was a confused crush that caused even more injuries to the gathered citizenry.

Angelo stepped away from Kavana and Clerak and bounded back down the stairs. His hand touched the guard's gun barrel and lowered it.

"What are you doing?" Angelo asked.

The guard shrugged. "You said by any means necessary. So..."

"I didn't mean open fire on the public on my wedding day," Angelo said.

"Well, you didn't say that. Next time, be more specific."

Angelo drew himself up. "Be more specific?"

He gave the guard a quick shove. The man was sent sprawling into the angry crowd.

The people went to work on him straight away, fists and feet flying. His cries and pleas quickly ended.

Angelo returned to his brides. Each took ahold of one of his arms as they entered the church.

BOOK 7: LOWER
LIGHTS

CHAPTER 1

Val hit the ground.

Hard.

Though, once she hit it, it barely resembled ground anymore. The soil was baked and pulverized, chunks of dirt and rock thrown in every direction.

The time of day didn't particularly matter, as the smoke of battle clouded out any natural light.

Dots of muzzle flashes crowded the horizon. All that could be seen of air support was glowing engine exhaust far overhead.

Rik, leading a handful of soldiers, rushed towards the crater created by their queen's impact. The rest of their battalion lay down suppressive fire.

The smaller commando unit found Val at the bottom of the hole, partially buried in vitrified mud, her armor still mostly on.

The left side of her torso was exposed, scorched, and bloody. Parts of it were missing entirely. The surrounding armored plating smoldered with a fading glow.

"Holy shit. Oh, God, holy shit." Rik pressed the comm device in his ear. "This is the queen's Guardian. We need evac at my position, immediately."

"Guardian, we're having a hell of a time getting anything even close to your proximity," General Farbo replied over-the-air. "Our fighters and transports are being blasted out of the sky."

"This is not optional, general. I don't care if you have to bring down every warship we've got, you will get here immediately. Is that understood?"

"Yes, sir." She nodded to Metch, who now piloted her command ship, before heading towards the chair in the center of the bridge. "We'll be there as soon as we can." She stopped short. "Guardian, what's happened?"

"Something I'm not going to discuss over an open channel," said Rik. "I'll see you when you get here."

"Understood," Farbo said.

The command ship pushed its way through the smoke. Several of its compatriots hovered nearby, shielding them as best they could.

Fighting on the ground continued. From the air, it was just a field of blinking dots illuminating the dense haze.

A smaller pod, large enough to hold at least a dozen people, dropped out of the underbelly of Farbo's ship. It thudded to the ground, a doorway automatically opening on one side.

Rik and several others, carrying Val's heavy armored form between them, hurried to the pod. The rest of his troops continued firing at the enemy.

The soldiers made it inside and, as gently as they were able, lowered Val to the floor.

"Go!" Rik said.

The pod sealed itself. The wide silver coil that tethered it into the larger vessel heaved, dragging them in within a matter of seconds.

With the cargo secured, the insurgent ships pulled back up into the sky, swallowed again by the fog of war.

The command ship found its way out of the atmosphere and kept going. Inside, Rik fumbled to get the pod hatch open again. At first pull, the release lever failed to engage. The pod wasn't properly docked yet. He tugged again and again, growling at the mechanism as it refused to give way.

Finally, the lock popped.

He and his team once again hoisted Val up between them, carrying her to an awaiting gurney. The accompanying medical team sprinted her away.

Rik followed closely.

As they rounded the first corner in the adjacent corridor, Trainer and Elle joined their rushing group.

"What the hell happened?" Trainer asked.

"You tell me," said Rik. "I thought the Crown made her indestructible."

"What fool idiot gave you that idea?" Trainer asked.

"Uh, pretty sure it was you."

"Then you must have mislearned the lesson," Trainer said.

"Oh, so it's the student's fault if the teacher can't teach?"

"If the student can't learn because he's impenetrable to wisdom..."

"Seriously? Can we please not do this now?" Elle asked.

"The Crown grants the wearer great resistance to physical injury," Trainer said, "but it doesn't make them invincible."

Rik gestured down at Val, splayed out on the cart.

"Did she know that?"

"Yes," Trainer said. "She chose to enter the battlefield anyway."

"And you couldn't have stopped her?" asked Rik.

"No more than I could stop the wind or the tides," Trainer said.

"Great," Rik said. "Just friggin' great."

"That's not helping either," Elle said.

"Well what in the hell is gonna help?" Rik asked.

They reached the infirmary. The doors butted open as Val was wheeled inside. Rik tried to follow but was blocked by Trainer's hand on his chest. "Let them work."

"Trainer," Rik said, "I could..."

"You could order me to let you inside, and I'd have to

listen," Trainer said. "But I'd hope you wouldn't do that. I know you care for her…"

"I don't think you do."

"Rik, I've known the both of you since you were children," Trainer said. "I understand what's going on."

"No, you don't."

"I do. That's why I have to act as your voice of reason now. Interrupting the field medics won't help anyone, least of all Val."

"Field medics?" Rik asked. "She's being worked on by field medics?"

"They're all we have onboard," Elle said.

"Why the hell aren't there any doctors here?"

"Warships are usually only supplied with field medics to stabilize the wounded for transport to a fully equipped medical facility," said Elle.

"Except we don't have any of those," said Rik.

"Well," said Elle, "hopefully she won't need one."

Rik turned away, trying to hide his face from the others. He was doing a lousy job controlling its expression, and he didn't want to show the kind of weakness he was feeling.

Looking down, he found that there was a noticeable trail of blood along the floor. It disappeared around the nearest corner, though it wasn't difficult for him to surmise where it led.

"God damn." He ran his palm over his head.

Trainer placed a broad hand on his shoulder. Rik very nearly flinched away.

"The Crown also has great powers of healing," Trainer said. "Hopefully it'll be enough."

"Yeah," Rik said. "Hopefully."

He walked away.

CHAPTER 2

Around the same time that one Kaian queen's life was dangling by the thinnest of threads, another made her way through the palace hallways back on the homeworld, dodging soldiers and workers who moved ordinance and various large cases out of the residence.

"Pardon me," Kavana said to no one in particular, "Has anyone seen the king?"

A worker, his hands full with one end of a long crate, nodded down the corridor.

"I saw him in the dining room several minutes ago."

"Thank you." She gave him a peck on the cheek and hurried up the hall.

Kavana entered the dining hall and approached the king's end of the great table.

Angelo set down his drink and quickly swallowed.

"Ah, my dear." He gestured at the seat next to him. "Please, sit. I'd sent my new vizier to find you to ask that you join me and haven't seen him since. I'm afraid he's not very skilled. Unfortunately, someone took the liberty of relieving my former vizier of his duties."

"That's what I wished to speak to you about," Kavana said in a hushed voice. "How aware were you of all his workings?"

Angelo lifted his goblet and gave it a swirl, watching the blood-colored liquid splash across the gilded rim.

"I suppose that's difficult to say. Only a couple of months ago, I'd never have suspected him capable of the things he helped me accomplish."

"Before he refused your orders, yes," said Kavana. "Did you think him capable of that?"

"What's the meaning of all this?" Angelo asked.

"I had another mage sent to me from Palan before the fighting started," she said.

"Did you?" he asked. "How come I wasn't aware of that?"

"I wasn't keeping it from you, I simply like having a mage on hand, and my most loyal one was killed in your service," she said.

"Again, I implore you to get to the point."

"She and I were performing some basic castings, to read the energy of the palace," Kavana said. "What we discovered hidden away, by the former vizier's hand, was troubling. I would ask that you come view our findings with all haste."

"You do seem troubled, my love." Angelo wiped his mouth and tossed the napkin on the table. He picked his scepter from where it leaned against his chair's arm and followed his young bride out of the room.

Elle looked around the hallway's corner. As she'd suspected, she found Rik in the shadows there, sat on the floor, his shoulders awkwardly pressing against the metallic wall.

"Hey." She approached slowly. "General Farbo's looking for you."

"I don't care."

She took a seat next to him.

"You kind of have to," she said.

"Make me."

"You know what I mean."

"No." He turned his head towards her. "What do you mean?"

"I mean, you're the queen's Guardian," she said. "With her, you know... incapacitated..."

"Knocking on death's door."

"Don't."

"Hey, I can..."

"I can't handle it," Elle said. "Okay? I just... I can't."

"Yeah, okay." They sat in silence for a moment. "You know she threatened to remove me as her Guardian? Maybe that's why I'm having a hard time, you know, being responsible."

"I don't think she would have actually done it," Elle said.

"She was pissed at me."

"She still worked with you. I know she still trusted you."

"And I was pissed at her," Rik said. "Mostly because she had the gall to be pissed at me."

"I don't want to take sides here."

"It's not about taking sides," he said. "It's... we've known each other since before puberty. I pissed her off, right or wrong. And if she dies, then that's how we left things."

"I don't... I mean, I don't think she'd die."

"You have no control over that. No one has any way of knowing right now." He took a breath. "You weren't in that rescue pod. It just smelled like burning and blood. I've never smelled blood that strong before. We were only in there, what, a minute or two?"

"It took just under twelve seconds to seal and retract the pod."

"Well, it felt a lot longer than that."

"I'm sure it did."

Rik sniffled and wiped at his eyes.

He got up.

"You said the general was looking for me."

He held out a hand. Elle took it. He hoisted her to her

feet.

"Yeah," she said. "She was on the bridge. But she might've gone to check on Val by now."

"The infirmary's closer," he said. "We'll look there, first."

Rik and Elle made their way up the corridor just as Trainer was exiting the infirmary. Farbo already stood waiting outside the doors.

"Sorry," Trainer said. "I had to help the medics get the Crown off of her."

"I thought the Crown was helping heal her," said Rik.

"The Crown's done all it can," Trainer said. "And all it's going to do. She needs to get to a real medical facility."

"Which we've already established we don't have access to." Rik turned to Farbo. "How the hell could you not have thought to bring any medical ships?"

"Watch your..." She stopped herself mid-snarl. "Oh, right, you outrank me now. When our forces split from those loyal to the false king, we were allowed to bring a proportionate amount of equipment and ships with us. The outpost at Carse represented the bulk of our medical holdings. Unfortunately, the twenty-four hours advance wasn't enough for them. They were intercepted before they could rendezvous with the main fleet."

"So far, we've gotten by with the field medics," Trainer said.

"Well, 'so far' just ended." Rik inhaled deeply. "Look, I'm sure the field medics are great, and I'm sure they're doing the best they can, but we need real doctors and real medical facilities. Not just for Val, but she's our priority right now. If we can't – if she doesn't pull through, then we have a coup on our hands without a new leader to install. That's got to be one of the dumbest things anyone could do."

"In the meantime, we've got a war to fight," Farbo said.

"That's why I asked to see you."

"What about?"

"We need to discuss tactics," she said.

"Look, Val trusted you to know best," said Rik. "I can do the same."

"It's not just about this campaign," she said. "We're trying to repel our former comrades from the entire Palan system. That doesn't just require orders, it requires permissions. I'm a general, not a monarch."

"Well, neither am I," said Rik.

"And that's what we must discuss."

"Which I'd be all for, but every second we spend discussing is one second Val doesn't have," Rik said. "She's more important than any of us."

"But is she more important than all of us?" Farbo asked. "If we save the monarch but lose the coup, is that any worse than winning the coup with no monarch to install?"

"I'm sorry, but until we have a plan for what to do about Val, I'm not going to be able to focus on anything else," Rik said.

"What about a refugee ship?" Elle piped in.

"Beg pardon?" asked Rik. "What?"

"Like one of those medical ships the Empire sends out to help civilians from war-torn worlds," Elle said.

"You want to put our queen on one of Angelo's own ships?" Rik asked.

"Security and I.D. standards are usually really lax," Elle said. "And they have doctors onboard. Lots of doctors."

"Crap," Rik said. "Great. I mean, yeah, if we could sneak her onboard, get her to a doctor, and get them to patch her up without anyone recognizing her or asking any questions."

"They don't usually ask too many questions on those types of ships," said Elle. "And as for recognizing her, well, look at her. You've known her since you were kids. Would you recognize her in this condition?"

Rik took a quick peek through the windows of the infirmary.

"Maybe not."

"The decision is yours, Guardian," said Trainer.

"Ah, dammit," Rik said. "And no one has any other ideas?"

"Communication with the Palans was disrupted days ago and still hasn't been reestablished," said Farbo. "With all the cannon fire in space, the fold drives are pretty much useless. It's two days to Palan without it, and that's if they recognize us as allies. Unless you want to trust her fate to some back-alley doctor on the black market..."

"No, I've seen the black market. We're not taking her there," said Rik. He looked to his friend. "Alright, Elle, prep a shuttle. Time is a factor here."

CHAPTER 3

A pair of medics loaded Val onto a shuttle, the same class G, 3rd model troop transport that she and her team had been using in the weeks before Farbo's fleet had found them. She lay on a gurney, wrapped in enough blankets and sheets to hide the extent of her injuries from a passing glance.

All of her friends, her travel companions, and those she'd met on her journey stood watching.

The merged Single and Three Point Crown sat in her palm. Trainer gently wrapped her fingers around it.

"Make sure she keeps this on her person," he said. "It will help preserve her for the trip."

"Got it," Elle said.

"You're sure you want to take her in this beat-up thing?" Metch asked.

"It's less likely to be noticed than a shiny new military shuttle," Elle said.

"And you're sure you don't want to bring an experienced pilot along?"

"Metch, we've got to do this as quickly as possible," she said. "The more people involved, the more questions they'll ask."

"I just… really don't like this," Metch said.

"The plan, or the shuttle?" Rik asked.

"Both, while we're on the subject."

"The debate's over," Rik said. "We already decided."

"I wasn't invited to the debate," Metch said.

"Did you have an idea?" Rik asked.

"No, but it still would've been nice to have been included."

Elle walked towards the shuttle. "I'm going."

Rik grabbed hold of her arm.

"Wait a minute." He looked to the others. "Can you give us a second?"

The rest of the crowd moved off a respectable distance.

He turned back to Elle.

"Elle, you know I'm trusting you with... something beyond our scope of comprehension."

"I'm aware."

"A couple months ago, we were all just soldiers," he said. "Now we're a queen, a Guardian, and..."

"Still a soldier?" she asked.

"You're our hope of pulling this off right now," he said. "I'm trusting you. Please, get both of you back here quick."

Elle peered into the shuttle.

"As quick as I can, given her shape."

"Yeah."

"Wish me luck?" she asked.

"I've kind of given up on believing in that."

"Well, okay."

She ascended the ramp. It rose behind her.

A few seconds after, the shuttle lifted, out of the cargo bay and away from the larger vessel.

The former vizier's chambers were dark, though that hadn't been unusual even during his life. He'd been a man with many strange habits, although no one was quite sure how many of them were legitimate quirks and how many were affectations used to manipulate his public persona.

The door swung open. Kavana entered first, followed by Angelo, and then her new mage. The Palan mage was the only one whose nerves seemed at all rattled.

Kavana flipped a switch on the wall, confirming that the room did possess functioning light fixtures.

She shut the door behind them.

"We noticed something of a mystical nature in the former vizier's quarters here," she said. "Knowing the kind of man he was, it bore investigating. We had a look around…"

"And you didn't think to come get me then?" Angelo asked.

"We did, but I felt a compulsion to know first what I'd be leading you into," Kavana said. "You're of course aware how strongly I feel to follow my compulsions."

That declaration did nothing to set the mage's nerves at ease.

Kavana nodded to her.

The mage moved to the far side of the room. Her hands took on a faint glow; as she waved them before her, the stones that comprised the wall slid away, one-by-one.

A whole other chamber was revealed. Technology was sparse within it, but tables and shelves were littered with artifacts of an arcane nature.

"This was hidden with a simple spell of concealment," said Kavana.

"I'm familiar," Angelo said.

"But of course the vizier was hiding things," said Kavana. "It was more what we found here that gave me cause to be disturbed."

She tapped on the lone computer screen, sat on a simple wooden table. A text file was displayed.

"I thought he left no written records," Angelo said.

"None relating to the Crown or the answers you sought regarding it," said Kavana. "This is something else. It's a spell of compliance that the vizier was working on."

"A spell of compliance?" the king asked.

"In short," Kavana said, "mind control."

Angelo looked concerned.

"He left no notes as to what, exactly, he planned to do with it," she said. "But it got me wondering, why did he wish to see you installed as king?"

"What?"

"You must have realized, certainly. Your brother and nephew's 'accident.' Sacrificing his order to give you the power to take the Crown. And then we find this." She gestured at the scrawlings on the screen. "Could he have been working to control your mind? Install you as his puppet servant? Or does the spell's incomplete state tell us that he was working to enslave your brother's mind and couldn't work out quite how?"

"Unfortunately, his untimely death means we'll never really have those answers," Angelo said. "You say the spell is unfinished?"

The mage nodded.

"Can it be finished?" he asked.

"I... uh, it doesn't appear so..." the mage stammered. "I wouldn't know how, anyway."

"Good. There's a reason these sorts of spells were outlawed in the first place. We should..." He caught notice of something at the bottom of the screen. "Wait... the time stamp on this file..."

Kavana and the mage crowded in to see what he pointed at.

"He didn't start working on this spell until after I'd already ascended to the throne. If he'd meant to control me, certainly he'd have started sorting out how before then?"

"Who knows?" Kavana said.

"I..." the mage peeped.

"What?" Angelo asked. "What is it? Speak up, girl."

"There appears to be another concealment spell," she said. "On the file."

She reached out. A series of glistening flashes floated

from her hand to the screen.

The display changed. More text and system information.

"A hidden sub-folder," the mage said.

Angelo squinted at the words on the screen.

"I can't read this," he said.

"I can't even tell what language it's written in," said Kavana.

"You can't?" They both glared at her. Her heart jumped. "There must be some kind of distortion spell on it. Anyone trained in the mystic arts would recognize and decipher it as second nature. It speaks of a gift for you, my king."

"The mind control?" Angelo asked. "That was his gift?"

"I don't believe it was intended for you, sire," the mage said. "And there's another spell. A key."

"A key to what?" the king asked.

Kavana nodded to the mage.

She reached out again, twisting the floating lights.

The back wall of the chamber slid away. A dull glow and rhythmic hissing emanated from the uncovered stall.

The mage swallowed hard. Her body shook.

"Is that..." Kavana's words, usually so boisterous and confident, faded to a dull mutter.

"Not one more word," Angelo said. He looked to the mage. "You're a nervous sort, aren't you?"

"S-sorry, my lord." Her mumbling was more expected.

He averted his eyes from her, looking instead at the head of his scepter.

"As am I."

The club swung down at the young woman's skull.

Elle's shuttle burst out of the nothingness of fold space. A large medical ship sat a short distance away from the exit point, like an entire hospital floating amongst the stars. The outer hull was all smooth curves and gentle lines, with a soft color palette. It stood in stark contrast to the dark, angular designs of Kaia's warships, in part to set visitors at ease, and to make it easier to pick out in a battlefield. It would violate every treaty on galactic conflicts to fire upon a hospital ship.

Elle watched it grow larger in her forward port, quickly encompassing the entire view, as her shuttle puttered towards it.

She dipped her craft down, skimming along the ship's underbelly. The med ship's hull became a blur of softly tinted metal and running lights.

The shuttle popped around the other side and slowed towards an airlock.

She gracefully set down on the surface, forming a seal around the hatch.

Elle headed to the back of the ship where Val lay undisturbed. She appeared to be at least as alive as she was when they left the insurgent fleet. Elle took the Crown from Val's hand and pocketed it in her own coat.

The rear hatch opened. Elle pushed the stretcher towards the exit. It only took her a moment to override the sensor on the med ship's maintenance hatch. Once done, she rolled Val into the adjacent hallway.

Like the outside, the interior of the ship was designed for comfort and function. The hallways were wide and rounded, with plush bench seating along every wall. The light being piped in was clean and bright, easy on the eyes.

Still, this particular ship seemed to be fresh from a rather large assignment. The hallways, pleasant as they were, were lined with the sick and injured. Elle guessed they were refugees, but there was no telling from where or by whose hand.

She had to do her best to ignore them and keep going.

Coming around a corner, she spotted a uniformed guard heading towards them. She quickly backpedaled, pulling against the gurney's momentum, and ducked into a darkened room. She waited in the blackness for the guard to pass, noticing in silhouette how shallow the movements of her queen's chest had become.

She peeked out, making sure the guard was well gone, before again pushing the stretcher back into the corridor.

Finally, she found what she had been looking for: someone in the white medical uniform.

Elle bounded frantically down the hall, working up a small frenzy as she ran towards him.

"Are you a doctor?"

"That's why I'm dressed like this." He tapped his coat. His eyes dropped as he let out a short sigh. "Sorry. It's been a long day. What can I do for you?"

"My friend here is hurt." She fought back tears. "She needs help right away."

"Why wasn't she assigned at intake?" the doctor asked.

"Things were crazy," Elle said. "I guess they somehow just skipped over her."

"That seems weird." He lifted the sheets covering Val. "Oh, my God. How the hell would they have skipped her?"

"I don't know, but she needs help. Please."

The doctor waved for a pair of nurses.

"You don't have to beg. This is our job." He pointed a bit down the hall. "O.R. five."

The nurses rushed off with Val.

The doctor touched Elle's shoulder.

"Don't worry. We'll do everything we can for your friend."

Standing outside the operating room, Elle got a feeling like she had been there before. She also felt like nearly every muscle in her body was contracting at once.

She peered through the small circular window on the doorway; she tried to keep focus on the window frame, the surgeons' backs, anything so she could keep track of Val but not allow herself to focus on all the blood pooling on the aerated floor. It was all she could do to stop herself from visibly shaking.

Security guards approached.

"Miss? Are you the one who brought in the woman they're operating on in there?"

"Yes." Elle didn't look their way.

"We have some questions about how she was processed," the first guard asked. "Or, rather, how she wasn't."

Elle remained silent, still staring through the window.

"It's just very unusual that someone in that condition wouldn't be singled out and assigned a priority spot upon entering the ship," said the second guard.

Elle still didn't speak, didn't so much as glance their way.

"Can we start by getting your name?" The first one pulled out a datapad.

Elle finally looked at them.

"I'm Commander Elle Roma of the Kaian Imperial Army. You should probably get ahold of King Angelo. That's his niece in the O.R., the insurgent leader Valentina." She patted the round lump in her coat. "And I've got something he wants."

CHAPTER 4

"While we all hope and pray for our queen's speedy recovery, we've still a war to fight," Farbo said. She had gathered ranking officers around the tactical station table near the back of the bridge.

Four raised its hand.

"I have a question."

"I... are we taking questions?" Farbo asked.

It took Rik a moment to realize he was being addressed.

"Oh, you're asking me? Uh, not usually, but since we've already been interrupted, Four, what's your question?"

"If the worst should happen to Val, who is next in line to the throne?" Four asked.

"Uh... what? I mean, they have a whole line of succession, and, I think, technically, if she dies, Angelo actually would be the legitimate king," Rik said. "Though, we're all opposed to that, because he murdered Joseph and possibly Andor and Thoome."

Trainer leaned over and whispered in Rik's ear.

"What? Seriously?" Rik leaned back. "No, Four, you wouldn't ascend to the throne."

"But I have one of the Crowns," it said.

"Yeah, but just having a Crown doesn't make you a queen," said Rik. "King? I wouldn't even know how to address a Syman monarch."

"So it's a good thing we don't have to worry about that,"

said Farbo.

"Only those who the Crowns speak to, who bond with them, may ascend," Trainer said to the robot.

"But I am bonded to the Crown," Four said.

Farbo, Trainer, and Rik looked at one another. Their eyebrows raised and their lips curled back.

"And wasn't part of the reason Val freed me from bondage so that I could explore my own personhood?" Four asked.

"Ah," Rik said, "I'm not sure..."

"I also am bonded to a Crown," Bontu said.

"Okay, but aren't you the most distant of cousins to the royal bloodline?" Rik asked.

"I have the same amount of royal blood in me as Val or Angelo or anyone else currently living," Bontu said. "And I have a Crown."

"But what I'm saying is, the further you get from the straight line of succession, the harder it's going to be to convince the people to accept anyone as a ruler," Rik said. "They're definitely not ready for a Syman leader, either."

"Ignore the robot," Bontu said. "My Crown has fewer points than its."

"What... oh God..." Rik held his head. "What does that have to do with anything?"

"The smaller the number, the higher the ranking," Bontu stated.

"What?"

"Like in a sports competition," Bontu said. "The person who comes in first is the best. Second is next, then third and fourth."

"But it's the Five Point Crown that the people have been following for centuries," Farbo said.

"Each additional point represents an additional level of power," Four said. "Four points is still greater than two. Like in a sports competition, as you say, the person with the higher number of points is the winner."

"Then give me your Crown, and I'll have six points," Bontu said.

"I'm not giving up my Crown," Four said. "It's what sustains my life."

Bontu slammed his ax down on the console.

"Then fight me for supremacy."

"Holy crap, guys, we are getting way off topic here," Rik said.

"Yes, the Guardian is correct," said Farbo. "What's our play here?"

Rik pointed to Bontu and Four.

"You mean with these two fighting, or…"

"I mean, with the war out there." She motioned out the viewport, towards the colony planet.

Rik looked at it, wide-eyed.

Fighters and warships darted past, exchanging fire.

"I have no idea," Rik said.

"Well, you'd better got one," said Farbo.

"I…" His face flared red. "Can I talk to you in private? Let's go to your quarters."

She followed him off the bridge.

They tensely rode a lift down several decks. Rik's focus was on nothing in particular, often darting around the ceiling. His lips remained pursed.

Farbo almost attempted to start a conversation several times but thought better of it. That wasn't easy for her. She wasn't used to holding her tongue, especially on her own ship.

Finally, they reached her quarters.

"Before you try anything," she said immediately upon entering, "I should let you know I'm married."

"No, that's not what this is," he said. "What the hell was that out there?"

"What was what?"

"You calling me out on the bridge." He couldn't keep his head from bobbing slightly.

"I wasn't 'calling you out.'"

"Look, I know I don't have the experience you do, but you don't have to point that out in front of everyone."

"That wasn't my intention."

"Then what was?"

"Exactly the opposite," she said. "I was trying to give you a chance to prove yourself."

"That's what you thought you were doing?" he asked. "That, whatever it was up on the bridge, that wasn't helpful. You know I'm new at this, and maybe I'm not prepared for it, but it is what it is."

"If you want my help, ask me for it," she said. "In private, or in front of the troops, I don't care. But don't just freeze up like that."

"Fine. Assuming I want your help, what are we dealing with?"

"We can discuss that on the bridge." She started towards the door.

"No, I want to discuss it right here," he said.

She stopped. "Alright, though I've often found it's better to let the process be made public."

"Well, I'm not there yet."

"Very well." She took a breath. "What we're dealing with is that we're losing the conflict around this colony. The royal navy is putting a lot of effort into it because they want to cut us down here. Our ships are trying to forge a path through to Palan, but it's slow going. We can pull ships back to our current position, help fortify our lines here, but then we lose any progress we've made."

"I was just down on the planet," Rik said. "Our ground game isn't doing too bad."

"It wasn't until Queen Valentina was taken off the board," Farbo said. "She was the tip of the spear for our ground forces. Without her, morale is suffering. Communication is difficult between positions. Our platoons can't even say hello to one another, much less coordinate attacks."

"Huh."

"What?"

"I've got an idea."

Elle leaned against the wall opposite the doorway to the O.R. Armed troops blocked the hall going in either direction. Nearby, the captain of the ship had words with the attending surgeon, his scrubs and gown still slathered in Val's blood.

"That woman in there is a known terrorist and fugitive from Kaian justice," the captain said, pointing sharply towards the operating room several times for emphasis. "I demand that you turn her over to the guard immediately."

"That woman in there is currently undergoing extensive surgery, with the goal of saving her life," the doctor said. "If you move her now, you kill her."

"So? Who cares? She's an enemy of the crown."

"What Crown?" Elle pulled Val's merged Crown from her pocket. "This Crown?"

"What the devil is that?" the captain asked. "And who the devil are you?"

Elle pushed off from the wall and stood before him.

"Me? I'm the person who got sucked into a rebel escape attempt when that woman in there and her brother tried to kill King Angelo. I'm the one who's had to work without detection, hoping to make it back to loyal territory. And now that I have, I'm someone who's invaluable to the king. Now, get the palace on the comms so I can give my report to Angelo, or whoever's in charge of the palace guard now."

"That won't be possible," the captain said. "The palace ship has left Kaia, and there's too much interference around Palan to get in touch with it."

"Around Palan?" Elle asked. "What the hell's the palace ship doing there?"

"You can ask your close personal friend the king when next you see him." The captain sneered. "As you've admitted to cavorting with enemies of Kaia, I should have you locked in the brig, if not outright executed."

"This is a medical ship," the doctor said. "We don't have a brig."

"Every ship has a brig if you try hard enough," the captain said. "Now, as for the pretender to the throne in there..."

"How do we even know that she is who this other woman is claiming she is?" the doctor asked him. "We can't get through to anyone in royal security to verify."

"She's admitting to associating with terrorists," the captain said.

"That's not quite it," said Elle.

"At any rate, both of you will be held for questioning until we're able to reach royal command," said the captain.

"The woman on that operating table is not going anywhere," the doctor said firmly. "This is a medical ship, and I am a doctor. I swore an oath. We will patch her up, and if her life can be saved, we will save it. Once she's made whole again, and we reestablish contact with the royal guard, then her fate can be decided. I'd err on the side of keeping her alive, in case the king has some use for her."

"Fine." The captain turned to Elle. "But as for you..."

She held up the Crown.

"As for me, once you've reestablished contact with the king, he can tell you he's spent weeks and dispensed entire armadas looking for this. And, I can tell him where to find the rest. Until then, you'll be treating me like a VIP. Got it?"

The captain stepped towards her until his fetid breath engulfed her face.

"I will not be ordered around by some little girl on my ship."

"This 'little girl' technically outranks you," Elle said calmly.

"And this isn't your ship," the doctor said. "You're here as a courtesy to the royal army, but you don't tell doctors which patients they should save, and you don't get to turn any room on this hospital into a makeshift brig. If you've a problem with any of this, take it up with the chief physician. The rest of us have actual work to do."

The doctor pushed through the doors back into the operating theater.

Elle smiled, trying not to laugh at the captain, who stood defeated, powerless on "his" ship.

Rik and Farbo reentered the bridge.

"Comm," Rik called out, "contact our forces at Union Pointe. Let them know that Queen Valentina is heading the charge at Whero Falls."

"Sir?"

"Do it," Farbo said.

"Then," Rik continued, "contact Whero Falls, let them know that Queen Valentina will be arriving at Canyon Bluffs shortly to take direct command of the forces there. Tell Canyon Bluffs she's heading to the outskirts of Lotella. Etcetera, etcetera. Got it?"

The communications officer grinned.

"I believe so, sir." He turned to his station and began his task.

A soldier approached Elle, who hadn't moved from her spot in front of the operating room.

"Commander?"

"Mm?" She barely noted his presence, still transfixed through the little window.

"The captain would like to see you on the bridge."

"Alright." She took one last, lingering look before following the soldier down the hall.

CHAPTER 5

The bridge aboard the hospital ship was unlike the military vessels Elle had served on. It was large, sure, but like the rest of the ship, rounded and less tactically oriented.

She entered and approached the captain, who stood near a railed ring towards the front port.

"You asked to see me?"

The captain looked up from the communication officer's station, just beside the ring.

"Yes, commander. We've not yet been able to reach the palace ship, but we have reached General Clerak of the second fleet."

"Clerak?" Elle asked. "I thought she retired."

"She did, but she agreed to be reinstated by her husband to help with the annexation efforts."

"Her husband?"

"Yes. The king."

"Holy hell, what have I missed while I've been gone?" she asked.

She positioned herself at the center of the ring. A pale, translucent projection of Clerak appeared before her.

Elle stood at attention.

"General."

"Commander. The captain has told me that you've been working undercover with the insurgents?"

"Pretty much, yeah."

"Odd how King Angelo hasn't mentioned anything about having a spy in their ranks."

"Does he tell you everything?" Elle asked.

"We have a very open relationship."

"Well, he didn't exactly know," Elle said. "When Val and Rik made their escape, I kind of just got caught up in it."

"You just got caught up in it?" Clerak's eyes and lips flattened.

"I was part of Commander Smit's unit on security detail," Elle said. "We got an alert and we geared up and went to work. No one really knew what was going on."

"Mm-hm."

"Look, I have valuable intel," Elle said, "but I'll only give it to King Angelo himself."

"Oh, I see," Clerak said. "And what if, I don't know, I speak to Angelo, and he tells me he's never heard of you?"

"I served under him for several years. He knows who I am."

"That's sort of what I'm driving at," the general said. "How 'under him' did you serve?"

"What?"

The hologram leaned in.

"I'm well aware that my husband had a weakness for the prettier soldiers under his command. He succumbed to it on more than one occasion, I'm told."

"I'm not... I don't even know..."

"Uh, do we need to be here for this?" the captain asked.

"Who said that?" Clerak demanded.

"I did," the captain said.

"Are there other people in the room?" Clerak asked.

"I'm the one who patched you through to the commander," the captain said.

"Of course there are other people here," said Elle.

"Well, they're outside the transcriber's range," Clerak said.

"We're on the bridge of a medical ship," Elle said. "You didn't ask us to clear it."

"I didn't realize that's where you were taking my transmission."

One of the staff nurses ran onto the bridge.

"Hold on." Elle turned her attention toward the nurse.

"Don't you tell me what to do," Clerak snapped.

"Sir." The nurse gasped for breath. "We have a situation with the, ah, the uh, woman calling herself Queen Valentina."

"Has she passed?" the captain asked.

"No," the nurse said. "In fact, she's made what you might call a remarkable recovery."

The doors to the bridge burst open. A pair of soldiers stumbled through.

Val followed them in, dressed in little else but her poncho and the purloined lower portion of a set of scrubs.

Elle spun around and quickly switched off the transmission.

Val kicked one of the soldiers away, then punched the other.

In one smooth motion, Elle tossed the Crown to Val, Val caught it, slid it on and armored up.

The captain and a few other soldiers drew their weapons and fired. Their attack didn't faze Val. She marched forward, batting the captain aside.

Elle shook with nervous energy as Val faced her.

"Where the hell are we?" Val asked.

"I can explain later. Our shuttle is attached to an airlock on deck six."

Elle ran for the door. Holding her left side, Val followed, her usually swift movement still hampered by a bit of a limp.

As soon as they made it to the shuttle, Elle planted herself in the pilot's seat and started liftoff procedures. Val settled for the chair next to her.

The shuttle jerked as it uncoupled and sped away.

"It doesn't look like we're being followed," Elle said after a quick check of the instruments. The medical ship wouldn't have had any weapons with which to affect a pursuit, anyway. "We should be able to go into fold-space in a few minutes."

She looked over at Val, who was slumped in her chair and breathing heavily.

"You alright?"

"Yeah." Val wheezed. "Apparently I got shot?"

"Yeah."

"And whose dumbass idea was it for me to go to a royal med ship?"

"Probably the dumbass who saved your life."

"Well, then I'll probably have to thank that dumbass."

"But, seriously, are you okay?" Elle asked. "I mean, you almost died."

"I'll be alright," Val said. "If I pass out, it's only because I need the sleep."

"Sure," said Elle. "I'm not a doctor, so I don't really know what that would actually mean."

General Clerak stood in the command position aboard her flagship.

"What the hell happened?"

The frightened comms workers stared helplessly at their workstations.

"Get her back!"

One of the comm officers turned to her. "I'm sorry, sir, but the problem isn't mechanical. No one on the other end is responding."

"Dammit!" Clerak threw her hand against the panel in front of her. "What the hell is going on over there?"

The communications officer perked up.

"Sir, we have an incoming transmission."

"Is it the medical ship?"

The younger woman shook her head.

"No, sir. Secure channel... they're saying it's for you, personally."

"Fine. Have it sent through to my quarters."

Clerak threw herself behind a small desk in a corner of her bedroom. Her fingers flew over the control pad, inputting her personal code and activating the holographic transmitter.

"Kavana?"

"Hello, my love."

"Now's really not a good time." Clerak sighed and leaned forward, bracing her forehead against her palms. "If this is about the mission, I already received the updated orders."

"It's not, no. It's about our husband."

CHAPTER 6

Val was dressed in just her palace guard uniform for the first time in over a month. It was clean, well pressed. It didn't smell of weeks aboard a cramped shuttle, weeks without access to any facilities to maintain proper hygiene. In fact, the only odor it gave off at all was a slight hint of laundry soap, the same kind used in the actual palace.

No. No, that wasn't true. That smell was just a memory, wasn't it? She couldn't actually smell anything at the moment.

Nor could she see much of anything.

"Um... hello?" she called into the churning darkness. "What, uh, what the hell?"

"Valentina."

"Yeah, you've said that before. It's gotten really old, actually."

She twisted around, trying to locate the sound's source. It wasn't easy when she couldn't really see her surroundings. There was almost no sensory input outside of her own body. She couldn't even swear she stood on solid ground.

"Valentina."

"Look, if that's all you've got to say, piss the hell off, okay? I don't need this."

Some color began to bleed into the blackened void.

"Valentina..."

"Yeah, I answered you."

"You must..."

"Well, that's new."

"Go back."

Through the spinning, tinted mist, Val began to make out a figure. She tried desperately to bring her vision into better focus.

◆ ◆ ◆

Val jolted awake.

Elle looked her over.

"Um... you'd tell me if you weren't alright, right?" Elle asked.

Val tried to rub her eyes but realized the Crown was still covering her face.

"'Cause if I made it all the way to a royal medical ship and back just to have you croak on me..." Elle trailed off.

"I'm fine."

"Yeah, totally," said Elle. "That's exactly how people who're fine always act."

Their shuttle was cleared and landed.

Trainer, Farbo, and Rik awaited its opening.

The rear ramp lowered.

Elle and Val walked out.

"I'm going to take the fact that you're walking out under your own power as a good sign," Rik said.

"As fine as can be expected, I'm guessing," Val said. "I'm told I had a hole in my torso not too long ago?"

"Ah, not so much a hole as most of the left side of you, you know, missing."

"Cool." She gripped the Crown and lifted it off. "I'm assuming it's safe to take this off now?"

"It was probably safe before you even left the med ship," Trainer said.

"Sure, but if my stitches popped open or anything, I wanted something there to catch all the blood and guts and stuff."

"Well, you made it back just in time," Rik said. "We've managed to secure the colony, but there's been some weird activity from the royal fleet in the last few minutes."

"Yeah. I figure."

Farbo, Rik, and Trainer gave one another a look.

"How?" Farbo asked.

"Long story, which I'd rather talk to Trainer about first." She held out a data slip. "Who gets this?"

"What is it?" Rik asked.

"Coordinates for where we're going next," she said.

Rik took the slip and inserted it into a pad. He showed the display to Farbo, whose face scrunched up.

"Don't look at me," said Elle.

Rik shrugged.

"Alright," said Farbo.

The group, save Val, began to walk away.

"Hey, Trainer," Val called.

He stopped and turned back.

"Val," he said. "Or, your majesty."

"Don't."

"Are you alright?" he asked.

"I heard it again."

"The voices."

"No. It's just the one voice," she said. "And I think I recognized it."

"Really? Who was it?"

Her brow straightened as she looked him in the eye.

"It's my mom."

Before Trainer could react, Rik had returned.

"Hey, uh, just double-checking, you're aware that the coordinates you gave us are outside the realm of claimed space, yeah?"

"Yes."

"So, where the heck is it?" Rik asked.

"The natives call it Earth."

BOOK 8: FINALE

CHAPTER 1

From one end of the street, a crowd came running. People along the sidewalks and crosswalks were caught up. Traffic came to a standstill as motorists abandoned their cars to join the fleeing mob that clogged the roads.

Until shortly after eleven in the morning, it had been a regular workday in Milwaukee. Now, warships from another world flew over the skyline, dropping landing parties of armed soldiers and tanks, unleashing heavy ordinance towards any resistance as cover.

Police officers fired back, to no effect.

The sidewalk around Officer Marissa Wessel erupted. Chunks of concrete and gravel soared several stories into the air. She and her fellow officers were thrown back to the ground; those not caught in the blasts directly, anyway.

Wessel held her shoulder and winced as she tried to get herself back on her feet, just at the edge of the crater that had previously been part of Wisconsin Avenue.

"Like our roads weren't bad enough." The sound that escaped her throat was intended as a grunt or a growl, something fearsome, but it came out as more of a wincing wheeze. "Goddamn aliens."

She stumbled through the smoke, unable to locate any of her compatriots.

The Kaian warship still hovered over her.

She sighed, loaded a clip, straightened up, and took aim.

The ship charged its cannons.

It fired.

Wessel squeezed her eyes shut and pulled her trigger. She'd swear she heard the impact of the bullets, but the earth-scorching rain of destruction she'd expected to swallow her didn't come.

She opened her eyes again to find that another ship, noticeably smaller, had drifted in between the warship and the ground, taking the brunt of the cannon fire. The smaller ship was shooting back. More surprisingly, it was winning. It was rocked by the blasts from the bigger craft, but held its own, giving as good as or better than it got.

It may have been that the commander of the larger vessel decided this fight was not worth the effort, but eventually, it pulled away.

The smaller ship descended. Once it was no more than a few feet from the ground, the rear hatch opened and a ramp lowered.

A small contingent of insurgent forces, headed by Val, Bontu, Elle, and Rik, streamed out. Val and Bontu were both in full armor. Val carried an extra device on her belt, small, silver in color, with a few buttons on it.

As soon as their group was unloaded, the ship headed back up and off.

Far up the road, the Palace ship descended atop the U.S. Bank Center, using it as an elevated landing platform to ensure that the palace would be the highest visible structure in the area. The overall height of the skyscraper was well more than doubled by the addition of the ship.

The Palace ship was what the name largely implied; a mobile recreation of at least a portion of the royal residence on Kaia, complete with similar amenities and architecture. Because of its size and impracticality, it was rarely ever moved.

"You're sure you want me to leave you here?" Metch asked over the comm channel. "I can get you closer."

"No ships are getting closer than this without getting

blown out of the sky," said Val. "And you've got other cargo to drop. Be careful."

"Okay, well, it looks like the Palace ship will be securely docked within a few minutes," Metch said. "They won't lower their shields or blast-plating until that happens."

"This is our best chance," Val said. "Angelo hasn't left Olivert since the coronation. He's barely left the palace."

"It doesn't even make any sense," said Elle. "Why would Angelo even waste the fuel getting to this backwater little planet?"

"Because my brother loved it."

Val looked to one side and realized that Wessel was standing, facing them, aiming her gun forward.

"You're a police officer?" Val asked.

"You're from outer space?" asked Wessel.

"No, nobody's 'from' outer space," Val told her. "I'm from a planet called Kaia."

Wessel lowered her gun.

"What the hell is going on?" she asked.

"Unfortunately, your planet's been caught up in a sort of civil war," Val said. "I'm really sorry about that. I'll try to put a stop to it as quickly as I can."

She stepped closer to Wessel, looking down at the human's pistol.

"Listen," she said, "the Kaians view this planet as underdeveloped. They won't attack you unless they perceive you as a threat. Even a minor one. My advice is to lose the weapon and focus on helping the injured. There's really no way we're getting through today without collateral damage. Probably a lot of it."

Wessel moved her gun towards its holster.

"Yeah. Okay," she said. "I'll..."

"No," Val snatched the weapon out of her hand and tore it in half, "you have to be completely unarmed. Let your fellow officers know that, too. No weapons on their person, in their cars, nothing."

"You ever try telling a city full of cops to throw out their guns?" Wessel asked her.

"Listen to me, or don't, I'm telling you how to survive today." Val looked down the street towards the Palace ship. "I can't personally ensure every single person's safety. I've got bigger things to focus on."

The group of Kaian insurgents started their way up the road, weapons at the ready. Wessel headed off in the other direction. This road, at least, was fairly free of civilians by now. They were all flooding in other directions to avoid the missing section of pavement, or had already made it past.

"Damn lady was gonna try to take on a Kaian attack cruiser with a handgun?" Rik asked.

"That's brave," Bontu said. "Insanely stupid, but brave."

"No, I get it," said Rik. "She wanted to go down fighting."

"I'd rather live to fight another day," said Elle.

"What was she gonna do?" Rik asked. "Outrun the fighter?"

"There was plenty of cover," Elle said.

"So they start shooting down buildings to get her?" asked Rik. "Nah, if we hadn't shown up, she'd be a smear on the ground. Better to go out with a weapon in your hand and facing your enemy, even if it's just symbolic."

"This is a fun topic of conversation," said Val.

"What do you want us to do?" Rik asked. "We're marching down the road, toward the enemy stronghold, with very little real cover."

"Anybody know any good show tunes?" she asked.

Elle's head snapped back.

"Seriously?"

"I was on Earth for a few weeks," Val said. "They have some really good musicals."

"Huh. Never would have pegged you for a musical type."

"That just shows how little you really know me."

"We spent a month stuck on a transport ship together," Elle said. "I know you as well as you let anyone know you."

"Great," Val said, "so now we're psychoanalyzing me?"

"You kind of open yourself up for it when you start talking about show tunes," Elle said.

"Rik, don't I love musicals?"

"Oh, yeah," her Guardian confirmed. "Always had a real soft spot for them. When you were a kid, you used to sneak into the royal box at the theater whenever the queen wasn't using it."

"Yeah, and you'd never come with me."

"I didn't like the theater that much."

"You were scared of getting caught."

"Yeah, that, too."

"Val," Bontu interjected, "can I speak with you?"

"Is it something you can't talk about in front of the others?"

"I'd prefer it be in private."

"Now's not really a good time for us to stop and chat," she said.

"I'll be brief."

Val stopped and motioned for the others to continue on.

"Okay, what's so important that it couldn't wait?" she asked.

Bontu removed his Crown and held it out to her.

"I've been thinking," he said, "and I think you should take this."

Val lifted it from his outstretched hands.

"Really?" she asked. "You don't want it?"

"I do. But now that I've seen how the Crowns can bond together like that..." he pointed to her face, "I realize that you stand a better chance against Angelo with more of them in your possession. Four can't give you its, but I can give you mine. I can still fight without it. I have my ax, and I'm getting pretty good with guns."

"You realize, even with all the other Crowns, I still won't be as powerful as Angelo," she said.

"I know," he said. "But the more you have, the smaller the

gap, right?"

Val looked at the Two Point Crown.

"I guess. You're sure about this?" she asked. "Once they merge, I don't know if there's a way to split them apart again."

"I'm sure," he said. "You with more power behind you is better than me with some power."

"Alright."

She moved the Two Point Crown towards her face. When it got within a few centimeters, it jumped from her hand. Her head whipped back at the impact. She righted it again as the third Crown interwove itself with the two she already wore.

Beneath her poncho, the armor mutated further.

The whole process took only seconds, and then she was ready again.

"Come on."

They hurried to catch up with their teammates.

CHAPTER 2

Angelo and Kavana stood at the doorway to the terrace, waiting for the defensive plating to finish lowering. In moments, they would be able to see their newest territory with their own eyes. Just the thought brought a smile to Kavana.

Once the plating was fully retracted, they stepped out onto the expansive balcony and took a look at the city.

"There's been some resistance from the natives," Angelo said, "but we always expect that."

"We didn't count on the insurgents reaching us so quickly," his queen said. "Who would have tipped them off about our plans?"

"I don't know," said Angelo. "It may not have been anyone; they may have simply reacted faster than we'd anticipated. I'd have liked to have had the local population subdued before they arrived."

"Your plans relied upon it."

"It shouldn't be anything we can't handle," he said, "especially with Clerak out there leading the fight."

Kavana squinted into the distance. She flattened a hand over her brow to block the glare.

"Some of those are Palan ships."

"It's not the ships that are at issue. I've complete confidence in our fleet and our defenses here. No, the only true threat comes from my niece. But without this..." He patted the

Crown that he cradled beneath his arm. "She hasn't a chance. Those poor facsimile Crowns she's been collecting are nothing against the true symbol of our people."

For effect, he hoisted up his scepter and gave the Crown a good tap.

"Let her try to come to me. If she makes it this far, I'll end it myself. Then Kaia can once again have its peace."

A group of rebel soldiers scampered between two buildings. Led by Hune, they included Four amongst their ranks. They weren't as brazen as Val's group, lacking any members wearing nigh-invulnerable magic armor.

Hune peeked around the next corner.

"Clear."

The group darted across the street, to the next bit of cover.

One of their members, a man called Drit, shifted impatiently.

"This is taking forever."

"Yeah, but it's what we need to do." Hune's voice was something of a whispered shout. "You're a soldier, right? Didn't they teach you patience in basic?"

"I'm actually not, no," he said.

"Wait, what?"

"I'm an airman," he said. "There just happened to be a shortage of fighter craft and a greater need for infantry, so lucky me, I got volunteered."

"Probably better for you."

"Please. Let me behind the stick of a fighter any day. Better than all this scurrying around like rodents."

"The fighters are the easiest targets right now," Hune said. "For now, they're ignoring the ground troops."

"Oh, cool," Drit said. "So we can wait even longer to die."

"Not really the kind of talk we need right now," she said.

"Gallows humor, lieutenant."

"That's only for when you're heading to the gallows."

"I said what I said."

Four forced its way in between the two of them.

"We should continue our movement," it said.

"And why the hell do we have a damn Syman with us?" Drit asked. "Thing's creepy as hell."

"The Syman is right here, and can hear you, and has a name," said Four. "And a gun."

"Four is different than most robots," Hune said. "It's self-aware. Some might even argue alive. Which begs the question, Four, what are you doing here? You fought to get free of that pit boss so you could explore your personhood. Rushing into a warzone doesn't really help you do that."

"It's really simple, Lt. Hune. I wish to be a good person. Queen Valentina was the first one in centuries to treat me as an individual, not a piece of property. She fought for me. I cannot do any less for her."

"Well, let's hope you live to regret it."

Four tilted its head curiously.

Hune peeked around the next corner.

"Alright, clear. Like Four said, we need to keep moving."

Val and her group made their way up the abandoned street, towards the building where Angelo had landed the Palace. They still had several miles to go yet, weaving as they did between empty automobiles and toppled street fixtures.

Elle's voice interrupted the uneasy silence. "What do you think are the odds that Angelo doesn't know where we are?"

"Not good," said Bontu.

"You hear that, too?" asked Val.

"Yeah," said Elle.

The group raised their weapons and braced themselves.

A battalion of royal soldiers rounded a nearby street

corner, already firing on the insurgent group as they came.

"Alright," said Val, "you guys know which way we're headed."

She charged at the enemy soldiers. Leaping into the air, she came down in the middle of a grouping, blasting ten or so of them away on impact. Her sword charged with energy, she hacked her way through the remaining troops.

Rik and the others opened fire, trying to cut enough of a path to follow.

"Hey, so, what's the first thing you're gonna do when you're queen?" Rik called to Val.

"What?"

"Assuming we win this thing and you become queen," Rik said, "what's the first thing you'll do?"

"You're assuming an awful lot," Elle said over the sound of gunfire.

"It's a hypothetical," Rik said.

"I'm going to have to take a serious look at succession laws," Val said.

"Nah, not laws and stuff." Rik pivoted and took aim at another assemblage of Angelo's loyalists. "I don't mean what's your first royal decree. I mean, what's the first thing you'll do? Take a big ol' dump in the golden toilet?"

"There's no golden toilet," Val said.

"There totally is."

"Why would anyone have that and why would you know about it?" Elle asked.

"Come on," said Rik. "Everyone's heard of the real golden throne."

"That's a myth," Val said. "And why would that be where your mind goes first?"

"It's not where my mind went first," he said, "but the first thing it went to is stuff you probably wouldn't do."

"Ugh." Elle grunted. She looked over her shoulder at Val. "Men, right?"

"I'm not sure what you mean."

"Maybe you and I really don't understand each other," Elle said.

"So what are you gonna do first?" Rik asked again.

"I'll give it some thought once we're there."

"Realistically, there's a good chance I'm not gonna make it," said Rik. "Or Elle."

"Hey."

"Or anybody who's not wearing a near-indestructible suit of armor," Rik added. "So I kind of want to know now."

"I've got news for you," Val said, "Not everybody wearing a suit of near-indestructible armor is making it."

Trainer waited near the rear ramp of the transport, mostly engulfed in shadows. He gripped an overhead strap for support as the ship swayed. Inside a planet's atmosphere, the flying wasn't nearly as smooth as it was in space.

An infantryman slowly shuffled towards him.

"Uh... sir?"

"Yes?" Trainer asked.

"Is this really, um, safe?" The soldier looked towards the center of the cargo hold they stood in.

"Angelo has tanks and troops," Trainer said. "And we lost a lot of our ground forces securing the Palan colonies. With the Palan reinforcements, we might have a chance of matching them in the skies, but on the ground, we need every advantage we can get."

A deep snarling echoed through the ship.

"Right," the infantryman said, "but, these aren't exactly tanks."

"You go to war with the army you've got, son."

"Uh, okay." The smaller man shifted closer to Trainer.

Trainer glared at him.

"You ever heard of personal space?"

The infantryman glanced back over his shoulder. "Given

the alternate, I'm staying as close as I can."

A pair of royal cargo ships descended into a clearing in the street, landing several blocks away from a fleeing mob.

The ship that carried Trainer dropped between the people and the royal craft, coming around and touching down with its rear facing them.

The bellies of the royal ships opened up, each dropping several rolling tanks onto the streets. Each was dark and easily larger than any Earth-based assault craft. They were heavier, too, with extra armored plating built up around vulnerable areas. The weight was carried on four engraved spheres, one embedded in the underside of each corner of the vehicle, allowing them to change direction nimbly.

The rolling batteries sped towards the insurgents, pummeling any cars, trucks, or other abandoned debris in their path.

As the tanks bore down upon it, the insurgent ship opened.

A pack of massive white bears stampeded out, charging the oncoming trucks.

The driver of the forward-most tank's mouth hung agape. His lips curled back and his eyes bulged.

The gunner crouched down from his post in the upper turret.

"Are those bears?" the gunner asked excitedly. "Where did they get..."

The bears threw their weight into the tanks, stopping their forward movement and lifting their front ends off the pavement.

Trainer jogged down the ship's exit ramp, leading a contingent of soldiers.

"And we're sure they're not going to try to eat us, right?" the nervous infantryman asked.

"Nothing in life is certain," Trainer said.

CHAPTER 3

The last of the insurgents' transport ships broke free of Earth's atmosphere and headed towards the command ship. It had to dart and dodge the fire that the larger craft lobbed at one another, and stay out of the way of the smaller, scrapping fighters, but with Metch at the stick, there was never any real danger.

The rear hatch opened soon after touching down in the command ship's launch bay. Metch ran out as maintenance crews headed towards the shuttle.

He made for a communication panel on the wall.

"General Farbo, it's Metch. The last of our ground troops are deployed."

Farbo's face appeared on the screen.

"Good work."

"Yeah, I'd have stayed down there to help out, but a transport ship's not going to be much good in a dogfight," he said. "Anyone been able to rustle up some more fighters yet?"

"The third wing is still on its way," Farbo said. "They have their own pilots, but I can have you assigned to a ship. If they get here before the fighting's over."

"Is that you being optimistic or pessimistic?" he asked.

"I'll answer that once this is done with," she said.

The screen went blank.

Metch huffed and leaned against the wall.

◆ ◆ ◆

Down the street from the action, police officers corralled pedestrian traffic in the Rave/Eagles Club. The crowds lurched up the front steps and impatiently pushed their way through the few sets of doors. The big brick concert hall was rated to hold over five-thousand people safely; those safety concerns were tossed aside for this day.

"In! In! Everybody in!" Officer Parker was a younger, slightly heavier man. His tightly cropped haircut did little to obscure his fading hairline.

"What're you doing?" Officer Wessel came running up the street towards them, weaving her way through the crowds.

"Getting these people to shelter," Parker said.

"Shelter?" Wessel asked. "Have you seen these things? They're knocking down whole blocks at a time. We need to get people away from the spaceships, not pen them in."

"Where's 'away?'" Parker asked brusquely.

She pointed to the Palace ship.

"See that? Go in the opposite direction from that."

Hangar doors on the outer walls of the Palace ship started opening. Kaian fighters swarmed out, like angry bees from a kicked hive.

Wessel turned to her fellow officers.

"And throw away your weapons," she instructed.

"What?" Parker balked. "Are you nuts?"

"She said they won't come after us if we're unarmed."

"Who said that?"

"The metal-faced lady!"

"You know how crazy you sound?" Parker asked.

"We're being invaded by space aliens. Everything is crazy!"

"Jesus..." Parker's muttering was indiscernible over the sounds of battle.

A rumbling in the air started low. Within seconds, it was

shaking dust loose from the buildings' mortar.

A group of insurgent fighters swooped over the street, heading for the palace ship and engaging the royal fighters.

"Jesus!" Parker screamed this time. He reached up to hold his hat down as the ships roared past before remembering he wasn't wearing it.

Wessel pointed farther down the street.

"Away from that thing!" she shouted to the citizens. "Away!"

The mob that had been packing itself into the theater turned and ran. Instead of moving as one mass, the crowd seemed to go in waves, as faster people further back caught up to slower people in front of them. Things began to logjam, leading to shoving and pushing.

"Goddammit!" Wessel climbed up onto the hood of a car and cupped her hands around her mouth. "Faster people to the left, slower people to the right! Just like when you're driving!"

As the crowd tried to sort itself out, some began stumbling. A few fell.

"Shit!" Wessel hopped down and ran into the fray. She looked back at her fellow officers. "Help those people."

Overhead and moving past the crowd fast, Metch sat behind the controls of one of the sleek insurgent fighters; the craft had been designed primarily for extra-orbital combat but were aerodynamic enough that operating within an atmosphere felt little different.

Though he technically had no authority in this squadron, Metch had moved to the lead position.

His gunner sat behind him, fingers ready on the triggers.

Metch flipped a switch, opening his communication channel.

"Alright, they're opening up to let the little guys out. That probably means they're not going to be firing the big cannons at us. Probably."

Their group angled down between the buildings. That didn't leave much room for maneuvering. They could pretty much only go straight ahead, directly into the oncoming squad of royal attackers.

"Uh, should we be pulling up?" one of Metch's squad members asked.

"No," he said. "They should."

Neither group changed direction. Neither slowed.

"Okay," the other pilot said, "but if they don't, and we don't..."

"I got no plans after this," Metch said.

"Do you have plans *for* this?" the other pilot asked.

The two groups of fighters would be on one another in a matter of moments.

"Yeah, but you're not going to wanna hear it," Metch told her. "I usually like to just..."

The imperial ships pulled up at the very last moment. A fraction of a second later, and their paint would've scraped off against their enemy's cockpits. Another half-second after that and they'd have collided head-on.

In inclining their flight path, the royal ships exposed their underbellies to the insurgents. No time was wasted in opening fire.

The few royal ships that weren't decimated scrambled to come about and head back to the safety of their main fleet.

"...wing it," Metch said.

"Ugh." His wingman groaned. "Who is this guy again?"

Along the same road, an imperial tank rolled its way along, scouting for any resistance from the local population or from fellow Kaians.

They weren't sure where Val came from. None of the personnel aboard saw her until she stood directly ahead of them, planting herself and holding out her sword.

As the tank rolled onward, the front face jammed itself into the edge of Val's blade. Rather than the woman or her weapon being moved, the tank was sliced up the middle, the force cracking the entire thing in half. Each side veered slightly in its own direction, around Val.

It had very little momentum left by the time it had passed her. The interior was completely exposed as it puttered to a stop on either side of the armored queen.

She gave a kick to the half to her left. It rocked over and clanged to the pavement.

Rik and the others rushed the halves of the tank. They quickly trained their guns on the royal soldiers trying to pile out.

"Hand over all your weapons and surrender and we might not be forced to kill you," Rik told them. The royal soldiers began tossing their weapons to the ground and stepping out of the destroyed vehicle with their hands up.

"There you go. That's the smart move here." Rik looked to Val. "Seriously, though. That was super badass."

In that moment of distraction, one of the royal soldiers drew a weapon from the back of his belt. Rik swung his rifle up and got off a single bullet into the man just as he pulled the trigger. The loyalist's shot flew harmlessly skyward as the man crumpled to the pavement.

His helmet rolled off. His eyes rolled back as he gasped for his final breaths.

"Tay?" Rik's voice had gone soft.

"You know him?" Val asked.

"Yeah, I know him," Rik said. "In a few seconds, I guess it'll be 'knew.' We were stationed together at our first post."

In his last moments, Tay's eyes tried to focus on Rik. His lips shook, but nothing came out save a dull hiss.

Elle gently placed a hand on Rik's shoulder.

"Come on," she said.

Rik slowly turned.

The group started on their way again.

"You never did tell us," Elle said, "if this golden toilet exists, how come none of us have ever seen it?"

"It, uh..." Rik cleared his throat. His voice strengthened with each word. "It's in the monarch's private bathroom. You wouldn't see it unless you were in the royal chamber."

"I've been in the royal chambers," Val said, "I never saw a golden toilet."

"Did you go into the private bathroom, though?" Rik asked.

"I have to admit I have not."

"Of course you wouldn't just be able to see it from the bedroom."

CHAPTER 4

Hune's team was the first to make it within spitting distance of the Palace ship.

"I almost don't believe it," said Drit.

"What?" Hune asked.

"That we're actually gonna make it." He let out a relieved chuckle.

"Goddamnit."

"What?"

"Do you even know what a jinx is?" Hune asked.

"What?"

They heard engine sounds in the air.

"Dammit," she said. "I hear airships."

Their unit circled up and scanned the skyline.

"Where are they?" Hune asked. "Anyone get a visual?"

Four raised its arm and pointed to a break between two tall buildings.

"Over there," it said. "Dropships."

"What are they dropping?" Drit asked.

"Whatever it is, it's your fault," Hune told him.

They raised their automatic rifles and fired at the four approaching dropships.

They managed to blow a wing off of one, sending it crashing into a building before it could drop its payload. The flaming remains of the ship, as well as a good bit of glass and steel from the structure, rained to the concrete below.

Hune's group kept firing.

The dropships passed overhead and released their cargo. Each deposited four pieces of hardware: person-sized robot crawlers with a turret for a midsection.

"Bug-tanks!" Hune shouted.

In actuality, the tanks only had four multi-segmented legs apiece, but the name had stuck.

Her group ran for cover, firing at the crawlers along the way, to minimal effect.

They managed serious damage to two of the tanks before the bugs were able to take aim and let loose a flood of bullets.

None of the organic soldiers were left standing.

Four rose up from behind the cover of a now-decimated automobile.

"So, you're those 'more efficient,' specialized robots I've been hearing so much about," it said. It reached down with its free hand to grab one of its downed comrades' guns. "Hello. I'm Four."

Four sprinted sideways, strafing the bug-tanks.

The tanks fire back, putting chinks and dents in Four's outer casing.

Four flipped into the air, dodging tank blasts while continuing to squeeze its triggers. Several of the bugs' legs were taken out from under them; another pair were simply shot until they stopped twitching by the time Four landed on its feet.

The Syman slid, its metal casing letting out a trail of sparks as it slipped under one of the tanks. The others held their fire.

Four threw its right arm up, using the pile driver embedded within to punch rapidly along the tank's belly.

It slid out the other end and threw one last powered punch to the front of the tank, splintering the outer casing. Four grabbed the legs of the disabled mech, hurling its remains towards its fellow weapons.

Four limped to the cover of a building. The fire from the other tanks chipped away at the brick and mortar. It held its shoulder and took stock of its injuries. Damage to its outer casing was substantial. Internal systems were becoming compromised.

Peeking around the corner, Four spotted Val a few blocks over, making her final dash for the Palace ship.

One of the bug-tanks also took notice.

Four gripped its guns and ran out again, peppering the farthest tanks, the ones pursuing Val, with gun blasts. This left it vulnerable to the closer bugs. They didn't waste the opportunity.

They advanced on Four, their repeating cannons ablaze.

Val could see all of this happening, but she was too far away. Even moving at top speed towards them, there was nothing she could do from such a distance as the tanks engulfed Four.

The robot, however, wasn't going down without a fight. It continued shooting even as the bugs overwhelmed it: picking them off, landing a lucky shot here and there, until there were only a few left.

The only thing Val could think to do was to reach down and scoop up a chunk of loose concrete. She charged it with energy and threw it straight through two of the three remaining bugs.

She continued on towards Four. The Syman lay on the pavement, its legs crushed and dangling, its torso broken and beaten in.

The last bug-tank stomped down, crumpling more of Four's midsection.

The lights in Four's optics started to flicker.

Four looked at Val. Its vision was failing, things blurring and scrambling.

It reached down and, with a bit of fumbling, pried open its chest plating.

It tore out the Crown. Pulled back its throwing arm,

taking aim at Val as best it could.

The tank leg came down again, breaking that arm off at the elbow.

Four lashed out with the other hand, grabbing up the severed limb and hurling the whole thing, Crown, arm, and all, towards Val.

Val's feet pushed down, carrying her high off the pavement, towards the U.S. Bank Center. She snatched the Crown out of the air as she went. Four's skeletal arm components were shaken loose, save for the Crown and the pile-driver attachment. She hooked the pile-driver around her forearm. The mystical suit she wore grew out around it, assimilating the new component. She pressed the Four Point Crown to her face where it merged it with the others.

Her jump carried her clear over the bug-tank.

She hit the side of the office building and kept going, vertically.

The tank swung its turret upward, locking her directly in its sight.

Just as it fired, it was tackled by a great white bear, sending the shot astray. The enormous furry creature and its pack made short work of the quadrupedal construct.

Val scaled the side of the building, leaping and flipping sometimes several stories at once, deftly avoiding any enemy gunfire from the ground or air.

Attack ships tried to stop her any way they could, but she was too fast, too agile, evading most of their fire. What little that actually managed to hit her did not slow her down.

The enemy ships also had to deal with engaging her fleet, which soon drew their attention from her completely.

One final leap sent her sailing up over the balcony's edge. She landed and ripped away her poncho. She didn't toss it back and let the winds flutter it away, but threw it hard to the floor.

She stood revealed, her armor encompassing the power of four Crowns.

The bronze and silver armor plating more fully covered

her, the dark undersuit less exposed. It was observably heavier than at the start of her journey, though she was still slimmer than Angelo, due both to the gauge of the armor and her own trimmer build.

Angelo, fully protected by the Five Point Crown, stood on the far side of the balcony. Kavana cowered behind him.

He turned back to her only long enough to utter a single word.

"Go."

With no hesitation, his young bride darted around the door frame, into the palace, and disappeared from sight.

Val strode towards the palace entrance.

"I'm going to walk into this palace now," she said. "When I do, I'm going to sit down on that throne, and all of this will be over. I'll be recognized as the queen, and I'll have to figure out what to do with you. I've given it a lot of thought, but I guess it just feels different when you're in the moment."

Just before she could cross the threshold, Angelo hurled his scepter towards her like a javelin. She ducked back swiftly. It narrowly missed her, embedding itself into the entry archway.

Val looked at him.

She turned, gripped the scepter, and pulled. It took a bit of force to yank it from the wall.

She threw it over the balcony edge.

"Oh, now that was just petty," Angelo said.

"I feel like I've earned it." Val stepped towards the palace door again.

"*Valentina.*"

Val grabbed at the sides of her head. "Ugh. No. Not now."

"*Val.*"

Val shook her head. She looked over at Angelo, who seemed frozen in place. His gaze was somewhere past her, inside the throne room.

Val turned, following his view.

She stepped back.

Inside the throne room, pushed back into an enclave, she saw a rounded metal box, sat in the middle of a nest of reservoirs and wire bundles.

A stasis chamber.

Only the head and shoulders of the occupant, hooked into an abundance of wires, tubes, and probes, could be seen through a transparent plate on the chamber's front.

A sickly, pale light from within barely allowed Val to identify the form floating inside.

"Mom?"

The queen's eyes, half-open, stared at Val.

Her mouth opened slightly.

"*Val...*"

"What... is this?" Val was stammering, disoriented.

"The vizier saved her," Angelo said, his voice frantic and shaking. "I'm going to make her whole again."

"Can't you hear her?" Val asked.

"I'm sure she'll be grateful once she understands what I've done," Angelo said.

"Can't you hear her?" Val stressed again. "Listen."

"*Please,*" the queen murmured. "*Let me die.*"

"This is obscene," Val said.

"You don't know," Angelo said. "You don't know what I've been through. Without a true peer. Generals and child princesses, they're nothing compared to what she and I could have shared. What we still might share."

"You killed her son," Val said. "You're keeping her alive and it's torturing her. You're sick."

She walked towards the archway again.

Angelo lunged, covering the full span of the terrace in a single leap and tackling her to the ground.

They grappled, rolling into the balcony railing, Val cracking its concrete-like material with the impact of her body.

Angelo was the first to his feet, grabbing her by the collar and dragging her up.

"I want you to know I truly regret this," he said. "Your

brother forced me to kill him. I was hoping you wouldn't do the same."

"You can lie to yourself." She growled out the words as best she could through her narrowing airway. "You can lie to the people. But I was there. I know how it really went down. You're a murderer."

"If I am, it will be twice-over now."

He threw her, hard, into the floor.

Rather than lying still, incapacitated, taking time to catch her breath or gather her strength, she immediately rolled to the side, springing to her feet and drawing her sword.

He stalked towards her. She charged him.

The sword, its blade crackling with the Crowns' power, slashed across his chest, but he was barely scratched. She swung again. He deflected it with his forearms.

She swung again. This time, he caught the blade with one hand. He brought his other down upon it, shattering the metal.

She tossed aside the useless hilt as he reached for her throat. She dodged back, barely avoiding his grip. Her legs came up in a flipped kick to his face.

That was the first time he really felt the impact, being lifted off his feet and sent sprawling to the stone flooring.

He got up, rubbing his chin. Val was already on him again, sending a series of flying kicks and punches into his body. The first few landed squarely; the rest he was able to deflect. Decades longer spent training under the man who'd tutored her. There was little she could do to surprise him when he was properly prepared.

She threw a fist at his face, activating the pile-driver component. Angelo staggered back, swinging his arms wildly to try to bat her away.

He finally knocked her arm aside and regained his footing.

He reached for her throat again, this time successful in grabbing it, and swung her about, slamming her into the wall.

The marble and mortar crumbled behind her.

"You're well trained, Valentina," he said, his voice savage and ragged, "but I'm simply stronger."

"And older."

He threw a fist into her gut.

"More experienced," he said. "With the Crown, I feel like I'm in the prime of life. You, on the other hand..."

She threw a punch towards his head. He grabbed her arm with his free hand, forcing it back until he heard a splintering crack.

Val screamed.

"I couldn't do that if you were truly a match for me," Angelo said. She was dropped, landing on her knees. He brought his foot back and then forward, punting her in the ribs and sending her into the wall again. "I couldn't do that if your Crowns were any match for mine."

She swung at him with her remaining good arm. He easily caught it and kicked her in the stomach, knocking the wind from her.

"You can never beat me," he said.

"No." She defiantly pulled herself to her feet. Unseen by Angelo, she clicked one of the buttons on her belt-mounted device. "You can't beat me. Because I just don't care."

She summoned up the last of her strength and dove at him. Her attack lacking any discernable strategy, he was taken off guard. She was not punching, not kicking, not going for any vital spots on his body, just flinging the both of them towards the balcony's edge.

She got them there, though, and they tumbled over.

A small shuttle zoomed up, its loading hatch open, and plucked the pair of them from the air.

It continued upward into the sky.

Inside, Val and Angelo were virtually immobilized by the G-forces pinning them against the rear wall.

The whole interior still stunk of more than a month's worth of continued occupancy by an armed battalion with no access to laundry or showers.

"What are you doing?" Angelo's teeth rattled within his helmet.

"You haven't figured it out yet?" Val teased. "I'm winning."

Angelo pried away from the wall and dragged himself towards the ship's cockpit.

"If you're trying to change course, don't bother." She showed him the device. "The heading can't be altered."

Angelo looked at the instruments.

"We're flying directly at this system's star."

"Yup. Feeling beaten yet?" Val asked.

"This isn't winning! You'll kill us both! Then who will rule Kaia?"

"I think I said already; I don't care," she said. "As long as it's not someone who murdered their own family to get to the throne."

"And what happens to the empire without the protection of the Crown?" he asked.

"I don't know. And, not to beat the same drum, but I really don't care. It'll survive, or it won't. Either way's better than where it is now."

"You stupid bitch! I'll kill you!"

Val laughed, a deep, hearty laugh that made her already sore ribs hurt even worse. "I've already done that."

Angelo released his handhold, allowing the G-forces to carry him towards her.

He drew back his fist.

His ears rang from the impact of his knuckles on the rear bulkhead.

The shuttle burned its way out of the Earth's atmosphere and entered fold space.

It came out of the fold just within the warm glow of the

sun's corona.

The air above the balcony distorted. Val was spat out less than ten feet from the floor. She impacted with the same speed she'd been traveling aboard the ship. The sound of it likely echoed for miles.

Rik and Trainer rushed to her side.

She groaned as she rolled to her back.

"What the hell?" she asked.

"Hey," Rik said.

"Hey."

"So, you're not dead."

"Yeah," she said. "What's the deal with that?"

From across the balcony, Yost smiled and waved.

Trainer and Rik helped her up.

"Ow. Ow." She winced. "Watch the arm."

"That is… kind of floppy," Rik said.

"I'll send for a medic," said Trainer.

"Hopefully that'll do, this time," said Rik.

"Yeah. And I've been holding this in, because I wanted to seem cool and badass, but…" Val let out the loudest pained scream anyone nearby had ever heard. She clutched at her swinging arm. "Good God this hurts!"

"That's very regal," Rik said.

"Shut the hell up. My arm just got snapped like a dry twig, I'm allowed to be in pain. And I got punched and kicked a whole lot. And that asshole broke my sword. Goddamnit all!"

She looked to Yost.

"Yost, you got any healing spells?" she asked.

"I've got a few that'll make it so you can't feel that your arm is broken," he said. "I mean, you won't be able to feel anything for a little while. But, pain is part of anything, so…"

"You know what, forget it," she said. "I don't need your weird drug magic."

"Okay, so, wait, you didn't know that Yost was going to pull you out of there?" Rik asked.

"No," she said. "What I knew was that I was going to die."

"And you were okay with that?"

"I just tried to keep my mind off of it so that it didn't sink in," she said. "But, I mean, it's not like Kaia really needs a ruler who doesn't care what happens to it."

"No," Rik said. "But I think it does need a ruler who's willing to die for it."

There was a pounding on the door. Before anyone in the throne room or on the balcony could react, a large contingent of royal guards burst through, all their guns pointed at the handful of rebels.

"Where's the king?" the lead guard demanded.

Val looked up at the sky.

"There's going to be a minor solar aberration visible in about 8 minutes," she said. "That's your king."

The guards lowered their weapons and looked at one another.

"Rik, get some guys and take their weapons," Val said. "We'll figure out who we can use and who's going to prison later."

Rik started for the door.

"And..." Val said.

"Yeah?" Rik turned back to her.

Val nodded towards the ledge.

"Somewhere down there are Four's remains," she said. "Make sure it gets a proper burial."

The others filed out, leaving Val alone in the outsized chamber.

She approached the rear alcove, tucked away behind the throne. With her good arm, she pulled open the paneling that covered it.

The Queen floated in her stasis pod, her eyes fixed on Val. A look of sheer pain, shock, and desperation was etched into every line of her face.

Val put her palm on the glass.

She looked around the room, her eyes falling on a loose staff. One of the honor guards must have dropped it. She picked it up, cradling it under her functioning arm.

The Crown's energy infused it.

Val took a deep breath and plunged the spear into the stasis pod's machinery.

The internal lights went out. She heard the mechanisms wind down.

The Queen slowly nodded and closed her eyes.

Val spun as she slumped back, leaning against the stasis pod.

She removed the Crown and clunked it down beside her. It seemed heavier than it ever had before.

Tears streamed down her face.

She sat and waited for the medics to arrive.

CHAPTER 5

Wessel stood on the sidewalk, staring at the U.S. Bank building. Or rather, what was atop it. She'd approached with such purpose only moments earlier, and now found herself virtually frozen to the pavement.

A Kaian guard exited the lobby and stood facing her.

"Can I help you?"

She couldn't understand the words.

"Huh?"

The guard started to turn away.

"Friggin' troglodytes."

"I'm looking..." She took a step towards him. "I was hoping to talk to the lady with the metal face."

Rik emerged from the building's lobby and called to the guard.

"Hey, be nice to the locals," he said. *"They've been through a lot today."*

The guard grumbled and headed back inside.

Rik let him pass and then approached the uniformed officer.

"I recognize you," she said. "From before."

Rik gave her an odd look.

"Yeah," she said. "You were with the, um... the lady with the..."

She gestured at her face, splaying her fingers out across

her forehead.

"Valentina," Rik said.

"Is that her name?" Wessel asked. "I was kind of hoping to talk to her. Because, I don't know, she seemed like she has her shit together. I mean, you guys parked a big spaceship on top of an office building. You had a war in our streets. Even just finding out that aliens exist. I'm not sure if I'm gonna go back to my apartment and pass out for a few days, or never sleep again. If I could talk to her, maybe I could get some peace of mind. Or if she could talk to our leaders, or something. I don't know, this is all just... way too much. For me. For us. For Earth, as weird as that sounds."

Rik stepped towards her.

"I'm sorry." He patted her shoulder. *"I really wish I spoke Earth... Earthian? Earthan? Earthel? I don't even know enough of your language to know what it's called. If you ever become part of the empire, or if the queen declares you a protectorate, maybe that'll change."*

Wessel stared at him, unblinking.

He forced a smile.

"The queen can speak your language. Did you want to see her maybe? Though maybe she's not really in a 'talking' place right now. She's had a hard day, too. I can check with her, if you want."

"Never mind." She backed away, her shoulders and chin drooping, and walked off. "Nice talking to you."

The guard poked his head out of the building again.

"What was that about?" he asked.

"Unfortunately, I don't really have any idea."

CHAPTER 6

Val sat, numb, on the throne. Her arms lay on the padded rests of the chair, one encased in a luminescent brace.

From her seat, she could stare out over the city skyline. The sun was just peeking over the rooftops.

Rik leaned against the door jamb.

He forcefully cleared his throat.

Val didn't look at him.

"You can come in," she said.

"About time." He walked towards her.

"You were standing there for about two seconds," she said.

"How would you know?" he asked. "You weren't looking."

Val reached beside her and lifted the Crown in her palm.

"Heightened awareness."

"Aw. That sounds like fun."

"You remember what it was like on that transport ship for literally weeks?" she asked him. "Try being hyper-aware of everything going on there."

"Uh."

"Yeah. Did you need something?"

"I was just going to let you know that the last of Angelo's loyalists have been rounded up," he said. "A lot of them are asking for a tribunal rather than pledging their loyalty to you."

"We knew that was a possibility."

"Yeah, but it's still disappointing."

"Honestly, I'd rather have people on my side who were there the whole time."

"So, does that mean my job is safe?" he asked. Val cocked an eyebrow at him and slowly shook her head. "I'm just saying, your options were kind of limited before. Now you have the entire empire to pick from. Anyway, I was also going to let you know that the palace ship has been prepped, so we can take off whenever." She didn't react to his news. "Come on, we can finally go home. And, you get the big room now. You can't tell me you're not at all excited. Or, relieved? I don't know. I don't know how hyper-aware royals feel about stuff."

"Yes, Rik, I'm happy to be going home," she said. "But there's one more thing I have to do before we go."

She hoisted herself up and headed past him, towards the exit.

"What's that?" he asked.

There was a knock on the door of the suburban house.

A woman - middle-aged, dressed casually - answered it. There was no peephole, no windows near the door, but the area was nice enough that she felt comfortable opening it in broad daylight without having to check who was there first.

Val and her honor guard stood on the porch in full uniform.

Curious at the lack of conversation several moments after he'd heard the door open, the woman's husband joined her in the entryway.

"Honey," he said. "What's..."

"Uh..." The woman kept looking straight ahead at the regal visitors on their stoop.

"You're Catherine and Jason Hammond?" Val asked.

"...yes," the woman said.

"Joseph Hammond was your son."

"Yes," Catherine repeated.

Val lowered herself to one knee, her head bowed, a fist at her chest. Her honor guard followed suit.

The pair of humans looked at one another, then back at the aliens in their doorway.

"Okay," Jason said, "I'm gonna need some context here."